EDGE OF AWAKE

EDGE OF AWAKE

DESTINED FOR DREAMS, BOOK 3

by

GINNA MORAN

1

KEEP IT TOGETHER

NADIA

WARM BREATH TICKLES my neck. I silently count as I breathe in—*one, two, three*—and then out—*one, two, three*—it's the only way to keep my breathing in rhythm with what it should be like for a sleeping person. My breathing is identical to my cellmate Camden Allister's, and it helps that his heavy arm drapes over my side and his chest presses into my back. I just wish he wouldn't breathe on me. It makes it hard to focus.

Because Camden's and my DNA reads human, the Human Preservation Agency determined it safe enough to house us together in their termination facility. Luckily for us, it also means the HPA won't be experimenting on us. They're only keeping us locked up because they believe we have information they can use to destroy the supernatural world. The information they think we have is what's also keeping us alive. Once we have nothing else to offer, we're dead.

I flop on my back and stare at the white sheet covering my face so they won't see I'm awake. The dull ache of hunger grips my stomach as my nightmare inflictor side begs to take control. Grinding my teeth, I try to think about other things. I can't invade Camden's dreams right now. It'd be too soon since the last time. If I inflict nightmares too often, I'll drive Camden insane. A person can only experience terror so much before they break. I couldn't live with myself if I hurt Camden—or any-one—with my ability. I'm not a monster despite what the HPA would think if they found out the truth about me. They want nothing more than to rid the world of creatures—and night-mare inflictors would be at the top of their kill list.

One. Two. Three. Breathe in. *One. Two. Three.* Breathe out.

I've never been so controlled in my life. It only took giving up my freedom to save my father, being thrown in a cell with a powerless enchantress's son, and the heavy weight of my imme-diate demise if I screw up to get to this point. I never thought I could be this strong and resist a dream, but here I am. It's not like I have a choice.

Despite the constant tears burning my eyes and the heart-ache clenching my chest, I manage to keep myself together. If it weren't for my boyfriend, Hunter Sullivan, visiting me every three hours during the day like clockwork, and staying for twenty minutes at a time, I don't know what I'd do.

When the HPA made the sudden decision to transfer my father from the termination facility to the HPA lab, I had to wing an unplanned rescue mission. Hunter and Jacqueline Matthews, the sin-eater posing as an agent, were part of the escort team, and because of this, I did something crazy. With the help of my best friend, Alyssa Callaghan, and my new friend, Evangeline Thompson, from my short enrollment at Northern Bell High School, we managed to run the HPA van transporting my father off the road.

After the car wreck, I tried to distract the agents, and it nearly got me killed. That single decision forced Alyssa and my father to flee without me. It was the only way to keep everyone alive—almost everyone—since the only possible outcomes were to fight to the death or to split up.

Evie and I stayed because Alyssa knew the board would think I was human since I'm only half nightmare inflictor, and she knew Evie would be okay because her mother is a doctor for the HPA. I'm not sure what's happened to Evie, but I know her life is forever changed—just like mine.

I don't despise Alyssa and my father for abandoning me, but I do regret Jacqueline had blown her cover by killing the agent who was trying to kill me. I was tranquilized before I could see her fate, but I know it wasn't a good one. Putting her in that situation will always haunt me.

As for Hunter—he kept his agent façade to protect me. He

watches over me in the termination facility, and I'm sure he, my father, and Alyssa are devising a plan to get me out of here. I just hope it's soon. I'm at my breaking point.

Camden rolls closer, tugging me from my thoughts, and slings his leg over mine in his sleep. I squeeze my eyes shut and grimace. I don't know how people sleep next to each other with the constant shifting and moving, the tug-of-war for blankets, the fight over pillows, and the heavy weight of limbs threatening to crush me. But I don't have a choice. I have to deal with this until I get out of here.

I sigh and sit up. I'll either pretend to nap later or act sleep-deprived. I just can't take it anymore. If I have to pretend to sleep for another minute, I'll go crazy.

Pressing my feet to the cool tile, I pad my way across the room to the desk. I don't wear the slippers provided for me because I can't risk messing up and accidentally gliding. I need complete control to keep the HPA's board from discovering my nightmare inflictor half. If the HPA discovers I'm not completely human, they'll murder me without a second thought. It's hard being under a microscope all the time, but as each day passes, I find it easier to pretend to be human. If I ever make it out of here, I'll never have to worry about fitting in with the human population again.

I flip open the sketchpad and stare at yesterday's drawing. It's a stick figure with vertical lines drawn over it like prison bars. I'm not the least artistic, but boredom has opened up a new world I never thought of exploring. That's the answer I gave Dr. Harvey, the scientist who pesters me for information, when he asked me about my sketches. Every few days, he has Hunter retrieve the sketchbook for the board to analyze. They somehow think its contents will reveal all my dark secrets.

I pick a black crayon from the box and draw sixteen circles, adding four lines to each to make it look like a crowd of poorly drawn people. I give some hair while leaving others bald, and then I write names under each figure—Mike, Jamie, Christopher, Ted—each figure is given an imaginary identity I'm sure the board will go nuts over. The board thrives on information, so I make it up and lead them nowhere. I'll play this game as long as they're willing to go on wild goose chases that'll always leave them sore losers.

A beeping sound echoes through the quiet room, and I get up and walk to the wall, leaning my back against it. It's a habit I've grown used to after these eight extremely long weeks. Today is the last day of another month. I can't believe I've already wasted so many weeks of my life here.

The heavy door cracks open. Dr. Harvey covers for Hunter half the week so he doesn't have to take as many double shifts until they assign him a new partner.

A new partner. My heart sinks into my stomach thinking about Jacqueline.

I cross my arms. "You're here early."

Dr. Harvey rubs his hand over his day-old stubble. His chiseled jaw tightens as he clenches his teeth, and his dark coffee eyes shift from me to Camden sleeping on the cot. He tucks his hands in his lab coat pockets.

I stiffen. "Where's breakfast?"

"I'm not here for that, Emily," he says.

My heart hammers a million miles a minute. I gave them my mother's name as my own, and I'll never get used to people calling me by it, but hearing her name also helps me keep it together. If she were alive, she'd want me to fight and not give up. She believed in the goodness of my father, including his nightmare inflictor side, and she'd believe I could make it through this.

I press my hand to the wall for support. This could be it. They could deem me useless and send me to the black zone where I'd be murdered. Hunter isn't even here to save me. I thought he'd fight to the death with me if it came to it. *You don't want that. You want Hunter to live.*

I want to live, too.

It takes me a moment to find my voice. "Then why are you here, Dr. Harvey?"

"Please, follow me," he says.

I shake my head, cold dread seeping into my bones. "Not until I have some answers."

"It's only for some tests and questions, Emily. Don't make this difficult." Stepping closer, he leaves the door open behind him, strutting my way.

It takes everything in me not to scream for Camden. Even if we could take Dr. Harvey out, we'd never make it far even with the door open. There's nothing I can do. If I fight, they'll relocate me to another zone, but if I don't they might kill me.

I swallow. "You could've just said that."

Dr. Harvey stops in his tracks and pulls out a pair of hand-cuffs from his pocket. "I have to restrain you."

"Why? I'm not going to run."

"Emily, hold your hands up." He sighs, waiting for me to raise my hands.

My fingers tremble as I hold them up. The cold metal cuffs cut into my wrists when Dr. Harvey tightens them. He jerks his head toward the door, forcing me to shuffle to it with him at my side, digging his boney fingers into my shoulder.

This is the first time I've left the cell since I was transferred from another one days after my arrival. But this time, I'm not walking thirty feet under Hunter's care. We walk in the opposite direction of the cell block, and I don't get a chance to look into the cells around me. I wonder how many others share my fate. I've only heard screams through the wall from the cell next to mine.

"Where are we going?" I ask, my voice echoing through the quiet corridor.

"Don't speak. Keep your eyes on the ground. If you disobey, I'll call for an agent to assist me, and they don't care about your wellbeing like I do." Dr. Harvey nudges me past a desk with a set of monitors toward an elevator.

I flick my attention up and back to the tiled floor. Dr. Harvey doesn't really care about my wellbeing. He only cares about what I have to offer—whether it's information or some new scientific breakthrough—and once I have nothing left, I'll only be a number on some scribbled notes buried in a file.

The elevator dings, and my eyes shift to a pair of black stilettos. A woman waits inside the elevator, but I'm too scared to look up to see her face. Dr. Harvey pushes me forward. Tension rolls through me, feeling the woman's gaze on me.

"It's nice to see you, Andrea," Dr. Harvey says.

"I thought I'd join you for the transfer and interrogation, Harvey," the woman says.

I crinkle my nose. Dr. Harvey is one of the few doctors that goes by his first name. I'm not sure what to think about it.

Dr. Harvey tugs my arm, forcing me to the wall and away from the woman. "While Human 9209 asks a lot of questions, she never gives anyone any trouble. Right, Emily?"

I don't open my mouth. He's trying to trick me. Instead, I just keep staring at the floor.

A hand reaches out and grabs my chin and pulls my head up. I slowly lift my gaze and stare into hazel eyes so familiar they almost shatter my blank expression. Andrea isn't just any doctor. She's Dr. Andrea Sullivan, Hunter's evil, heartless mother who was willing to give up Hunter's soul for information about creatures, and the woman I want to kill most in the world.

HUNTER

I tie on the leather bracelet with a small engraved coin on it that Alyssa gave me three days after Nadia had given up her freedom for her father's. It's the only way to get past the spelled walls surrounding the non-human portion of her neighborhood. Without it, I'd constantly walk past and never find Dmitri's house again. He's tripled his security measures since losing Nadia, and I don't blame him.

Alyssa stands on her front porch, her red hair hiding under a fleece hat. She hugs herself, running her gloved hands up and down her puffy jacket. I raise my hand and wave. She motions for me to hurry, so I jog the rest of the way to her.

"You have ten minutes," she says.

My brows furrow. "What are you talking about? My shift doesn't start for another two hours."

"Will you ever catch on that Alyssa is a seer?" Jacqueline's voice rings in my ears.

I blink. "What did you see?" I add.

It's funny how our roles have been reversed. I never thought I'd ever host a soul, especially Jacqueline's. She didn't have a choice but to body jump into me to save herself after preventing Agent Rob from murdering Nadia. I'd let Jacqueline hitch a ride forever if I had to, because I could never repay her for her selfless actions.

"We'll just call it even, Hunter," Jacqueline says, hearing my thoughts.

Unlike the time I spent in her head when my mother traded my soul to Jacqueline in a deal that would grant Jacqueline amnesty from the board, Jacqueline can now hear everything that goes on in my mind. I haven't learned to conceal my thoughts—haven't really tried either—but it's not as annoying as I thought it'd be.

Jacqueline is basically like my strongly opinionated conscience. She walks me through everything, like my own personal, annoying guardian angel, and helps me make good decisions about the board and Nadia. But, one thing she's made clear, is that if I even think about telling anyone, including Alyssa and Dmitri, about her, she'll make my life more hellish than it already is. I don't know what her plan is, but as long as it doesn't consist of fighting for control over my body, I'll do what she asks.

"They're going to ask you to go in early," Alyssa says, pulling me from my thoughts. "The board decided to interrogate Nadia. She'll make a very clear decision that'll leave people unhappy."

Alyssa opens the door, and I follow her in. Dmitri sits on the couch, leaning his elbow on his knee. He presses his cell phone to his ear and glances at me before dropping his gaze to the carpet. Alyssa shrugs out of her jacket, struts to the kitchen, and returns with a steaming cup of tea.

I bring the warm mug to my mouth, the heat defrosting my face, but a chill remains in my stomach as I think about Nadia. I wish Alyssa would tell me more, but I know she's already moved past the topic. If it were something serious, she wouldn't be so put together. Her confidence is the only thing preventing me from running out the door and back to Nadia.

Nadia's going to be fine," Jacqueline says.

I exhale through my nostrils. "Are you psychic, too, Jackie?" I think.

"If you think anything other than that, then you don't know her at all."

I clench my jaw. "I can still wo—"

"Hunter?"

I rub my hand over my eyes and meet Dmitri's stare. "Sorry, what?"

He sets his phone on the table. "I asked if there was any change in the situation?"

Shaking my head, I say, "The board is still interested in Nadia. I'm more concerned that they're a little too invested in her. The scientist assigned to her constantly watches the monitor over my shoulder."

"I don't like this," he says.

I cross my arms. "I won't let them hurt her, Dmitri. Trust me."

Alyssa comes up next to me, bumping my shoulder with hers. "He does."

"Ask him about his plan."

I force Jacqueline's voice away. "What about your plan? How's it coming along?"

Dmitri stands, towering a good six inches above me. He runs his chalky white hand through his inky black hair and puffs air through his lips. "I need another week at least. The council refuses to leave the compound."

"And then what?"

Alyssa flicks her eyes from Dmitri to me. "It's not the right time to tell you, Hunter."

I sigh. I hate being left in the dark, but I'm not going to argue. The last time I did, I ruined the plan to get Dmitri away from the termination facility. I refuse to ruin Nadia's chance, too. "Okay."

Dmitri reaches out and grabs my shoulder. "As soon as everything is set, I'll tell you. Just keep me posted about Nadia."

He turns away from me, ending the conversation. His phone rings, and he waves to me as he answers it, then walks to the kitchen, leaving me alone with Alyssa. She shifts her weight from one foot to the other and pulls a napkin from her pocket.

She holds it out to me. "Give this to Nadia after nine o'clock tonight but before breakfast."

I shove it in my pocket. "She misses you guys."

"I know." Alyssa flings her arms around me, and I keep my hands at my sides.

"It's okay to pat her back, Hunter. She's not going to bite."

"Shut up, Jackie," I think.

Alyssa pulls away and walks to the front door and holds it open. "You have three minutes, Hunter. I'll call you later if I can."

I leave without looking back. As soon as I'm out of the neighborhood, I untie the leather band from my wrist and tuck it in a hidden pocket of my jacket. Running the rest of the way to my car, I climb in and start the engine. I stretch my achy, still tender hand. I got the cast off only a few weeks ago, but the memory of nearly getting beaten to death during Dmitri's failed rescue mission still lingers in my mind. I regret getting involved. If I hadn't, everyone would be free, and I'd be away from the board now.

I pull away from the curb and drive. I want to be as far away as possible before the board contacts me. I wish I didn't have to answer to them. I wish Dmitri would hurry up with his plan. I don't know how much more I can take.

NADIA

Dr. Harvey leads me into a small room with two couches and a coffee table. A folding table with a coffee pot, cups, and a plate of muffins rests against a wall with framed portraits. Along the opposite wall are floor-to-ceiling cabinets secured with combination locks.

Dr. Sullivan points to a spot on one of the couches, and Dr. Harvey pushes me toward it to sit down. I contemplate asking to stand but instead lower myself onto the worn, green cushion and rest my cuffed hands in my lap.

I listen to the clicks of Dr. Sullivan's heels as she crosses the room. "Would you like some breakfast?"

My stomach knots. I want nothing more than to be escorted back to my cell. I don't want to sit here and watch Dr. Sullivan and Dr. Harvey eat breakfast. My heart hammers in my ears, and I swear it's loud enough for the doctors to hear.

Dr. Harvey clears his throat. "Dr. Sullivan asked you a question, Emily. It's okay to speak now."

I keep my eyes trained on my trembling hands. "Yes, thank you." It's the expected response for someone who hasn't eaten food since last night. I'm guessing it'll also mean I'm going to be in this room for a while.

Dr. Sullivan saunters to the couch opposite me and sets the plate of muffins and two cups of coffee on the table between us. I draw my eyes up enough to watch Dr. Sullivan flip through a stack of papers on a clipboard.

Dr. Harvey sits next to me, setting his own cup of coffee on the table. He reaches for my arms and removes my cuffs, but I keep my hands in my lap. I don't attempt to grab for the muffin I don't really want. Instead, I rub my wrists.

Dr. Sullivan clicks her pen. "You must be wondering why we brought you here."

I twist my lips to the side. "I'm more interested in why you're keeping me here."

I glance from Dr. Harvey, who's sipping his coffee, to Dr. Sullivan, who now studies my facial expressions like I'm merely a subject of her experiments. She pushes her gold-framed glasses up into her brown hair, a shade lighter than Hunter's, treating them like a headband.

Dr. Sullivan taps her pen against her chin. "Well, dear, what did you expect would happen?"

"I didn't do anything wrong," I say, glaring.

She smirks. "The reports say otherwise."

I roll my eyes. I can't help it. "Dr. Harvey said you were going to perform some tests." I can't sit here and argue about why I'm here. I know the real reason why I'm here.

"We will get to that as soon as you answer a few questions," she says, shifting on the couch.

I peer at Dr. Harvey, who stares into his half-empty cup of coffee and purse my lips. Straightening my shoulders, I don't give in to my desire to sulk. To groan under her scrutiny or relent and answer whatever she wants. Because no matter what I say, it'll never get me out of here. "Then I guess you can take me back to my cell. I don't answer questions for anyone."

Dr. Harvey clears his throat. "What about Agent Hunter?"

I shrug. "What about him?"

Dr. Sullivan sighs and stands up. "Dr. Harvey is insinuating that you answer questions for Agent Hunter. Must we spell things out?"

I hold my serious expression. I've struck a nerve with Dr. Sullivan. If I keep it up, she might transfer me out of the green zone just to demonstrate her sadistic power. I lick my lips. "Hunter doesn't interrogate me and treat me like I'm less than human."

Dr. Sullivan exhales through her flared nostrils. "Dr. Harvey, please restrain Human 9209 and escort her back to her cell. I need to make a phone call." She shifts her eyes to mine. "I'll be seeing you later."

2

OVER THE EDGE

HUNTER

I TAKE A deep breath as my HPA cell phone rings and answer it through my stereo. "Agent Hunter speaking."

Static buzzes through the speakers before a voice blares through. "I know today's your double, but I need you to come in early." Dr. Sullivan sounds annoyed. Over the last few weeks, our relationship turned even more strenuous for me to maintain. Any semblance of a mother-son bond has long since died. I'm only cordial because I need to stay on Dr. Sullivan's good side for Nadia's sake. I must obey and pretend to be a good, loyal agent or else the board will transfer me out before Nadia is freed. If that were to happen, all bets are off, and I'd fight our way out. It'd be the only way. I've thought about doing it a dozen times, but Dmitri insists there's a better way—one that will guarantee both Nadia and I will survive.

I drum my fingers on the steering wheel. "Sure thing. Give me forty minutes."

"You have thirty."

I sigh. "Mind telling me what this is about?"

Dr. Sullivan sighs through the line. "One of your charges isn't cooperating, and I need you to put her in her place."

I grimace. "All right. See you soon."

Speeding to the termination facility, I zone out, thinking about Nadia, knowing she's the reason I'm racing. I can't stand the thought that I'll have to "put her in her place" according to Dr. Sullivan. The only place I want to put her is in my arms, holding her to me where I can protect her from the true monsters in the world.

Phillip waves from his desk the moment I enter the lobby to the termination facility. Crossing the lobby, I enter the already waiting elevator, taking it down to the green zone. I march the distance of the short hall, forcing myself not to run, to the viewing station I spend most of the time while at work. Dr. Sullivan and Dr. Harvey stare at the monitor and only glance up when I come up next to them.

Dr. Harvey assists me in the green zone so I don't have to work sixteen or more hour days, seven days a week. I'd gladly spend all my time here if it wouldn't make the board suspicious. Until the board decides to assign me a new partner, Dr. Harvey helping is more than I could've hoped for. He's better than an agent and getting a new partner. The board takes assigning partners seriously, so hopefully, I'll be gone before they do.

Dr. Harvey yawns without covering his mouth, looking like he stayed the night last night with his facial scruff and wrinkled lab coat. I'm pretty sure the shirt he's wearing was the same blue button-down one from yesterday. The board has been working everyone twice as hard lately, and I'm surprised they haven't added a wing for apartments. Then we'd never have to leave.

"He looks awful. You should tell him to go home and take a break," Jacqueline says.

I lift an eyebrow. "The board overworking you too, Dr. Harvey? You look like you need a vacation."

He straightens his back, blinking the sleep from his eyes. Dr. Sullivan glowers in my direction, because I basically called her out in front of a subordinate doctor, breaking my agent façade and showing that I might be able to get away with saying something because I'm Dr. Sullivan's son. Raising my hands up, I step back, smiling.

"He was just about to leave, Agent Hunter." Dr. Sullivan adjusts her gold-framed glasses and scoops her clipboard from my desk.

"You sure you don't need my assistance, Andrea?" Dr. Harvey asks.

She shakes her head. "I'll call you when we're ready for testing."

He nods, and I watch him stride to the elevator and hit the call button. I wave as the door closes and then turn back to Dr.

Sullivan. Her lips press into a tight line, the wrinkles at the corner of her eyes deepening with her serious expression.

"She looks ready to kill someone," I think to Jacqueline.

"Be careful what you say. It might be you."

I sigh in my mind. "Better me than Nadia."

Dr. Sullivan struts away without giving me any sort of direction. I follow behind her, knowing she just expects me to obey her silent, implied command. And I do. I stay right on her tapping heels like a shadow, close enough that I skid to a stop when she halts to keep from knocking her down. Peering into the window to Nadia and Camden's cell, she grumbles something to herself and brings her eyes to mine.

"Go in, restrain Human 9209, and bring her out here," Dr. Sullivan says.

I nod and enter my pass code. It kills me having to enter Nadia's cell with Dr. Sullivan breathing down my neck. I wish I knew what to expect. There's no way I'm relocating Nadia to a new zone. I'll tranquilize Dr. Sullivan and risk the security team to escape. It's not how I want it to go down—I want to save as many people as I can—but I'll do what I have to.

I crack the door open, and Nadia moves from the desk to the corner of the room with her back to the wall. Camden sits on the edge of his bed, twisting his lips to the side at the sight of me. I step in, shutting the door behind me, and glance over my shoulder at Dr. Sullivan staring at me through the window.

Reaching for my metal cuffs, I slide them from my weaponry belt. "I have to put these on you, Emily." I stare at Nadia's glistening eyes. She peers from me to Camden and back to me. The pout she offers me screams how much she hates that I'm standing here in this position, sending my heart into my stomach. Because she's thinking about how I'm feeling and now the other way around. Touching her soul before, now in tune with her every gesture, every hidden meaning, leaves us closer than ever. We could never use our voices again and still understand each other.

She crosses her arms, sucking in her ever kissable bottom lip. "What if I say no?"

"Tell her you'll tranquilize her," Jacqueline says, cutting through the torture Nadia's eyes unintentionally inflict on me. I really wish she'd stop telling me what to do. I'm not her puppet.

I step closer, swallowing. "Don't make me tranquilize you and drag you out of here."

Nadia's jaw quivers, nearly cracking my steely façade, and my chest tightens because it hurts to see her scared and uncertain. She shouldn't ever be afraid around me. It kills me that I can't pull her into my arms, hold her, and kiss her trembling lips. All I can do is apologize with my eyes and beg for her to stay strong.

Straightening her shoulders, she pads to me, holding out her arms. I flick the cuffs on without tightening them, the gesture too much to handle. She waits until I nudge her toward the door, sinking against my hand on her lower back. It's not often I'm within feet of her, and even touching her like this nearly makes me lose it.

"Don't even think about doing anything stupid," Jacqueline

says, forcing my swirling thoughts to disappear.

I touch the doorknob while keeping my hand on Nadia, sliding my fingers on her side for a second to pull her back a bit to open the door.

"Where are you taking her?" The worry in Camden's voice intensifies my own doubt.

I peer over my shoulder to meet his gaze. "I'd tell you if I knew."

I'm not sure why, but Camden's concern for Nadia bothers me. It's obvious he genuinely cares about her, but I can't tell if it's only friendly affection. It's hard ignoring my jealously of Camden, and if Nadia's love for me didn't resonate from her when I look at her, I'd worry even more. I know she's trying to survive. It's what I want, too. I just wish I didn't have to watch their interactions so often.

"It's okay, Camden. I'll be back in a little while," Nadia says. The way she says it sends heat up my neck. Not because I believe she's interested in Camden but because it should be me who she's reassuring.

"Take a breath. You're going to give yourself away. Don't take anything personally, Hunter." My head pounds as Jacqueline's voice nags at me. She's the voice of reason I've never wanted.

Dr. Sullivan gazes at Nadia for a second, looking her up and down like she can somehow find answers in her physical assessment. Finding nothing as always, she turns on her black stilettos and saunters back to the viewing room. I gently hold my fingers against Nadia, guiding her, and follow Dr. Sullivan to the elevator. She calls for it, and I step on before her.

Dr. Sullivan swings her gaze from her clipboard to me. "I expect full cooperation from Human 9209."

I nod my head. "Did you hear that, Emily?"

Nadia doesn't say anything while staring at the ground.

I tap my index finger on her back. "Emily, do you understand?"

She stiffens under my touch. I hate that if she doesn't answer, I'm going to have to threaten her. And she knows this. But she also knows complete compliance isn't what's keeping her alive either.

She glares at the ground. "Yes, Agent Hunter."

My stomach flips at the sound of my name on her lips, her voice cutting through me sharper than the knife on my weaponry belt. I wish the elevator door would open already. The tense air suffocates me in a mixture of my own sweat and the citrusy scent of Nadia's shampoo. Having Nadia this close to the most evil woman in the world affects me more than it should. I never knew someone could despise their own mother as much as I do.

Dr. Sullivan clicks her pen. "Good."

The elevator door dings open and cool air drifts around me. I take a deep breath, filling my lungs, getting another whiff of Nadia's hair. Pushing Nadia out first, I hang onto her shirt to keep her from walking forward. She bumps into my chest on purpose, making me steady her on her feet. I release a small breath into her hair, just feeling her so close.

Oblivious to our connection, Dr. Sullivan strolls past us and into the narrow hallway of the interrogation rooms. I haven't been in this section of the termination facility since the first time I laid my eyes on Jacqueline and lost my soul to her. We pass interrogation room six, the room where Dr. Sullivan had made a deal with Jacqueline, and I clench my teeth at the faint memory. This is where it all started.

"Oh, look. It's where you snatched my soul, Jackie," I think. "Funny how it's you in my head now."

"I don't need the reminder."

Dr. Sullivan stops in front of us, drawing my attention back to the situation at hand, and I tug on Nadia's shirt again. She tilts her head back, her pale blond hair touching my chin, before she straightens her shoulders and looks at the tiled floor.

"Take a seat on the couch, Emily," I say.

Nadia shuffles forward and eases onto the couch, crossing her legs at her ankles. I take a moment to drink her in. Under the harsh lighting, shadows darken her indigo eyes yet a mixture of stubbornness and strength light up her face in the beauty of her nightmare inflictor side she hides from the board. Two red hearts, drawn in crayon on the knees of her white cotton pants, pulls my attention away from the gaze she locks me in, allowing me to breathe. I plop down next to her, just out of reach, and she eyes me in her peripheral vision.

Dr. Sullivan grabs a tray of muffins from a folding table and sets them on the coffee table before sitting down and crossing her legs at her knees on the green couch across from us. She pulls her clipboard from under her arm and positions it on her lap, flipping a few pages.

"You may remove Human 9209's restraints, Agent Hunter," Dr. Sullivan says without looking up. "I expect this will go more smoothly this round."

My forehead crinkles. "I'll remove them once Emily answers your first question."

NADIA

It's hard to breathe no matter how deeply I inhale through my nose. I imagine the air leaking from the room, though I know it's in my head. It's what being so close to Hunter in his HPA uniform does to me, leaving me breathless in a bad way. Because I miss him—touching him, kissing him, seeing the sun shine on his dark hair outside these prison walls. I miss how perfectly I fit in his arms, how he feels unguarded and open to me without the HPA locking away everything I love about him from me.

Fear's cold hug, an unwanted replacement for Hunter's embrace, tortures me, reminding me how much of Hunter's warmth I miss despite him sitting close enough that if I were brave enough, I'd scoot over and let my leg brush his. But I'm not brave in that way. Daring.

I'm only brave because I have no other choice if I'm to keep myself together as everything else rips at invisible seams to send my world scattering through this concrete and bulletproof glass fortress. Bravery is facing Hunter and not reacting—maybe it's the sheer will to keep us both alive. Without having to hear him say it, I know Hunter would risk his life for mine if all our options were destroyed. If I mess up, it doesn't only put me at risk but him. So now, I'm brave for the both of us.

Hunter clears his throat, flicking his serious hazel eyes in my direction. "Now, don't be difficult."

The harshness deepening his voice provokes a chilling emptiness within me, stabbing at the steel barricade I imagine protecting me, turning it into glass. I feel like I'll shatter at any second. *It's his job,* I think. The more I tell myself that, the more I believe it. If it weren't for his comforting touch on the way over, I'd have thought I lost him to the HPA.

I lick my lips. "I said I'd cooperate."

The side of Dr. Sullivan's mouth twitches up into an almost smile. Pulling her pen from her pocket, she taps it on her clipboard. She scribbles something down and then brings her eyes to mine.

Dread runs its slimy fingers down my back. Dr. Sullivan's eyes might look like Hunter's, but they lack the life and strength that shine through his. Where he is love and adoration, she is cold and calculated. Dr. Sullivan's world is black and white and empty, and Hunter's is vibrant and colorful, full of everything that makes him good. They couldn't be more different.

"Now where did we leave off?" Dr. Sullivan knows exactly where we left off. It's why I'm back in this room again, only this time with Hunter instead of Dr. Harvey. She taps her pen on her clipboard again. "Oh, yes. I have a list of questions I need you to answer before transferring you for some more blood tests."

I blink. "Go on." I can't stop the terror from knotting my stomach. They haven't tested my blood since my arrival, because my DNA read human. *Why now? Did I mess up?*

"You stated you are human," Dr. Sullivan says.

"Because I am." I wring my hands together in my lap. I hope I didn't sound too defensive, but I think if I were fully human, I'd still hold strong to the idea, knowing what the HPA is looking for. I just don't want to give them reason to dig deeper, search harder.

Hunter nudges me. "Let Dr. Sullivan finish."

It takes all of my willpower to keep my face from giving anything away, my heart aching.

"You stated you're human," Dr Sullivan repeats. "But what I want to know is who sent you to interrupt the transfer of one of our most interesting subjects? Obviously he was someone special to go through the trouble. No one has ever done what you did. The board also thinks you know who was responsible for the attack that happened a few days prior. If you'd tell me, things would go more smoothly for you."

I blink again. She's referring to my father and just thinking about him sends my heart racing. No one has inquired about the accident since the intense interrogation during the first week. I'm not sure what's triggering the board to ask about it again. "I don't know what you're talking about. No one sent me. Your dumb van rear-ended my friend, and some man tried to kill me."

Dr. Sullivan shifts on the couch. "Your friend?"

Oh, no. I shouldn't have used that word. "My acquaintance. I barely knew Evangeline." Which is true. I wasn't in school long enough to grow our friendship into one like I have with Alyssa. I wonder what Evie is doing now. I wonder if the HPA got to her yet. "I already told you people all this. Why ask again? Why keep me here. This is against the law." Acting human is hard. I don't know much about human law considering I spent most of my life under Creature Council law, but I'm pretty sure after watching a few TV shows with Alyssa, this wouldn't happen in the human world I'm claiming to be a part of.

"Emily," Hunter says, his tone not as sharp as before, but still hard enough to make me wince.

I crinkle my nose and glare at him.

Dr. Sullivan shifts. "It's all right, Agent Hunter. It's a fair question." She turns her eyes to me, and I drop my gaze back to my hands. "I figured you'd had enough time to clear your head. You can't possibly want to spend the rest of your life here, do you?"

It's a trick question. It has to be. I don't know how to answer it so all I do is shrug.

Dr. Sullivan scribbles another sentence on her paper. "Now getting back on topic. You knew Evangeline enough to convince her to drive you. Did anyone else help you?"

I press my lips together. If I answer too quickly, she'll know I'm lying. I'd never mention Alyssa, who managed to get away with my father unnoticed. Who knows what the HPA would do to someone with Alyssa's ability. They'd try to use her for sure. The creature world would be doomed with a seer in the HPA's hands.

Hunter nudges me again. "You need to respond."

I glower at Hunter again. I can't help it. Being under Dr. Sullivan's scrutiny is hard enough, but now with Hunter, probably freaking out over every word I'm forced to offer, things are worse. He's counting on me not to mess up, but I don't have the sort of training to get me through this. I'm not my dad. He'd know what to say.

Clearing my throat, I say, "You promised to remove the restraints if I answered her first question."

He tugs my hands from my lap, locking his fingers around mine, and unlocks the metal cuffs that were loose enough to slide my hands out of if I wanted to. He's playing tough for Dr. Sullivan, but the slight tremble of his fingers screams how much he would prefer to continue holding my hand rather than pushing me away. He does so anyway. "Now respond to Dr. Sullivan or they go back on."

I jerk my head toward Dr. Sullivan and scowl. "I paid her to take me to the mall."

Dr. Sullivan raises an eyebrow. "The nearest mall was thirty miles from the scene of the accident."

"So what?" Anger rushes through me, shadowing my vision. Dr. Sullivan's interrogation claws under my skin and puts me more on edge than usual. I'm losing control. All I can think about is the glint of the knife Agent Rob held to my throat, the look on Hunter's face when he thought I was going to die, and watching Jacqueline charge to fight as the world closed in on me. I hate reliving that day so much. It's the second worst day in my life since watching an agent murder my mother.

Dr. Sullivan slams the clipboard down on the coffee table. "You're lying!" Her threatening voice echoes through the room, causing me to flinch as if her words slapped me. She points her pen at me. "I know you're working with the council."

Tears cloud my eyes, my vision blurring. I can't keep up with her. I can't think of responses fast enough.

I need to get out of here.

Dr. Sullivan will push me over the edge. I'm going to lose control of my nightmare inflictor side, and it'll reveal me as the monster they make me out to be. I want nothing more than to fly across the table and wrap my pale fingers around her neck, proving her right. The HPA doesn't find monsters among creatures. They turn them into monsters through places like this. They make us want to hurt them.

Before Hunter has a chance to grab me, I stand up and strut around the table to Dr. Sullivan, clenching my hands into fists at my side. Rage courses through my veins in hot waves. If it weren't for Hunter rushing up behind me, I'd do something that would get me killed.

"Are you crazy!" I scream. "I'd never work for the council. They've done nothing but ruin my life as much as you have."

I turn to glance at Hunter. Fear rims his beautiful hazel eyes as he stands in shock. If I'm to die right here in this room, he'll be the last one I see before death can wrap its cold arms around me and take me to a place where I can forget about everything.

HUNTER

"Hunter, stop her!" Jacqueline's voice yells in my head, her fear magnifying my own.

Nadia stands two feet away, staring down Dr. Sullivan with eyes full of hate. I stiffen, preparing to watch Nadia kill Dr. Sullivan in front of me.

Shock and disbelief course through me at Nadia's revelation about her spite toward the Creature Council. And now, I'm not sure what'll happen. Something in Nadia broke. I can see it in her angry indigo eyes, and I wish I had the courage to fight our way out of here right this second, but it'd be a death sentence for both of us. The morning shift starts soon and agents will swarm the place, getting their assignments. I couldn't possibly take them all.

"Use your tranquilizer!"

Jacqueline's voice kicks me into action. Drawing my tranquilizer gun from my weaponry belt, I aim it at Nadia and pull the trigger. A dart whizzes through the air and sinks into her arm, causing her to cry out. Pain and despair sweep across her face, shattering my strength into a million pieces. I close the distance between us and catch her before she falls onto the coffee table.

Easing her limp body to the cold tiles, I glance up at Dr. Sullivan peering at Nadia on the floor. She turns her attention to me, her eyes shining with mixed emotions—annoyance, relief, pride, something indecipherable.

It takes all my willpower not to pick up Nadia from the floor. Instead, I plop down on the couch next to Dr. Sullivan. "Are you all right?"

She grins. "I'm better than all right, Hunter. We've just had a breakthrough. I wish you hadn't tranquilized her, though. She wasn't going to hurt me."

She moves her hand from her lap to pat my knee, and I

close my eyes for a second to control myself. I'd slap her hand away if I could.

"Tell her you were following protocol." Jacqueline's smooth voice loosens the knots in my stomach.

"I was following protocol. You know it's mandatory to sedate subjects who get agitated."

Dr. Sullivan smiles. "I guess I'll have to make an exception with Human 9209." She stands up and touches my shoulder. "Good work, though, Hunter. Return Human 9209 back to her cell. We'll try again tomorrow."

Nodding, I press my lips together. I was afraid of this. Nadia's outburst has inspired more intrigue from Dr. Sullivan, which means more interest from the board.

Dr. Sullivan saunters from the room and leaves the door open behind her without saying anything more.

I bend down and scoop Nadia's unconscious body into my arms, holding her tighter than I should. This is the first time in weeks I've been able to put my arms around her. It takes everything in me not to kiss her pale blond hair, to snuggle my face into the nape of her neck.

I drag myself from the room, walking slower than I should, to give me time to soak everything in about my soul mate. "I'm sorry, Nadia," I think to myself. "I hope you can forgive me."

"She already does," Jacqueline says, interrupting my personal thought.

"Seriously, Jackie?"

"If you hid your thoughts better, maybe I wouldn't comment."

"Not everyone is as good at hosting souls as you."

Nadia stirs in my arms as I take the elevator to the basement. She struggles in my hold, swinging her head wildly, and then she snaps her eyes open and meets my gaze. Blinking a few times, she relaxes and closes her eyes, sinking against me in a way that makes me want to attempt to walk out of the facility with her in my arms.

Without saying anything, she subtly buries her head in my shoulder. Her cool breath tickles my neck, and I swallow a few times, desire rushing over me with her unintentionally teasing me. I release a quiet moan in my throat, holding utterly still. Using her hair to veil her face, she shifts, acting like she's coming to from sedation, unaware of what's happening and risks kissing my collarbone, driving me insane.

I automatically shift her away and dig my fingers into her side, telling her how much I wish things were different right now, how much I need her. She responds by pressing her chin into my shoulder. I keep my eyes trained on the elevator door instead of reacting, watching it ding open. Forcing my legs to move, I carry Nadia the rest of the way back to her cell as she pretends to stir from sedation.

I sling her over my shoulder and punch in my pass code, kicking the door open with my boot. Camden glares as I ease Nadia onto her cot, and I do my best to ignore him and how much concern he has for my girlfriend.

My boots squeak on the tiles. I peer around once, watching Nadia peek at me through her half opened eyelids, and head toward the door without saying another word.

Before I close it, I hear Camden say, "Oh, God. What did

that monster do?"

The door clicks shut behind me, cutting off Nadia's response. If it wasn't for her sitting in that cell, I'd be rushing toward the door and out the building. I don't know how much more of this I can take before I break. If Dmitri doesn't tell me a plan soon, then I'll come up with my own plan. He doesn't see her like this. If he did, he'd do the same.

3

WORTHLESS

NADIA

"EMILY?"

I keep my eyes shut, savoring the memory of feeling Hunter's arms around me for as long as possible. It's the first real touch we've shared in weeks. My heart aches so badly to be with him.

"Emily? What did they do to you?"

Camden pulls me into his arms and brushes my hair from my face, inspecting my face. I squeeze my eyes shut tighter and purse my lips, before finally peeking through my lashes to meet his worried gaze.

Leaning closer, I rest my head on his shoulder. "I messed

up." My voice comes out inaudibly to anyone except Camden with my lips nearly touching his ear. "They know I know about the council. I couldn't control my anger."

He stiffens, leaning back to stare at me. His narrow eyes shift from mine to the door and back to mine. We study each other for a long moment, both of us tense and quiet, a million unsaid words swirling between us.

I press my lips together, watching him gather his thoughts. Camden knows the truth about my ability—I couldn't keep it from him because I needed him to know about my nightmare inflictor side. He needed to know his nightmares weren't his own doing but mine. It's what brought us closer together yet keeps me guarded with him, because he not only faces the threat of the HPA but me.

He licks his lips and leans toward my ear, his beard tickling my neck. "What exactly did you say?"

I shiver. "That I hated them."

He shuts his eyes and takes a deep breath. A million thoughts crinkle his forehead. I'm not sure what I expect him to say. All I know is I screwed up and the HPA may deem me useless. What good is a prisoner if they're not working for the enemy? What good am I if I don't have connections to the council? My information is worthless.

Turning away from him, I stare at my hands. Camden reaches up and touches my chin, guiding my head up so I have to look at him. Even though he's technically human, the blood of the Enchantress Sisterhood flows through his veins and gives him a sixth sense of how to read people. He can't manipulate them like enchantresses, but he is an accurate judge of character.

"This isn't necessarily a bad thing," he finally says after a minute. "But it's going to be tricky."

I blow air through my lips. "Not bad? I'm of no use to them."

"That's not true. You still know the council."

I suck in my top lip. He's right. I didn't think about it that way. I was trying my best to appear as an uninvolved human, but maybe I was going about this the wrong way. I wish I could talk to Alyssa for five minutes to see what she thinks. *She'd tell you she couldn't tell you unless you make some sort of decision.*

I nod. "You're right. It doesn't make me feel any better though. I hate this."

He wraps his arms around me, his comforting touch the only thing I'm now used to after so many weeks. I lean against his chest for a moment before pulling back and sliding off his lap, putting space between us. As much as I could use the comfort, I can't jeopardize my resolve and allow him in. Moving to the desk, I plop down in the seat. I open my sketchbook and notice the drawings I did this morning have been ripped out.

Smiling to myself, I look at Camden still sitting on my cot.

"A doctor took them," he says, responding to my silent inquiry.

I force a loud sigh even though I knew someone would take my meaningless drawings. "You should let me finish them sometime!" I yell at the camera.

Camden turns away and smirks at me. "You're funny," he mouths.

I continue to glare at the camera. "Can you at least bring them back when you're done this time?"

Huffing, I get up from the desk and throw myself onto Camden's cot since he's on mine, rolling over to face the wall. I need to collect all my thoughts to figure out a plan. I need to make a decision. Camden's even breathing trickles to me, and I feel his eyes on my back, watching me.

Without wanting to talk anymore, I pretend to fall asleep.

It's all I can do to keep calm and in control.

If only I could really lose myself to my own dreams. Because right now, I have no reprieve.

HUNTER

I TURN MY gaze away from the video feed of Nadia's cell when she flops on the bed away from Camden and look over the other video streams. I have twelve cells filled with sixteen charges in my zone—five humans, six shifters, one forest nymph, and four unidentified species—at least that's what my log says. In actuality, there are three humans, an enchantress's son, a forest nymph, seven shifters, two pixies, an adolescent ogre, and Nadia, a nightmare inflictor. I had seventeen charges, but a pixie threw his glitter dust in my face and there was nothing I could do to save him. I didn't even know his name.

I study each cell for a second, then lean back in my chair and lace my fingers on the back of my head. This is the boring part of my job, sitting and watching, but it's necessary to please the board.

If I visit the cells too often, they'll become suspicious, so I visit each cell six times a day—three to drop off meals, two to ask questions, and one to hand out extra water. Occasionally I'll visit an extra time but only when instructed to do so. I can't make special trips, and it sucks. I want to visit Nadia every few minutes to ask her if she's okay even if I can see that she's managing.

"There's nothing going on between Nadia and Camden," Jacqueline says, invading my thoughts.

I press my lips into a line and think, "I know that."

"But you're jealous."

"And? It should be me comforting Nadia."

"Then give up your freedom and join her in a cell."

"What a fantastic idea." Aggravation swells in my mind, and I imagine shoving Jacqueline into a void like the billion times she did it to me.

She laughs. *"You'll have to try harder."*

"Do you seriously want me to shove you into the void?"

She sighs. *"No, not really."*

"Then maybe keep your thoughts to yourself. I'm trying to work."

"I was only trying to help. I can feel how hard this is on you."

Leaning forward, I bring my gaze to Nadia's cell again. "But it's a thousand times worse for her."

The elevator dings open, and Malory Banks, Dr. Harvey's laboratory assistant, steps out. Her light brown hair hangs behind her in a hair tie, looking messier than usual, and an unidentifiable brown stain decorates the front of her lab coat. She pulls a manila folder out from under her arm and waves it as she greets me with a straight smile. I don't smile back but only nod.

"The lab wanted to return these to Human 9209," Malory says, handing me the folder.

I open it and look at a couple sloppily drawn stick figures with random names, what appears to be a prison scene, and a sunset. I lift my eyebrows. "What for?"

She shrugs. "I guess she asked."

I glance from Malory's green eyes to the monitor. Nadia faces the wall, still lying on a cot. "And when do you guys ever do what the subjects ask?"

She laughs. "Haven't you heard? The board wants us to comply to her demands as best we can. They think she holds the answers to information they think can help them give us the upper hand in this war."

War? The board thinks we're fighting a war? It's hard not to roll my eyes. "I guess my memo is running a little late. I'll give them to Emily when I distribute lunch."

Malory clears her throat, and I shift my gaze from the monitor to her. "They said immediately."

The chair creaks as I stand. "Fine. I'll see you later then." I walk from the monitor and leave Malory at the viewing station. The click-clack of her shoes echoes as she heads back to the elevator, but I don't look behind me to watch her go.

I tap on Nadia's cell door and pound in my pass code. Peering through the crack, I catch sight of Camden looking up at me from Nadia's assigned cot.

Camden crosses his arms. "Kind of early for a visit."

Entering the room, I flick my gaze to Nadia still pretending to sleep and to the camera in the corner of the room. "Apparently this couldn't wait."

Nadia sits up on the cot, flinging the sheet off her face. "What's so important? It's impossible to sleep around here with everyone always bothering us." She rubs her eyes as she looks at me and holds my stare for a moment before dropping her gaze to her hands.

I hold up the manila folder with her sketches. "You asked for your sketches back."

She crinkles her nose. "Well, thanks. They're important to me."

I clear my throat to stop myself from laughing. "You're quite the artist, Emily. Maybe you can draw me something sometime."

She blushes. "I'll think about it. You have a lot of making up to do for tranquilizing me, Agent Hunter."

I glance at Camden, rubbing his beard. For a second, it felt like I was alone in the room with Nadia. "Yeah, dude, that was cold."

"You don't know cold," I say, more threat in my voice than necessary.

Sliding off the cot, Nadia shuffles to me. She snatches the manila folder from my hand, but before she walks away, I reach out and grip her shoulder. She meets my gaze, a mixture of surprise and fear in her eyes, causing me to flinch.

She must see the pain in my eyes, because she relaxes under my touch. "What? You going to tranquilize me again?" Even though she doesn't smile, her voice does.

"No, I only wanted to apologize, Emily, but it was your

own fault."

She blows strands of hair from her face and shakes out of my hold. Swaying her hips just enough to send my heart racing, she struts to the opposite wall and leans against it. She tucks the folder under her arm and then says, "No, actually, it wasn't. But thanks for apologizing."

I nod and shift my gaze to Camden, who watches Nadia. "You two need anything while I'm here?"

"Yeah, some entertainment," Camden says.

"How about some music?" Nadia asks.

I raise an eyebrow. "Seriously?"

"You know they don't mess around." Jacqueline was so quiet I almost forgot she was in my head. Almost.

Camden pulls on his beard. "Do we look like we're joking?"

I shrug. "All right. I'll see what I can do."

NADIA

I smile at Hunter. "Yes, please do. You don't know what it's like being stuck in a box with nothing to do." As the words escape my lips, I immediately regret them. Being trapped in another person's mind wasn't easy for him, and he knows what being trapped is like. I think I'm better off than he was. At least people know I'm here, and I don't have to rely on a stranger to get me out.

He frowns for a second. If I wasn't studying him so intently, I would've missed it. The corner of his lips twitches up, and he runs his hand through his dark, curly hair that hasn't been cut since I was taken. "I guess not."

Turning from me, he strolls out the door. I wish I could chase after him to tell him I wasn't thinking. I hope he understands. *Of course he understands. You're not supposed to know his history.*

Camden shuffles up next to me and tugs the manila folder from under my arm. He flips it open, stares at my stick figures, and then tosses it on the desk. We gaze at each other in our peripheral vision before he slides his arm over my shoulders.

I turn into him, wrapping my arms around his neck. "That was weird," I whisper.

He touches his lips to my ear. "Why would the board return those?"

From the way we're hugging, no one watching us can tell we're having a conversation. It looks like Camden comforts me, and it's the only way we can have private conversations. The board probably thinks there's more to our relationship, and we won't let them know otherwise because it seems to work. They think we'll slip up eventually. *Like you already did.*

Pushing the thought away, I whisper, "Whatever the reason, it can't be good. Maybe it has to do with my slip up."

Camden's breath tickles me. "I don't like it."

I rest my head on his shoulder. "Me either. I'm scared."

He rubs circles on my back, reminding me of Hunter. I wish I was having this conversation with him instead. I wish my arms were around his neck with his lips against my ear. I'm afraid I won't ever be with him again. What if no one can save me? *Then you'll save yourself.*

HUNTER

Dr. Sullivan waits at my desk when I emerge from the cell block. Her brown hair hangs loosely over her shoulders, her glasses resting on top of her head. She smiles when she sees me, and I hold my expression neutral.

"Well, if that isn't the smile of the devil," Jacqueline says.

I chuckle in my mind. "I think the devil would be afraid of my mom."

Dr. Sullivan touches my arm when I close the distance between us. "Did Malory come by yet?"

I nod. "Yeah, what's the deal with complying with Emily's demands?"

"Isn't it obvious, Hunter?" She raises her eyebrows and waits for me to answer.

"You want answers?" I ask, rubbing my chin.

She clicks her tongue. "It's more than that. You see, Emily's hatred toward the council is extremely useful to us. We need to find out why and figure out a way to get her to see the bigger picture. It should be easy enough to convince her. Maybe even make a deal."

My jaw twitches. This is bad.

"They want Nadia to join them. They think they can convince her that humanity needs to be saved from monsters. Training a new recruit already involved in the creature world, one fearless like Nadia, is far easier than pulling in a random person off the street."

I exhale a long breath through my nose. "Except Nadia isn't really human," I think. "And she'd never risk the lives of people, even if she hates the council."

"We're going to start with small sessions like the one today," Dr. Sullivan continues. "Get a better feel for things. Gauge her interest. I think she might like you, you know. We can use that."

I clear my throat, uncomfortable with the way the direction heads. "Sounds like a plan."

Her eyes shine. "It's a good one. I can feel it. I think as long as I keep you involved, she'll be compliant. There's something about you the subjects trust. We have to take advantage of it."

"Yeah, because we're not the enemy," Jacqueline says. I imagine her telling that to Dr. Sullivan's face and the shock and fear that would follow.

I focus my attention on Dr. Sullivan and say, "It might be because I call them by their names."

Dr. Sullivan presses her lips together. "Among other things."

"Yeah, like treating people, even creatures, like people and not monsters or experiments."

The elevator dings open, and a server from the kitchen rolls a cart with covered trays of food. He parks it just outside of the elevator and doesn't say anything as he gets back on and stares at the ground when the door slides closed.

I strut to the cart and wheel it to my desk. "If you don't mind, I have some work to do."

Dr. Sullivan grabs her clipboard from my desk and tucks it under her arm. "After you deliver lunch, why don't you take a few hours off? I'd like to schedule another session tonight, and I know how overworked you are. Maybe you can give Mason a call. He's been complaining about you not hanging out with him."

"I know you're going to argue, but don't. Agree with her."

I nod even though Mason is not one of my top people I'd like to see when I'm not at the facility. "Sure, I'll do that. Maybe he'll help me catch up on some laundry."

Dr. Sullivan laughs and shakes her head. "Good luck with that. I'll see you tonight, Hunter."

"Hurry up and pass the trays out. We have somewhere to be."

I don't have to ask. For the first time in weeks, things with Nadia have changed, and I need to tell Dmitri. I just wish they'd have changed for the better.

4

UNCERTAIN

HUNTER

I PARK MY BMW wagon on the corner of Northern Bell Road and Sacada Lane, a block away from Northern Bell High School. Even after everything that happened, Alyssa still chooses to attend school. Things are different though. Evie, Nadia's only other friend at the school, suddenly transferred out the day after Nadia was taken. I've never asked about Evie, but I know the board was involved in her situation. She's probably living with her mom now, being force fed inaccurate information about the supernatural world—maybe even had her memories manipulated to overwrite any sort of friendship she had with Nadia.

Funny though, if only the board spent more time scrutinizing Northern Bell, they'd have discovered the truth about Nadia and Evie's friendship. Luckily, they think because they have Nadia, they're one step closer to any information they seek.

Alyssa steps from the brick building and pounds down the steps. Hugging her jacket tighter around her, she jogs through the slushy snow melting on the school's lawn. I don't drive closer but wait as she strolls in my direction. I can't risk being seen here in my uniform. It would only mean trouble.

Leaning over, I swing the door open for Alyssa. She tosses her backpack on the floor and climbs in. "I called Dmitri. He's going to meet us at the park near my house. He has some people over, and it's not a good idea if they see you."

I put my car in drive and pull away from the curb. "Have you seen anything?"

She stares at me while I stare at the road. "No one has made any decisions about Nadia, if that's what you're asking."

"Alyssa will only tell you things that are important."

"Think she'll tell me when I'll get rid of you?" I think to Jacqueline.

"Don't worry. You'll be the first to know."

"I'm starting to think you enjoy spending every moment with me."

"Oh, shut up, Hunter."

I grin at my reflection in the rearview mirror. "Yeah, that's what I'm asking," I say to Alyssa. "Things are changing, and I'm not sure if it's good or bad."

She holds up her hand. "Dmitri should be the first to hear

it from you."

Pressing my lips together, I turn on the radio. We only listen to one song before the park comes into view, and I see Dmitri leaning against his black pickup truck. He wears a tan trench coat and black slacks. Dark sunglasses hide his onyx eyes, and he crosses his arms over his chest. When I park next to his truck, instead of waiting for us to get out, he slides into my backseat.

I leave the engine running to keep the air warm. Unbuckling my seatbelt, I swivel in my seat so I can meet his eyes. He tugs off his sunglasses and tucks them away in his coat and then leans on his elbows.

"What changed?" Dmitri's voice low voice rumbles over the engine, like he's on edge, and I don't blame him. "I thought you worked a double today."

I tap my fingers on my knee. "I was given the afternoon off, but it's not important. I'm here because Nadia slipped up. She was being interrogated and let them get to her, letting her emotions get the best of her. She screamed she hated the council."

He shifts his gaze to Alyssa. "So, they know she knows the council. Nothing else." It's not a question but a thought.

Alyssa stares off into space before looking at me. "What aren't you telling us, Hunter? I saw Nadia in a different room. It had a green couch."

"That's the interrogation room. Nadia's going to be there a lot. The HPA considers Nadia's outburst a breakthrough. They think they can use her against the council."

Dmitri's brows furrow. "That makes perfect sense."

"A human who knows and hates the council—they probably think they've hit the jackpot. I bet they hope Nadia will be wearing a uniform soon." Alyssa grimaces as she looks at me.

"The council would never trust Nadia as an agent. Her story about freeing Dmitri and working with an agent against the HPA will never add up. You know that's the truth." Jacqueline's anger swells in my mind and rubs off on me. It's hard to separate her emotions from mine.

I shake my head. "Doubt it. Unless she can spin a story that puts all the puzzle pieces together for the day she was taken, it'll never happen. And then there's Evie. I haven't heard about her, or from her, since her mom picked her up, and she knows the true story. If the board pressures her enough, she'll crack."

"Evie won't tell," Alyssa says. "She's scared of what the board will do to her. I've seen her make the decision to keep her mouth shut anytime the topic is brought up by her mom."

Dmitri's phone rings and draws my attention away from Alyssa. His eyes cloud with his own thoughts, and I wonder what they're about. He's always calculated and in control, only talking when it's important.

He holds his finger up and answers. "Yes? That's right. I can be there in ten." Hanging up the phone, he turns to me. "Keep in touch with Alyssa. I'm meeting some people out of town later and will be harder to reach."

I frown. "What if something happens before you're back?"

He stiffens. "You'll figure it out. I trust you to protect my daughter."

Opening the door, he gets out. Cold air trickles in when he shuts it, and I turn to look out my windshield without looking at Alyssa. If something happens while Dmitri is away, we're going to be screwed. Every time I try to come up with some foolproof plan to save Nadia, I come up short. I can't fight dozens of agents alone, and Jacqueline isn't exactly up for helping. If it came down to it, either Nadia or I aren't going to survive. Maybe we'll both die.

"You might not think so, but I'm not useless without my body. I'm a fighter, and I'm not letting you give up so easily. You can't die until I'm ready to body jump."

I rub my temples and think, "Nice to hear the old Jackie I know and appreciate."

"Hunter?" Alyssa nudges my arm. "Did you hear me?"

I shake my head and glance at her. "Sorry, I was thinking about how Nadia and I will survive if something goes wrong."

She offers a small smile. "It won't. At least not today. Do you still have that napkin I gave you earlier?"

I nod, pull it from my pocket, and hand it to her. She grabs a pencil from her backpack and scribbles something else on it. I don't peek over her arm to see. If she wanted me to know what was on the note to Nadia, she'd tell me, and I can't break her confidence in me even though I'm curious as to what she has to tell Nadia.

She hands me the note. "I need you to give this to Nadia before seven now but not with dinner. You'll have to figure something out."

I shove the napkin in my pocket. "I'll try."

She grimaces. "Just do it. It's important."

I sigh. "Okay, I will." I glance at the rearview mirror. "Where to now?"

"Back to my school. Mr. Augustine is waiting for me."

NADIA

I lie next to Camden on the small cot, and we stare at the ceiling together. We haven't moved in what feels like forever. I wonder why Hunter hasn't stopped by. He usually passes out water bottles before dinner, and because I hear Camden's stomach growling, I know it'll be here soon. I hope nothing bad happened to Hunter. It's torturous enough staying here as it is. It would be my own personal nightmare without him.

"What are you thinking about?" Camden asks.

I roll to my side to look at his bearded face. His aqua blue eyes shine in the fluorescent lighting, and he doesn't meet my gaze. "How much I miss the stars." It's a lie, and the way Camden stares at me in his peripheral vision shows he knows it, but as long as we're in here, I'll never tell him the truth about Hunter.

Camden shifts on the bed and faces me. "It's funny how you don't really think about those things until you don't have them anymore, huh?"

Reaching out my hand, I tap my finger to his nose. "What do you miss?"

"Besides good food?" He laughs. "I don't know."

I roll my eyes. "You have to miss something."

He twists his lips to the side in thought and then after a moment smiles. It lights up his whole face, and the simple expression makes me smile. It feels weird to do it, but I can't stop myself. "I got it. I miss driving."

I laugh. "Yeah, I definitely don't miss that. I prefer walking."

"Really?"

I lick my dry lips. "No." I actually hate walking now. It's not fun having to calculate every step I make. I miss gliding. How much faster and freer the movements are. I lean close to Camden and press my lips to his ear.

My pale blond hair veils our faces, and I whisper, "What I really miss is being me."

Camden shifts and slides his arm over my side. His lips brush my cheek, and I pull back. I offer him a small smile and turn to look at the ceiling again. It's strange how comforting it is to lie here next to him. We've bonded over our circumstances, and it's better than being alone. But, even when I look into his aqua blue eyes, I imagine Hunter, and guilt sweeps through me. It's not his fault he can't be with me. I wouldn't want him in this cell anyway.

A knock bangs on the door. I get up and move to the wall like I always do. Crossing my arms over my chest, I glance from Camden, who sits up and throws his legs over the edge of the bed, to the door. It cracks open, and Hunter peeks in, sending my heart thudding faster. It's like he knew I was thinking about him. I lean my back against the wall so I don't step closer like my feet want to do.

"Sorry I'm late with the waters," Hunter says, setting four bottles on the small table by the door.

He brings his gaze from the table to me. His brows pinch together, his forehead crinkling with worry while his hazel eyes seem duller than usual. He slides his hand into his pocket and just stares at me, like he expects me to read his mind.

I study him, reading him the best I can. Spotting the corner of a napkin sticking out from his pocket, I realize he has a note for me, but he can't just pull it out and give it to me. Alyssa times these things perfectly, but today, something is different. She's making Hunter risk exposure to give me a message.

"What was the hold up?" Camden asks, drawing my attention away from Hunter and the note.

I'm glad someone says something, before things got too awkward with Hunter standing there.

Hunter breaks his stare with me. "None of your concern."

Stepping away from the wall, I stroll to the desk, raking my teeth over my bottom lip, hoping Hunter lingers for as long as he can while I come up with a reason to approach him. "It's never our concern, Cam," I say, sitting at the desk. I flip open my notebook without looking up.

Hunter hovers in the doorway. "Do you two need anything else?"

I raise my arm, waving it out. "Yeah, wait a second."

Peeking up, I meet his gaze for a second, a smile playing on my lips. He shifts his wait, shoving his hands deeper into his pockets.

"Hurry up, will you?" he asks, trying to sound annoyed but relief laces his words.

I tilt my head up and glare, pointing my finger at him.

"Please."

Without responding, he watches me with hot intensity, probably wondering what I'm planning. Pulling a blue crayon from its box, I sketch out the waves of the ocean. I add black clouds and a brown pier, and then scribble a circle with a few lines on the pier. My five-second drawing of the second time Hunter and I met in Jacqueline's dream world is pretty bad, but I need an excuse to go to Hunter. He's the only one who'll know what it means, and I hope it'll make him smile.

I jump up from the desk and jog to him, stopping close enough that his minty breath blows strands of hair from my face. "Here's the picture you wanted. You still owe me some music, though." In the spot we're standing, we're just out of view from the camera positioned on the wall. Hunter slides his hand with the napkin from his pocket and reaches out to grab the sketch from me. I crumple the napkin in my hand and turn away, strutting back to the desk. "And I want it soon. We're so bored."

Hunter's eyes smile despite his serious expression. I wish I could see him smile again. "I told you, Emily, I'll see what I can do." He exits the cell, closing the door behind him, staring through the window for a moment before disappearing.

My heartbeat pounds in my ears, and my hands stay clenched as I hold onto the napkin note. It's been two weeks since I got one, and I wasn't sure I'd ever get one again. It's a huge risk for Hunter—a huge risk for both of us.

Taking a deep breath, I turn toward the tiny bathroom. It doesn't have a door to prevent us from locking ourselves in and contains only a toilet and showerhead. I shuffle across the room, and before I enter the bathroom, Camden gets off the bed and walks to the door. We try to give each other as much privacy as we can.

I smile and sit down on the toilet lid. It takes a moment to get up the nerve to open my hand. I'm both excited and terrified to read the note from Alyssa. I'm excited because it gives me a thread of hope that it'll tell me she's going to rescue me, but I'm terrified it'll have bad news instead—like the HPA caught my father again or something, or she had a premonition that someone will die. It's the uncertainty that always has me on edge.

I stretch my fingers out and straighten the napkin on the palm of my hand. My heart sinks into my stomach. It's not a note telling me I'm being rescued. It's a sketch—a beautiful, detailed sketch of me pressing my forehead to Camden's. What pulls at my heart isn't the image itself. I know who my heart belongs to, but there's a note written along Camden's jawline. It says, *Careful, his love for you is going to get him killed.*

I swipe my hand across my watery eyes. I was not expecting to hear anything like this. I need to put a stop to this. Camden wasn't supposed to fall for me. He was aware of how we needed to act so the HPA wouldn't question the sporadic times we share a bed. Why didn't I see it happening? Maybe I can get Hunter to transfer me.

Folding the napkin in half, I blink the tears away. I notice the sketch isn't the only thing written on the napkin. Along the edge, written in pencil, is a note that says, *Trust yourself to get you through the next few days.*

I ball up the napkin and toss it into the toilet before flushing. I wish Alyssa would spell things out. How can I trust myself, someone who is so uncertain about everything? What if I make the wrong decisions? What if it's impossible for me to get myself through this? I've always relied on my family and friends to help me through things. What if I'm not strong enough?

I shake the thought from my head. *You can do it. You've always managed before.*

But what if managing isn't enough to keep me alive?

5

FIGHT FOR HER

HUNTER

"MOM SAID YOU were going to call me. What gives?" Mason isn't even a foot out of the elevator before he starts interrogating me.

I turn away from the monitor. "Sorry, bro. I got busy."

"Right." Mason strolls up next to me and pulls up a chair.

I should've called him, at least to say hi, but I didn't feel like it. There's no point in maintaining a relationship with him since the HPA already got to him. He'll only be around here for a short while longer, and then—I'm not sure. He'll either be dead because he wasn't strong enough to survive the genetic alteration the HPA asked him to be a part of, or he'll be on a special division of the Special Abilities Task Force—which is basically like being dead to me as well.

I shrug. "You try working sixteen hour days and tell me if you still want to hang out."

Mason taps his fingers on my desk and stares at the video feed of the cells. "I could offer to help."

I lean forward. "You're an intern at the lab. It's better to stay there. You'll learn more."

"You could teach him things, too, Hunter. Your brother isn't lost to you yet." Jacqueline's voice swirls through my mind.

I stare at my hands and think, "He'll be soon enough."

"You don't know that."

I sigh but don't respond to her. The thing is, I do know he's lost to me. He's been lost to me for months. I can't ever trust him because he doesn't see any fault with our mom. He doesn't see how she manipulates or how she puts the HPA before everyone. Who knows, maybe Mason does, too. It's why he's willing to put his life on the line.

Mason swivels back and forth in his chair. "Well, the offer is open if you need me."

I roll my shoulders and bring my attention back to Mason. "Cool."

Leaning forward, I stare at the video feed of Nadia's cell. My chest tightens as I watch Camden stare at her. Even through the fuzzy feed, his eyes shine with intensity, like he's staring into her soul. I don't like it.

I pull my gaze from the monitor and add, "You should probably get out of here before the board complains I'm not working. I have a few things I need to do."

"I'll help," Mason says.

"No, really, it's okay."

Mason furrows his brows. "What's your problem, Hunter? It feels like you don't want me around."

His sudden outburst surprises me, causing anger to slither through my veins. I have a few choice words for him, and I grind my teeth to stop myself from yelling the real reason I'm acting like this.

"Careful what you say, Hunter," Jacqueline says.

I ignore her.

"Are you still hung up about the SATF? I thought you'd be over it by now," Mason adds.

I shake my head and glare at him. "It was never about that, Mase."

"Hunter!" Jacqueline screams.

I snap my mouth closed before I lose control.

"Then what is it?" Mason asks.

I inhale a long breath. "I have work to do. You should go." I point to the elevator as I stand up.

Mason frowns and pushes to his feet. "Okay. See you around then." He strolls to the elevator, and I sit back down in my chair when the door slides shut.

"You almost ruined everything," Jacqueline says.

I squeeze my eyes shut and think, "You don't have to tell me that."

"But I do."

"Whatever, Jackie. Just leave me alone for a minute. I need

to prepare myself for Nadia's interrogation." I don't need this from Jacqueline—especially not right now. I need to focus and figure out an escape plan if something goes wrong while Dr. Sullivan is here.

"Everything will be fine, Hunter."

"Seriously, Jackie."

"Shutting up now."

Blowing out a breath, I focus on Nadia's cell. Watching her gives me the strength to know that as long as she's on my side, we'll get through this.

We don't have a choice otherwise.

NADIA

I perch on the edge of my cot and stare at my hands. Camden sits across the small room on his and watches me. I peek through my hair veiling my face and study him. His blue eyes try to capture me, like he tries to read my thoughts. I wish he'd look away. He's waiting for me to acknowledge him, and I don't want to. Maybe if I ignore him long enough, he'll start despising me.

It's not like I can tell him about Alyssa's vision without giving Hunter away either. He knows I'm a nightmare inflictor and not a seer, so I can't play it off like I'm the one who predicts the future.

He sighs.

I press my lips together. *Don't do it. Don't look at him.*

His cot creaks when he moves. My heart races, hearing him step closer. I squeeze my eyes shut, willing him to stop in his tracks, or willing myself to disappear. The thin mattress shifts, and then Camden touches my knee.

I stiffen. Not because I'm uncomfortable with him being so close, but because I'm trying to resist melting into him. Feelings for Camden have never really crossed my mind until this moment. I don't know if it was the image Alyssa put in my head, or if it's the thousands of morbid thoughts swirling through my mind, but I'm scared for Camden. I'm scared for me. I wouldn't be so conflicted and on edge if I didn't care about him—and I do. *You love Hunter. He's who you belong with.* I know it in my very soul, but what if I can't be with him? What if I never get out of here?

Camden brushes my hair behind my ear. He leans in and whispers, "Something wrong?"

I lick my lips and bring my gaze to his. Tears rim my eyes, my chest tightening. It makes it hard to breathe. I swallow and suck in a breath. "I've been thinking..." My voice trails off.

His brows knit together, lining his eyes with worry. "You're making me nervous."

I run my fingers through my hair. "The thing is—" I close my eyes for a second. "The thing is I'm scared for you."

He touches my chin so I face him. A small smile plays on his lips, and he tilts his head. "For me? It's you the HPA's interested in."

"Exactly. They're crazy. What if they hurt you to try to break me? I couldn't live with myself if something happened to you because of me. I think we need to back off some."

Pulling back, he shakes his head. "They'll do something regardless."

I cover his mouth with my hand. "Shhh!"

He tugs my hand away and holds it in his. "They don't scare me."

I wipe spilled tears from my cheeks. He doesn't get it. He'll never get it unless I tell him the truth. My lip quivers as I gather my strength. I need to tell him that even if I had feelings for him, it'd never work out because every time he falls asleep, I want to invade his dreams. I yearn to be his worst nightmare. His sanity will break because of me. I already see it. It's not obvious, but his aqua blue eyes look haunted when he's lost in his own thoughts.

"Seriously, Cam, you need to think—"

Before I can get the words out, Camden cuts me off with a surprise kiss. His hands run in my hair, pulling me closer, and I automatically react and lean into him. His soft lips taste of fruit, and his beard tickles my chin. I don't move. He surprised me, and all I can think about is how safe I feel. But that's it. Safe. Nothing like what I feel with Hunter even being in the same room. Hunter stirs a million emotions through me, hot and cold and everything amazing in between. My soul screams and begs for Hunter, and my heart would love nothing more than to escape my chest and break through all the impenetrable walls of this prison to find him.

The door beeps, sending hot fear twisting through my chest and stomach, making me ill knowing that everyone who was watching saw the kiss, including Hunter. But the same camera blinking freezes my face. I can't react as much as I want to—and all I want to do is cry my eyes out for being in this position. For unintentionally letting things get too far.

Pushing Camden back, I jump up and spin on the balls of my feet to face the door. My heart feels like it smashes to the floor only to crawl away from me, trying to escape to be with the boy who frowns in the doorway to my cell. Hunter's sad hazel eyes flick from me to floor, like he can barely even look at me in this moment.

I squeeze my eyes shut, my hands trembling at my sides. I don't know what else to do. I can't just scream out that it's not what it looks like because it's exactly what it looks like. Camden kissed me, and I let him.

It didn't mean anything, I think. *Please, please know that, Hunter. I love you. I love only you.*

He clears his throat. "Dr. Sullivan would like to visit with you again, Emily. Please hold up your arms so I can restrain you." An edge to Hunter's voice sends panic through me, stabbing me through my soul.

I don't move. I just stand there with my eyes shut, willing the stupid prison to disappear, for the unbearable nightmare my life turned into to just end. Because I can't take this. I can't handle this.

But I don't have a choice. None of this is going away. I'm already awake and not hovering the edge of the nightmares I create.

"You guys can't wait until tomorrow?" Camden asks from behind me.

Tears spill on my cheeks, his voice doing nothing but making me feel worse. "It's fine, Cam." My voice sounds so small and empty. I'm not even sure if I said the words out loud.

Boots thud on the tiled floor, drawing closer to me. But still, I don't look.

Warm fingers graze my wrist, vying for my attention, but as quickly as the heat of Hunter's hand came, a cold handcuff replaces it. Swallowing back the agony stealing my breath, I force myself to open my eyes. Hunter locks me in a staring match, his eyes softer than a second ago, and he adjusts the cuff on my other wrist. I will for him to understand. I need him to understand.

I open my mouth, preparing to blow our cover. But something changes in Hunter's eyes, and the words are lost on me. I'm not sure I'll ever find the right words to say and if it even matters.

HUNTER

I blink a few times, my jaw tight. I don't know what to think or feel. The image of Nadia kissing Camden etches in my mind. She stands a foot away, her indigo eyes burning into my soul, tears branding pink lines on her pale cheeks. She looks so fragile, like at any second she'll break, but I'm too shocked to do anything. A thousand thoughts circle my head, and a knot forms in my stomach.

If Nadia wasn't standing in front of me, I'd strut over to Camden and punch him for making a move on my girlfriend, putting her in a position that obviously brings us both agony.

Clearing my throat to stop my voice from cracking, I gaze over Nadia's shoulder and glower at him. "Don't bother waiting up. Emily's going to have a long night. Someone will bring around dinner shortly."

"You need to calm down, Hunter," Jacqueline says.

"Shut up," I think. "Don't tell me what to do."

"No, I'm not going to shut up. You're hurt and angry. But you have to realize that this is no one's fault. I doubt Nadia wanted to kiss Camden, and you know he doesn't know about you. They've been stuck in a box for two months with no one else to really interact with. You can't hold it against them."

I place my hand on Nadia's lower back, gently nudging her. She resists, letting my press my hand more firmly to her. Her love for me radiates from her, like a thousand light bulbs set aglow all at once, and I relax. I never doubted her love—our love for each other—but it's still painful seeing her like this. She has to play games to survive. I drum my index finger on her, and she turns to look at me as I walk her into the corridor.

Her eyes cloud with tears and desperation, and I force a small smile. She doesn't need to stress about this right now. She needs a clear mind. Dr. Sullivan will do anything to knock down Nadia's walls to discover her secrets. She needs to keep herself together because it's the only thing protecting her.

"You need to say something to her, Hunter. Anything."

I turn to look at Nadia, catching her gaze. "Don't be afraid."

Her eyes widen for a second. "I'm not."

"Your hands are shaking."

She twines her fingers together. "I'm just hungry, all right?"

I nod. "Okay."

The elevator door dings open, and I guide Nadia into the

empty corridor. She strolls next to me, my hand still touching her back, and then I stop in front of the same interrogation room I brought her to this morning. Entering my pass code, I open the door.

We're greeted by the plain, empty room. Dr. Sullivan isn't here yet. If it weren't for the camera, I'd wrap my arms around Nadia and pull her to me. She looks like she could really use a hug from me—and I could use one from her. Seeing Camden with his hands in her hair rocked me. I don't want to lose her.

"Then you need to fight for her." I shake Jacqueline's voice from my head. It's crowded enough as it is with both of our emotions mixing together.

Guiding Nadia to the couch, I unlock her cuffs and plop down next to her, leaving a few inches between us. I rest the restraints on my knee, dying to say something, anything, but I can't think of the right words without blowing my cover.

She shifts on the couch, her knees touching mine as she turns. "I want to apologize."

I wish I could reach up and touch her lips, kiss her. Instead, I frown. "You have nothing to apologize to me about."

Her shoulders relax. "You're right." She glances at the door. "I guess I should save it for Dr. Sullivan."

I know from the way her eyes still shine with unshed tears that it really is me she wants to apologize to, and I wish we could have a moment to talk. I hate having so many unsaid words between us.

I hear the door click and shift away from Nadia to watch Dr. Sullivan enter. She carries a brown paper bag that smells like fries. Standing up, I touch Nadia's shoulder to keep her sitting and force myself to smile at Dr. Sullivan.

Dr. Sullivan sets the bag on the coffee table and shrugs out of her lab coat. She lays it on the back of the couch across from us and unlocks a cabinet to pull some paper plates from it. She beams a smile at Nadia, who stiffens, and then Dr. Sullivan sits down.

Opening the bag, Dr. Sullivan pulls out three paper-wrapped burgers and a large cup full of fries. "I thought you might be hungry, Emily."

I press my lips together. I've never heard Dr. Sullivan refer to anyone in the cells by their names, only by their assigned numbers, and she must've thought about what I said to her earlier. She's acting like we're all good friends just meeting for dinner instead of an interrogation. I don't know who she thinks she's fooling, but it's neither Nadia nor I.

Nadia leans forward and looks at the fries. "Is this a trick?"

Dr. Sullivan glances at me before meeting Nadia's eyes. "No, not at all. Help yourself. I think we got off on the wrong foot."

"This is weird," Jacqueline comments.

I grind my teeth. "Tell me about it," I think. "Who knew my mom and girlfriend would ever have dinner together."

Nadia reaches for the plate of food Dr. Sullivan offers. "Yeah, I agree. I wanted to apologize for yelling this morning. I don't know what came over me. I just—" She takes a breath. Dr. Sullivan leans in, hanging on her words. "I don't want anyone to think I associate with the Creature Council. They've done nothing but wronged me."

My vision darkens as her words echo through the air. Sweat beads on my neck. I feel light headed. I want to kiss her to get her to be quiet. I don't know what she's planning, but it makes me nervous.

"I don't believe it."

My hand shakes as I take the plate of food from Dr. Sullivan. I think, "I don't either, Jackie."

NADIA

I glance from Dr. Sullivan to Hunter. He pales, the color draining from his cheeks, and looks like he's going to black out at any second. Dr. Sullivan doesn't notice because her stare bores into me, trying to see past the imaginary brick wall that hides my secrets.

Something about her changed since this morning. She called me by my fake name, smiles more instead of scowls, and gazes at me like she probably gazes at her most prized possession. Maybe that's what I am to her now. But that's not necessarily a bad thing. People cherish their most valuable possessions instead of tossing them out like garbage. Who knew our one commonality might be what it takes to save my life. But just because I hate the council doesn't mean I'll befriend the evil doctor anytime soon.

"If you don't mind sharing, I'd like to hear what they did to you," Dr. Sullivan says.

I shake my head. "It's really hard to talk about it. Maybe some other time."

She reaches across the table and touches my knee. "I understand. I know what it's like to have been wronged by people you trust."

It takes all my strength not to roll my eyes. She's lying through her teeth. The only people who've been wronged were wronged by her and everything she stands for. She doesn't know how it really feels to be let down by people you thought cared.

I shrug. "It sucks." I take a bite of my burger even though I'd rather just leave it untouched on my plate.

Dr. Sullivan wipes her mouth with a napkin. "So, if you don't want to talk about what the council did to you, how about we talk about something more pleasant. Tell me about your family."

I drop my gaze. "I don't have any."

Dr. Sullivan sighs. She's annoyed by my lack of answers, but I'm not going to give away things so easily to her. I've resisted this long. She'd be suspicious if I just started spilling my soul to her—even if they're all lies.

Hunter clears his throat. "How about you tell us something about yourself?"

Dr. Sullivan smiles at Hunter. "Yes, Emily, I'd love to know more about you."

Pursing my lips, I think for a moment. "I'm seventeen. Maybe you can throw me a party on my eighteenth one coming up."

"I have two boys around your age, she says, flicking her gaze to Hunter for a second, ignoring my birthday remark.

I tilt my head to the side, surprised she told me something truthful about herself. She doesn't know that I know Hunter is her son, and I doubt she'll ever tell me. But it doesn't really matter because Hunter already disowned her. I don't care to ever know her as his mother.

Hunter knocks his knee against mine when he shifts on the couch. "They're pretty cool."

Dr. Sullivan raises her eyebrows. "Now, Hunter, don't get so carried away. This is supposed to be about Emily."

I touch Hunter's shoulder. "But I'd really like to hear about them," I say, smiling before dropping my hand back to my lap. "I bet you're a great mother. Nothing like my parents were."

Dr. Sullivan straightens her shoulders. "What were they like?"

I puff air through my lips. "Uncaring. All they were ever concerned about was their stupid jobs. My own mother pawned me off on—" I cover my mouth, faking surprise.

Dr. Sullivan sits on the edge of her couch.

I raise my hands up. "I'm sorry. I shouldn't burden you with my problems. Let me just say that no good mother would ever give up their child to some monster because she thought it'd help her in the end. But you know what? It didn't help her. It got her killed."

Dr. Sullivan's face turns red with my words. I'm risking a lot, weaving my lies the way I am, but I'm not backing off. Maybe it'll be good for her to hear what a horrible person she really is when it's put into someone else's perspective.

Hunter squeezes my arm. "You need to calm down, Emily."

I stand and move to sit on the couch next to Dr. Sullivan. Hunter stands over me a second later but doesn't move. Reaching out, I touch Dr. Sullivan's arm. She stiffens like I carry some incurable disease.

"I can't calm down. I get so angry thinking about her." I stare at Dr. Sullivan. "You'd never do something so awful, would you? You seem like a decent person."

Hunter grips my shoulder. "Emily."

I shrug out of his grip and wave my hand at Dr. Sullivan. "Well, aren't you, Dr. Sullivan?"

She clears her throat, looking at me and then shifting her eyes to Hunter. "I think we should stop here for tonight."

I clench my fingers into fists. "But I just got here. Please, don't send me back to the cell. Please."

Dr. Sullivan stands. "I'll see you later."

I reach out and grab her cool hand, trying to stop her from leaving. "Don't leave! I'm not finished."

She yanks her hand away and saunters to the door. "Sedate her, Agent Hunter."

When she exits the room, I meet Hunter's surprised eyes. He reaches for a tranquilizer on his weaponry belt and sticks me in the arm with it. Stumbling forward, I fall into his arms, letting him catch me. He scoops me up, cradling me, and I stare into his beautiful hazel eyes before the darkness claims me.

6

BIGGER THAN US

HUNTER

"I DON'T WANT to take her back to her cell," I think. Nadia rests in my arms with her pale blond hair veiling her face. She looks like she's losing color and will need to inflict a nightmare soon, but my jealously gets the best of me. The last thing I want is for her to share a nightmare with Camden despite knowing it'll never be like the dreams we've shared.

Jacqueline sighs in my mind. *"Then move her into a cell with someone else. Just remember it's risky because another person will have to know the truth about her."*

I grind my teeth as the elevator door dings open and force my legs to work. "Why do you always have to be right, Jackie?"

Nadia stirs in my arms, fluttering her eyes without opening them. She presses her cheek to my shoulder, her breath warming my collarbone. Then she kisses the nape of my neck, causing me to inhale a ragged breath, straightening my back. She releases a tiny puff of air against my skin, and I gently tilt my head to tap it against hers, making it look like I'm adjusting her weight.

When we arrive at her cell, I shift her over my shoulder and then unlock the door. Even though it's not as late as I expected, Camden lies asleep on his cot. Nadia stiffens in my arms, making me squeeze her a little tighter. I know the urge to inflict a nightmare torments her being this close to a dreamer. Sucking up my ego, I cross the room and lay her next to Camden against my heart's will. I only hover for a second before turning on my heels and leaving the room. Instead of going back to my desk to watch the monitors, I stroll down the hallway to check on my other charges. The rest of my shift will drag on for eternity. If only I could get Nadia out of here already.

NADIA

My heart aches for Hunter as he leaves me on Camden's cot. I wait a few seconds after he leaves before I shift under the white sheet and wrap my hands around Camden's neck until I'm in a position where I can touch his temples.

The world melts away, and my stomach drops as I invade his dream. I should've resisted another day. It's only been four since the last nightmare, but the sedation and constant fear I've experienced today has drained my energy. *His love for you will kill him...*

Opening my eyes, I push the words floating through my mind away and glance around the empty cell identical to the one we're in from the real world. My mouth falls open. This dream is different than all the other ones Camden has had over the last few months. Before tonight, his dreams always took place in the city and all revolved around agents killing his sister, Liv. Something in his mind has changed.

I glide to the metal door and grip the handle. It melts under my touch, sending dream dust floating in the air as I destroy Camden's dream. The door explodes on its hinges. Touching my boots to the floor, I move forward, each step leaving seared black spots on the tiles. I make my way down the cement corridor and to another door. I press my hands against it, sending it crashing to the floor with a bang. I find another empty cell with another door, and I know Camden is close by. I'm in a maze of repeating cells and corridors as Camden's mind only creates what he's seen in the real world.

I stomp through two more corridors and two cells until I reach a red door. Stopping, I peek through the window. Camden sits on his cot with his head in his hands. He wears a tan jacket with a flannel shirt underneath, dark washed jeans, and boots. Without his beard, he looks years younger, closer to my age. His short blond hair lies styled to the side with gel, and his aqua blue eyes sparkle with tears in the fluorescent lighting when he looks up.

"There's nothing you can do to stop me." I tilt my head to the side, my own voice echoing around me, but it doesn't come from my mouth.

Camden stands up and reaches out his hands. Moving in front of the window for a better view, I spot a dream version of myself cross her arms. She takes a step back to put distance between herself and Camden, and then my gaze falls on my outfit. My dream person wears an all black uniform with a weaponry belt like the one Hunter always wears. It's something I never thought I'd ever see, but Camden has imagined me to be an agent.

"They're using you, Emily. Can't you see that?" Camden rubs his eyes. "You're better than them."

My dream persona smiles. It's a smile without warmth and love. It's a smile lacking life—cold and empty and broken. I watch myself tuck my pale blond hair behind my ear. "So what? Maybe they're right about the world. The council isn't who they portray themselves as. They're the real monsters. You think they'll ever try to save us?"

Go in there and put an end to this. You've been here too long. Shaking my head, I push the thought away. I can't help it. I want to know the fear that lies in Camden's conscience.

Camden sighs. "What happened to you?"

My dream persona laughs. "I learned the truth."

Reaching over, he touches my dream persona's shoulder. "Not that. I thought you loved me." His eyes crinkle in sadness. "I know you loved me."

I press my lips together. I can't stay here any longer. It's more than I can take, even if it's only a dream. I touch my fingers to the door, causing it to explode on its hinges and fall forward. Sucking in breath after breath of strawberry tasting dream dust, I stomp forward.

Camden's eyes widen, and he stumbles back. "Please, don't do this, Agent Hunter."

I don't know why I'm shocked. It wouldn't be the first time someone was afraid of Hunter, and it's not the first time I appeared as him. My dream persona smiles at me, and I clench my jaw. I can't help it. It's unnerving.

I reach out and cup my dream persona's face. She explodes in a glittering cloud of dream dust. Camden calls out, drawing my gaze toward him. "How could you do this to her? How could you turn her against me?"

I don't answer because I need the nightmare to be over with now. I shouldn't have listened to what Camden was afraid of and shouldn't have lingered so long, because now I'm going to have to face him when he wakes up. I don't even know what I'm going to say. While dreams are made from the imagination, there are truths to be found among the chaos and terror of nightmares.

Gripping Camden's shoulder, I close my eyes as he explodes in my arms. I pull myself from the crumbling nightmare and bury my face in the pillow. I inhale long, shuddering breaths and then shift to hold Camden as the effects of the nightmare wear off.

"Shhh, it's okay. It was only a nightmare," I whisper. "It wasn't real. You're okay." I comfort Camden as he moans into his pillow. I do it because I don't know what else to do. I can't run from the cell like I would do after inflicting a nightmare in the outside world, and the one time I tried to do nothing, I felt guilty. More than guilty—I felt like a monster.

Camden's eyes flutter open. I stare at him, tears rimming my eyes, and he hugs me. He presses his lips to my hair and I let him, hugging him back as his erratic breathing evens and he gets himself under control.

"That was intense," Camden says after a moment. He brushes the hair from my eyes. "I thought I lost you." Shaking his head, he blinks his eyes, still disturbed by my nightmare inflicting.

"No..." My voice trails off, and I press my face into the pillow.

He pushes up on his elbow and presses his lips to my ear. "You're shaking. What's wrong? Did they do something?"

I squeeze my eyes shut, shaking my head. "It's nothing. Let it go."

"Okay, fine. If you want to talk, I'm willing to listen," he says, turning to look at the ceiling.

Pushing off the bed, I get to my feet. "It's better if I don't." I cringe as my voice echoes through the room and pad across the cool tiles, falling onto my own cot. I need to put some distance between me and Camden. I've taken this game too far. It's better this way.

Then why do you feel so bad?

HUNTER

Yawning, I stare at my ceiling. I left the facility two hours after I returned Nadia to her cell. I couldn't stand to check on her and risk seeing her with Camden, so I just turned off the monitor and left without making a round to say goodbye to those still awake.

I feel myself dozing off, and I let sleep take me. I need to escape reality and go to a world where I'm in complete control.

Sitting on the roof of a six-story building, I dangle my feet over the edge. The sun sets in the distance, casting a fiery veil of red and orange light over the empty city I've recreated to replicate the one I first met Nadia in while being stuck in Jacqueline's head.

The air shifts, and I feel a familiar presence. Jacqueline shimmers into view next to me, appearing as the dark, curly haired girl she was when she held me captive before she body jumped into Agent Camille and then into me. Her skin glows golden brown in the warm sunset, and she rests her hands on her knees.

"I realize now why Nadia invaded my dreams," Jacqueline says. "When you're not the dreamer, it's so amazing. Like nothing I've ever experienced."

"Controlling my dream world is a great trick I learned in your head, Jackie. Who knew it would ever come in handy." Rolling my shoulders, I stare at the city. The sun doesn't sink lower but hovers in the sky, frozen in time.

She laces her fingers together, and I watch her in my peripheral vision. "It does make my time without a body more bearable."

"Speaking of, how much longer do you plan on staying?" I ask, kicking my heels against the building.

Turning to face me, she touches my hand. "To be honest, I don't know. I need to find a new body to anchor myself to. I think it's better to wait until you leave the HPA. We'll find someone ready to go."

I blow out a breath. "Seriously? I didn't think about having to kill someone. Camille's body still haunts me, you know. And it's not like you're even dead." Who knows how long I'll be pretending to work for the HPA. What if these months turn into a year? What if Dmitri never comes up with a great enough plan? And if that happens, what if Nadia refuses to fight her way out with me? That's a long time to be hosting Jacqueline.

Jacqueline laughs. "Your purity's showing."

I glare at her before jumping from the building, landing in the middle of the empty street. Within a second, Jacqueline's at my side again. There's no escaping her, even if I just want to be alone for a minute. She's like a shadow dead-set on haunting me instead of trailing behind me, unnoticed.

"It's not purity, Jackie. It's called morals. Don't you feel a little bad about killing someone?" I stroll to the wall of an abandoned building and sit down with my back against it.

She doesn't follow me but instead stands in the street and crosses her arms. "No, I don't, because the people I've killed are ones meant only for nightmares. Do you remember when I body jumped into you? How you saw my life flash before your eyes?"

I nod. "I could never forget."

"Imagine that but with the faces of all the innocent people who were affected by these bad souls. In the end, I'm doing the bad guys a favor. I help them find peace."

"How do you even know?" Jacqueline's never really been

open about who she is, and I'm going to take advantage of the opportunity while she's willing to share. "Do you escort them into a white tunnel or something?"

She laughs, shaking her head. "It's hard to explain. I just know. It's kind of like how we can feel each other's emotions. They never die in despair but relief. And Hunter, it's not like I have to do it. I don't live on sins like Nadia survives on nightmares."

I rub my chin. "I see."

"I'm not a bad person."

"I know, Jackie. I never really believed you were," I say, staring into her lavender eyes.

The ground shakes, and a few pieces of concrete fall into the street next to me. Something disturbs my sleep, messing with my dream. The sky cracks, clouding the world, and Jacqueline disappears. I pull out of my dream and jerk upright on my bed.

My cell rings on my nightstand. It's an unknown number, and I pick it up and press it to my ear. "Agent Hunter."

"How is she?" It's Alyssa.

"I don't know." My voice low voice sounds hoarse as I speak. I shift and tilt my head against the wall. "It's been an interesting day."

She breathes into the receiver. "You sound weird."

"I'm tired. Is that all you wanted to know?"

"Don't take out your pain on Alyssa."

The line buzzes with static from her breathing. "I'm sorry for today."

I rub my hand over my hair. "Why?"

"You know why."

I don't say anything for a moment, staring at my wall like it's the most interesting thing in the world, and then finally get the nerve to speak. "So you knew. Why didn't you warn me, Alyssa?"

"Because you would've stopped it."

My brows furrow. "She's my girlfriend!" I snap my mouth shut, my voice echoing through the room. I knew I was angry and jealous—hurt—but it didn't hit me as hard until now finding out that Alyssa let it happen. She knew Camden was going to kiss Nadia, and she knew I would see. She could've prevented the pain I saw in Nadia's eyes. The despair Nadia saw in mine.

"Hunter..." Her voice comes through the line as a whisper. "I'm sorry. It needed to happen."

I tap my fingers at my side, listening.

"Because if it didn't happen, Nadia would've accepted the offer your mother is going to propose to her tomorrow. She would've done it to try to escape, and she would've failed."

My eyebrows knit together. "What offer?"

"I can't tell you."

"Then why bother calling me?" I ask, sighing.

"Because you're my friend, and I wanted to make sure you were okay."

I'm not exactly okay. I haven't been okay for weeks. As each day goes by, I'm losing hope in my ability to change things. I've always found my hope through Nadia and seeing her hopeless tears me apart. Incapable of showing my love while some other guy, a guy on the right side of her world, can comfort her, hold her—kiss her—well, it kills me.

"I won't be okay until Nadia is free," I say.

"It'll be soon. I promise."

"You keep saying that, but it hasn't happened. If it were you in that cell, you know Nadia would've had you out by now." I switch the phone to my other ear.

Alyssa blows a breath into the phone. "That isn't fair, Hunter. Nadia is one of two people that are my only family left. I'd gladly trade my place for her, but this is bigger than me and her. It's bigger than you. You always talk about changing the world, well, Dmitri is so close to doing so."

I grimace. "I don't understand."

"We're not only planning on getting Nadia out. This is much, much bigger. We plan on seizing control of the city again. We're going to stop the HPA from terrorizing us."

"How?"

"I can't tell you everything, but if we can't change the board, we're going to do the only thing we can do. Dmitri is going to reform the council."

7

AFRAID

NADIA

THE DOOR TO our cell swings open earlier than it should for breakfast and in walks Dr. Harvey. He's bright-eyed and clean shaven, wearing a salmon pink dress shirt with black slacks under his lab coat. He smiles when I sit up. Staring at his dark coffee eyes, I imagine how he could've been a model or actor in another life. I wish he were in this one because then it'd mean the show would be over soon, and I could get back to reality.

"Good morning, Emily," he says as he struts in the room, leaving the door open behind him. I wonder how many people escaped under his watch. If I let my nightmare inflictor side have control, I'd glide past him faster than he'd be able to react.

If it weren't for the stupid elevator and armed security team, I might even make it out if I tried.

"There's nothing good about this morning." I fake a yawn and stretch my arms.

He laughs. "You'll feel differently about it soon enough."

I raise my eyebrows. "I doubt it."

Reaching into his coat pocket, he pulls out a pair of metal cuffs. He motions for me to stand, and I get to my feet, crossing my arms. He meets my gaze and presses his lips together. He should know by now that I'm not going to jump up and do whatever he asks without question.

He steps closer. "Please hold out your arms. I need to restrain you."

I comb my messy hair with my fingers. "Where are we going?"

"To the infirmary. I didn't get a chance to draw your blood for retesting like I wanted to yesterday."

I hold up my hands, and he tightens the cuffs. The cold metal bites into my skin. I glance away from him toward Camden, still asleep on his cot. I hate that he's going to wake up without me here. I hope he doesn't think his nightmare came true, but I'm also relieved to get out of the cell. The emotions between us are too intense, and I don't feel like dealing with Camden right now.

"Will I be back for breakfast?" I ask as Dr. Harvey escorts me out of the cell. He shuts it and locks it behind him, and I watch Camden sit up on his cot through the glass before getting tugged away. No one sits at the desk, and I catch the time on the wall. Five o' clock is two hours before Hunter's shift. I wish I'd be left alone until at least the morning shift starts.

"Don't worry. Someone brought in bagels." Dr. Harvey calls for the elevator, and we get off on the ground floor. My mouth falls open when I see the front door, unguarded this early, and it takes a lot of convincing myself to stop from jumping on Dr. Harvey's back, stealing his tranquilizers and keys, and getting out of here. *You'd never make it.*

"Yum." My voice falls flat.

Dr. Harvey grips my arm, leading me into the lobby and past the front desk. I peek over my shoulder at the front door again before we enter a locked door that leads to a sterile, white hallway.

Slowing my pace, I look at Dr. Harvey. "This isn't the infirmary I was taken to when I first arrived here. These walls are white. The other ones were blue."

"Very observant of you. You were in the lab then, but we're not running the exact same tests as last time. Before, we ran the standard creature test which tested you for abnormalities. Today, we're testing you for compatibility. We keep all creature testing separate from everything else." He punches in his pass code at another locked door, and we enter a spacious room with a row of hospital beds and medical equipment stationed behind them against a wall.

I swallow when Dr. Harvey points toward the last bed with a tray of syringes, vials, needles, and other sharp, shiny objects on it meant to prod me with. I sit on the edge of the bed, feeling queasy and frightened, and swing my legs on and lean back.

Dr. Harvey removes the cuffs, and I rest my hands in my lap.

I'm terrified of whatever tests he plans on performing. What if he discovers I'm not completely human after all? And what about what he said about compatibility? What does that even mean and for what? I don't know what I'll do if he's preparing me to be transferred to their main laboratory. I refuse to live the rest of my life as an experiment. *They won't if they believe you're human. The lab's for creatures.* I imagine Alyssa whispering in my ear and take comfort in knowing that my thoughts ring true.

I clear my throat, my hands trembling, and resist the urge to run. "You said you had bagels?"

Dr. Harvey nods. "You can have one after I get what I need."

Grabbing a rubber tourniquet from the metal tray on a rolling stand, he ties it around my arm. He hands me a small ball to hold, but before he can prepare the needle, I swing my legs and jump off the bed. I can't do it. I can't let him draw more blood for testing.

He rushes around the bed, reaching for my arm. I stumble back out of his reach. Fear slices through me and shadows my vision as Dr. Harvey runs to the wall, slamming his hand on a red button. A buzzer rings in my ears, but I don't stop. I walk backwards, away from him, and he holds his hands up in a non-threatening position.

"It's okay, Emily," he says, his voice smooth and even, the least threatening tone I've ever heard.

"Please, just stay back," I say, covering my ears.

Turning my back on him, I jog toward the door. My bare feet slap the cold tile with purpose as I concentrate on preventing myself from gliding. Dr. Harvey forgot to close the door, just like he did in my cell, and he yells out as I cross the threshold into the corridor leading to the lobby.

"Emily, stop!" His voice echoes around me, my head pounding with each step I take.

I glance over my shoulder. "I can't! I'm scared Just leave me alone. Let me go back to my cell." My head screams for me to stop and think about what I'm doing, but my feet lead me out of here. It's like my body knows this might be the only chance I get at freedom, and I have to take it.

My vision blurs as tears rim my eyes, and I crash into a familiar agent. Dressed in the board-issued uniform, the woman stands a few inches taller than me with a muscular build. Her sharp cheekbones look fierce with her brown hair styled in a pixie cut. Her wide eyes narrow on me, stopping me in place. She was one of the agents in charge of transferring my father. Her strong hands grip my shoulders, and she flips me around, pressing her chest into my back as she yanks my hands behind me.

Dr. Harvey rushes to us, staring into my wild eyes. "She's just frightened, Agent Rosaline. If you hold her for a second, I'll sedate her."

I struggle in Agent Rosaline's grip and flinch when Dr. Harvey sticks a needle into my arm. Tears burn my cheeks as the world blurs in and out of focus, and my body starts to feel heavy. I regret resisting Dr. Harvey. Because now, I'm afraid I won't ever wake up.

HUNTER

"What's she doing here?" Jacqueline asks.

I turn my gaze to Agent Rosaline standing next to Phillip's desk in the lobby. Her short hair flies in every direction, and her eyes water when she sees me. After Jacqueline killed her partner, Rob, before he could kill Nadia, Agent Rosaline requested to leave field work for a while. I haven't seen her since then until now.

"Agent Hunter!" Agent Rosaline offers me a wide smile that takes up the bottom half of her face and rushes to me, flinging her arms around my shoulders. I keep my arms at my sides and look past her at Dr. Sullivan stepping from the elevator. "It's so good to see you. The last few weeks have been pretty lonely for me."

I step back and shove my hands in my pockets. "They have you pushing paperwork?"

She laughs. "Not even close. Remember the driver of..." Her voice trails off. She doesn't even have to finish her thought because I know who she's referring to and why it's hard for her to talk about it. It's hard for me to talk about the day Nadia was taken, too.

I frown. "Dr. Thompson's daughter?"

She nods. "I'm her guardian."

I twist my lips to the side. "Why in the heck would she need a guardian and from who? I thought only board members and high ranking scientists were offered protection."

"Her mother believes the council set out a hit on her. After we released Evie from the green zone, Dr. Thompson sent her to live with her aunt in Texas because she didn't think her father could protect her here. She wasn't at her school more than three weeks before a troll infiltrated her high school as a teacher and tried to kidnap her and another student."

My eyes widen. I can't help it. It sounds so ridiculous and almost unbelievable. "Whoa. That girl has been through a lot."

Agent Rosaline looks over her shoulder. I follow her gaze and end up staring Evie straight in the eyes. I didn't even notice her seated in the sitting area. Dr. Sullivan talks quietly with her, but Evie doesn't take her eyes from mine. My chest tightens and dizziness washes through me. No one knows Evie and I were acquainted before the day everything went wrong.

"I have a terrible feeling about this, Hunter." Jacqueline's been quiet up until this moment, and she has the same feelings I do. Why would the board bring Evie back here? Why would Evie agree to come?

"That makes two of us, Jackie," I think.

"I know," Agent Rosaline says, cutting off my inner conversation with Jacqueline.

I break eye contact with Evie and shift my gaze back to Agent Rosaline. "You staying long?"

Agent Rosaline shrugs. "No idea."

"Well, find me before you go. I need to go start my shift." It's not like I get in trouble for being late or anything, but I need to get out of here. I need to have a moment to myself to pull my thoughts together to think through everything. I need to figure out what the board's up to and why Evie is here. What if she gives us all away? I can't let that happen.

I pat Agent Rosaline's shoulder and slide past her, heading to the elevator. When I reach my desk and glance at the monitor, my stomach knots. Nadia isn't in her cell, and no one filled out the log that's supposed to inform me where my charges have gone.

I pick up the phone and call the front desk. It doesn't even ring before I hear Phillip's voice. "What can I do for you, Agent Hunter?"

"I'd like to know the location of one of my charges, Emily, Human 9209. Someone forgot to log her out."

"Oh, hmm, Emily? Let me call—"

"She's in the infirmary with Dr. Harvey." A voice echoes over his. It's Agent Rosaline.

Phillip breathes into the phone. "Oh, wait, Agent Hunter, she's in the—"

"I heard," I say, cutting him off. "Send a message to Dr. Harvey to call me when he's available, all right?"

"Got it."

A thousand thoughts whirl through my head. Agent Rosaline said the infirmary, but why would Nadia be there? I've never once seen anyone other than agents in the infirmary. They take prisoners to the lab. I tap my fingers on the desk. I can't just go over there and find out what's going on, so I have no choice but to wait for Dr. Harvey to call.

"Act normal, Hunter. You need to do your job and be patient."

I glare at the screen and the fifteen people who are expecting me to check on them any minute. "Easy for you to say, Jackie," I think.

"Nadia's not the only one counting on you."

Even though she's right, I don't have to like it. The first stop I have to make is to Nadia's cell. I'm not looking forward to talking with the dude who's putting moves on the girl I'd risk losing my life to see happy. I know it's not his fault—he doesn't know how complicated everything is—but part of me blames him for putting Nadia in an awkward position. She has enough to worry about. She doesn't need to worry about hurting Camden's feelings, too.

I roll my shoulders and straighten my back. Heading to the corridor, I force myself to knock and enter in my pass code. Camden sits at the desk and flips through Nadia's sketch book. He looks up when I enter, and I cross my arms and lean against the door.

The air feels different in here without Nadia—sadder, emptier, more intense—and it's not until this very moment that I see what effect Nadia has on people. The effect she has not only on Camden, but on me, and I bet even more than us. Her soul radiates with all that is good in this crappy, HPA-infested world I can't get away from.

It's Nadia's strength and light that will change things. I can feel it in my bones. But, her ability to change people opens her up to being changed. I've seen her change. I'm afraid if the HPA gets to Nadia, gets under her skin, in her head, her essence—the change we need to have a life together won't ever happen.

"They won't get to her."

"How do you know? Alyssa said the HPA was going to offer something," I think, watching Camden without saying a word to him.

"She said she won't consider it because of—"

"Him."

Camden shifts on the chair. "Dude, you're being creepy."

I shake my head. "Need anything before breakfast?"

Standing up, he twines his fingers on the back of his head. "Nadia. What the hell are you people doing to her?"

I frown. I hate being included in his hate of the HPA. "I don't know what you mean."

He paces. "You know exactly what I mean. You're changing her."

"Hunter, you need to get out of here. Something's wrong with him."

I press my lips together to keep my mouth from falling open. I'm shocked that it's like Camden sensed my fear and confirmed it. He glowers at me and struts to the wall to lean his back on it.

"I'm serious. Get out of here. He's acting out of character. He's acting like—like I did after a nightmare."

"I'm not doing anything," I say, touching my hand to the doorknob.

"Then where is she?" His voice echoes around the room.

I open the door and step into the hallway, locking it behind me, resisting the urge to rest on the door and sink to the floor. Instead, I peek through the window. Camden rushes the door and bangs his fist on the metal. The sound resonates through me, and I turn my back on him. I hope he's wrong about Nadia. I need him to be wrong.

99

8

THE HEART CAN'T BE PERSUADED

NADIA

WHITE LIGHT BREAKS through the darkness. It's like I'm no one and then someone in a matter of seconds. The white fades to red, but I don't open my eyes. I'm not ready to deal with the world yet. The only reprieve I get from everything is when I inflict nightmares on Camden, and I didn't even catch a break last night. The HPA haunts every aspect of my life. I'm afraid they'll break me.

"Emily?" Dr. Harvey's smooth voice wraps around me.

I peek through my lashes but don't say anything.

"It's okay, Emily. I'm done. You can open your eyes."

I purse my lips and squeeze my eyes shut.

A warm hand rests on mine. "Please, open your eyes...Emily. I didn't travel all the way from Texas to watch you ignore Dr. Harvey."

My heart nearly explodes at the sound of a voice so familiar, I'm almost afraid it isn't real. Snapping my eyes open, I sit up. Evie stands next to my bed, looking different than I remember. Her hazel eyes shine against her golden skin, the red streaks now gone from her dark brown hair, cut short and curling around her chin. She traded in her glasses for contacts and looks older—like the last few weeks were years.

I meet her gaze, and my heart falls into my stomach. Something else is different with Evie. Her eyes don't shine with the same light they used to have. She's guarded and untrusting with the way she crosses her arms, only offering me a closed lip smile. Evie looks haunted. I know deep in my soul that the HPA got to her, and I've lost her.

"I'll give you two a moment," Dr. Harvey says, scooping up a file. He heads to the door and disappears.

I don't know what to say. While I hoped I'd see Evie again, I didn't think I would, and I definitely didn't think it would be while I was locked away in the termination facility.

I rest my hands on my lap, taking a long few moments to find my voice. "Guess you figured out your mom lied to you when she said my mom was going to pick me up, huh?"

"She's not the only liar." Evie's studies me, her lips twisting to the side.

With the sharp edge of her words, the little color I have in my face drains away. My heart sputters and then races, sending sweat prickling on the back of my neck. This isn't the heart-warming reunion I was praying would happen. It's heart-wrenching and scary, and I wish Evie would go away.

She leans forward and touches my hand. It takes everything in me not to jerk away from her. "You look ill. Are you okay?"

I swallow the lump in my throat. "I've been through a lot."

Her eyes crinkle in the corner when she frowns. "Me, too. You changed my life, you know."

I cringe. "I'm sorry, Evie. I really am. I wish I could rewind time and do things a little differently."

She shrugs. "I didn't say for the worst."

My brows furrow. "I guess that's good."

I exhale a long breath, forcing the conversation harder than it should be considering I've been faking it for weeks. I sense a million thoughts swirling around Evie's head. Sitting on the edge of my bed, she takes both my hands into hers. I glance around for a camera but don't see one. It must be hidden somewhere.

She leans forward and whispers, "You're still my friend, Nadia, and I want to help get you out of here."

I open and close my mouth, fear slicing through me at the sound of my name. But somehow, it's strangely comforting, too. I'm so confused. I don't know what to think. "You can get me out of here?"

She shakes her head. "No, but you can."

Puckering my bottom lip, I say, "I'd be out of here already if that were true."

"Things are different. The board is fond of you."

Icy dread runs its fingers down my spine. She mentions the board like they're someone she trusts instead of the group of people she should fear. No wonder Evie is different. The board got to her and is trying to get to me through her. Whatever friendship we had doesn't exist anymore.

Tears burn my eyes, so I close them and lean back. "I don't feel so good. Can you call Dr. Harvey?"

Evie presses her lips together and gets up. She doesn't say anything as she turns her back on me and heads toward the door.

My breathing comes fast and hard, and it feels like the world closes in on me, threatening to swallow me whole. This can't be happening. A tear escapes my closed eyelid and rolls down my cheek. Grief and pain swells in my chest as I think about the death of a friendship that could've been what helped change the world for me and Hunter.

It's not over. I shake the thought away. It feels like it is. Deep in my heart, I know everything I once knew is lost.

HUNTER

The phone on my desk rings. I pick it up and cradle it on my shoulder. "Agent Hunter."

"Phillip notified me you called. Sorry about not logging Emily's relocation to the infirmary. I didn't expect it to take so long," Dr. Harvey says.

I press the phone harder to my ear. "Everything okay?"

A muffled voice sounds out through the line. It takes a minute for Dr. Harvey to say, "Yeah, it's great. Want to do me a favor and retrieve Emily? Dr. Sullivan wants to see her in thirty, but I have things I need to do. She can wait in her cell until then."

I close my eyes for a second in relief. "Yeah, sure. I'll be there in two."

"He seemed a little too happy," Jacqueline says.

I ignore her as I walk to the elevator and take it to the lobby. Evie and Agent Rosaline are gone, and Phillip sits at his desk drinking a cup of coffee. I nod, strolling past and enter the infirmary. It's quiet and sterile, and I'm nauseated from the memory of the few terrible times I've been in a hospital setting.

Dr. Harvey flips through a stack of papers. Nadia sits on the edge of the last hospital bed and lifts her gaze to mine. I hold her stare as I strut closer. Her pale blond hair hangs loosely over her shoulders and half veils her face. Her indigo eyes shine red and glassy like she's been crying made obvious by the tear stains glossing her cheeks in the bright lights. She shifts, straightening her wrinkled shirt and pulls her bare feet onto the bed, bending her knees to her chest. My heart aches seeing how broken and lost she looks.

Dr. Harvey glances up from his paperwork. "Emily is a little weak from testing so you can grab a wheelchair from the storage closet if you want." He moves toward a rolling tray and lifts an envelope from it. "Also, can you deliver this to Dr. Sullivan? It contains Emily's results."

"Sure thing. And I'll just carry her. Easier than restraining her to a chair." I walk toward Nadia and study her face for a moment before lifting her into my arms. She slides her arms around my neck and rests her head on my shoulder.

Dr. Harvey raises an eyebrow, and I shrug with one shoulder. He doesn't say anything as I turn on my heels and carry Nadia from the infirmary. Phillip doesn't even look up, and when I step into the elevator, Nadia snuggles closer.

She breathes on my neck a moment and then whispers, "I don't know how much longer I can take this."

I don't respond. I can't. I hug her tighter and wait for the elevator doors to open. Strolling through the viewing room, I glance at the video feed. Camden paces the cell from my monitor as I pass my desk. Stopping a few feet from the door, I set Nadia on her feet. I peer into the window without Camden seeing me and then turn to look at Nadia.

"Your cellmate is a little anxious today. Don't hesitate to yell for me if you need anything," I say.

Nadia studies my face with furrowed brows before nodding. I enter my pass code and crack the door to peek again. Opening it wider, I guide Nadia inside. Camden stops pacing and rushes to her, slinging his arm around her and lifts her a few inches off the floor.

I step back and watch them for a minute.

"I was so worried when Dr. Harvey took you," Camden says.

Nadia pulls away and tucks her pale blond hair behind her ear. "Well, I'm fine, really. It was just a few tests."

"I just—I'm—" He sighs.

Nadia touches his shoulder. "You look tired, Cam. You should lie down."

Turning, I walk out before my hovering becomes too obvious that I'm intentionally eavesdropping. I can't help it. Camden has me on edge. I don't want Nadia in his path if he breaks. I shut and lock the door and head to my desk. Nadia's whispered words echo through my mind, and I wipe a hand over my forehead as I sit in front of my monitor.

"She's stronger than you both realize. She's going make it through this," Jacqueline says.

My jaw clenches, and I think, "I just hate that she has to. I hate that I have to watch her and can't do anything about it. I'm supposed to protect her."

"She doesn't need protecting. What she needs is to believe in herself and know that you trust her to make the right decisions, even if it bothers you."

I don't respond. I do trust Nadia. I trust her with my life. I know she'll do what's right for her, but a part of me hopes that what's right for her is what's right for us. In the end, I just need her to have no regrets.

NADIA

Camden's aqua blue eyes hold a new wildness I have never seen in them. He runs a hand through his scruffy beard before dropping his arm to his side. Blinking a few times, he marches to my cot and plops down, rolling to his back to stare at the ceiling.

I kneel next to him and veil us with my hair. "The nightmare got to you," I whisper in his ear.

He shudders, feeling my breath. "It's more than that. I see it. I know how they work. They're going to turn you against me."

I press my fingers to his lips. "Shhh. Not so loud." Slowly,

I move my hand to his cheek. "That won't happen. You have to trust me. What you're afraid of is all in your head."

He shifts to his side to look me in the eyes. "And what if it's not? You're already acting differently."

Covering my face with my hands, I sigh. Alyssa was right. Camden's love for me is going to get him killed, but not in the way I thought. Maybe it was a mistake to change my behavior. Maybe I should've just pretended with him. I care about Camden and don't want him to wind up dying because of me, but it hurts so much to think of the pain Hunter endures when he sees us together. Things would be a lot less complicated if I were just in a cell alone. *But you wouldn't be able to hide your nightmare inflictor side for long...*

"That has nothing to do with the HPA," I finally say after a minute. "It has everything to do with me and only me. You have to understand where I'm coming from. I care for you and don't want anything happening to you. It's a weakness the HPA will take advantage of, and I can't let them. I need to be selfish right now because I don't want either of us getting killed." I hope he'll accept my reason and just let it go.

"You're wrong," he whispers. "That's what they want. They want us apart because we're stronger when we're together. We fight harder for each other. It's what'll keep us alive."

I frown. "I don't know. I just don't know, Camden. What if—" I take a breath as the thought comes to my mind. It's not the first time I've had it, and it probably won't be the last, but it makes me doubt everything. I shake my head. "I can't have feelings for you. You'll just get hurt in the end because I don't know how much more I can take. What if I'm not meant to get through this? I sometimes feel like I'm supposed to die like my mother—like it's my fate."

Tears burn my eyes as I think about all the times I cheated death. When I was seven and hid under the table as my mother died at the hands of an agent, and then in the elevator of Trinity Hope Hospital when Jacqueline took a knife for me, and when Agent Rob tried to kill me. It has to mean something. *Yeah, that you're lucky.*

Camden laughs, surprising me. "I don't believe in fate."

I close my eyes and rest my head on his shoulder. I can't argue with him.

The door beeps as it unlocks, and I draw my gaze to it. Hunter pushes the door open, hovering on the threshold. His hazel eyes line with worry, and he reaches for a pair of metal cuffs on his weaponry belt. I push to my feet and walk over to him with my arms out. I don't say anything to Camden as Hunter guides me from the cell. There's no point. The heart can't be persuaded.

HUNTER

"Now's the time to show her you trust her," Jacqueline says.

I tap my fingers on Nadia's lower back and think, "And how do you suppose I do that?"

"Tell her what she needs to hear."

I clench my jaw. I don't know what she needs to hear or how to say it without sounding suspicious. I just need a minute alone with her without the cameras.

An idea comes to me, and I'm not sure if it's a good one,

but it may be worth the risk.

"You're crazy. Don't even consider it."

I ignore Jacqueline and turn to Nadia and say, "Let's stop at the bathroom for a minute. Dr. Sullivan said there was going to be a guest and you look ready to pass out. Some cold water to the face always helps me."

Nadia's eyes widen, but she doesn't argue. "Okay."

I lead her to the short hallway with the single bathroom and open the door. "I can't let you go in alone." Following her in, I let the door swing closed behind us, but I don't lock it. Instead, I press my back to it.

Nadia turns on the faucet and spins around to look at me without a word. My heart pounds in my ears, thudding faster than ever just staring at her. It's like the world inside these walls stops. I open my arms, letting her close the distance between us. She falls into me, sliding her arms around my waist. She stands on her tiptoes, and I bend down to kiss her, stealing what feels like the best and most important kiss of my life—a kiss that fills me up while giving everything I have to Nadia to push her forward, to help carry her.

She sniffles, tears splashing on my face, and I pull away and smear them away from her eyes. Leaning in again, I kiss her once more, hugging her so close I can feel her whole body through the thin cotton of her shirt.

I pull away and meet her sad gaze. "We have only a minute, and I can't ever do this again, but I need you to know I love you and I trust you to do what you have to do. Don't feel guilty for trying to survive."

"Hunter, leave now."

Nadia brings her cuffed hands to my face and kisses me again, hungry, desperately, like I'm the only thing she needs in the world. My hands trail over her sides, sliding around her waist, and I dig my fingers into her hips.

It takes everything in me to let her go. Her eyes shine with more tears, killing me, but I offer my best smile to give her as much hope as I can. Turning away, she quickly splashes water on her face. I hand her a paper towel and open the door again, pushing her into the hallway. I expect a few agents to be waiting in the viewing area, but it's empty.

When I guide her on the elevator, her eyes meet mine, and for the first time since she's been here, she looks confident and put together. She looks like the beautiful nightmare inflictor I fell in love with.

9

PLAYING GAMES

NADIA

HEAT CRAWLS UP my neck with the memory of Hunter's kiss fresh on my mind. It's like he knew I needed him and was willing to risk everything to reassure me. He's helped me clear my mind, and I believe I can figure things out. I *will* figure this all out.

Hunter opens the door to the ugly room with the green couches, and my stomach knots as my gaze locks on Dr. Sullivan sitting on the couch with her legs crossed at her knees. She wears burgundy slacks with a black silk top under her white lab coat and her gold-framed glasses perch on the tip of her nose. Her light brown hair is pulled back in a bun, and her hazel eyes squint when she smiles.

She stands up. "It's so good to see you, Emily." She turns to Hunter. "Please, remove her restraints."

Fear slithers up my back like a thousand tiny spiders. I tense my shoulders to stop the shiver from ripping through me. Hunter unlocks the cuffs, and I drop my hands to my side and force my mouth to work. "Thanks," I say to Hunter, rubbing my wrists as if they bother me.

Hunter nods and reaches into his back pocket, pulling out the envelope Dr. Harvey gave him and holds it up for his mother to take. "You requested these."

Dr. Sullivan's eyes light up, and she motions toward the couch. "Oh, yes, thank you. Please, take a seat. It'll only take a minute to look over these."

Hunter nudges me toward the couch. Dr. Sullivan stays standing in her spot, tearing open the envelope like a kid opening a present. Her gaze shifts over the single sheet of paper and something changes in her expression. Her fake smile melts into something real. And it's terrifying.

Sliding the paper back into the envelope, she clips it on top of the stack of papers on her clipboard. She settles on the couch and pulls her pen from her pocket. The thick air clouds with a mixture of emotions—the love and strength radiating from Hunter and I and something darker, wilder, like unsettling convictions and self-assurance from Dr. Sullivan. She nearly bursts with satisfaction. It awakens a storm of panic in my heart.

"I heard Evangeline Thompson visited you in the infirmary," she says, shifting her gaze to me to gauge my reaction. But I don't give her one. I was expecting her to question it. Dr. Sullivan's predictability is one of my only saving graces.

"I'm sure you watched the show live." I tug at the ends of my hair and drop my gaze to the empty coffee table.

"This might come as a surprise, but we don't have cameras in primary staff locations. I trust you'll keep that information a secret." She smiles again like she provided me with highly classified material with the capability of ruining the board when all it means is that there's one way in and out of the infirmary, and no one wants to break in somewhere they can't easily escape from.

I don't know what to say, so I nod and suck in my bottom lip, thinking for a moment. After a few long seconds I say, "I was surprised to see her. I didn't expect her to visit a girl she barely knew."

Dr. Sullivan sets her clipboard down and leans her elbows on her knees. "You have a way of making quite the impression on people. I, for one, am one of those people. Dr. Harvey as well."

I grimace. "Why?"

Hunter clears his throat next to me. "Watch the tone, Emily."

Dr. Sullivan smirks. "It's fine, Agent Hunter. Emily has a right to ask and feel the way she does." I feel her eyes on me and force myself to look up. "It'll help you see we're not the bad guys."

I'd love nothing more than to roll my eyes. "That's something the council would say."

Dr. Sullivan stiffens, her lips disappearing as she presses them together. Her face reddens, and I imagine steam shooting from her ears, but she takes a breath and composes herself. "The Human Preservation Agency is nothing like those monsters. Let me prove it to you."

I narrow my eyes. "How?"

A knock on the door cuts off our conversation. A second later, it swings open, and Evie steps in.

HUNTER

I don't know why I'm surprised Dr. Sullivan brought Evie here to talk to Nadia. After talking with Agent Rosaline this morning, I knew the board had plans for Evie, but I didn't think they'd want the two near each other. They must be absolutely confident that Evie is on their side, and it makes me uneasy because Evie knows the truth. She knows about my love for Nadia and what happened that day, and her presence is dangerous. I should've never let Nadia trust her.

"Don't beat yourself up, Hunter. Nadia's mind was set. She's about taking action and it's action that creates change. I don't think we need to worry just yet. Remember what Alyssa said?"

I don't take my eyes off Evie while I think, "Thanks, conscience, but you know how things can change in an instant."

Jacqueline doesn't respond. I pull my stare away from Evie to gaze at Nadia. She holds a smile but doesn't move. She and Evie don't break eye contact, even when Dr. Sullivan touches Evie's knee. I wish I could hear the silent exchange of thoughts Nadia and Evie share.

"Agent Hunter, have you met Evangeline?" Dr. Sullivan

asks.

Three pairs of eyes fall on me. I clear my throat but can't find the words.

"You're the guy from the lobby this morning," Evie says, extending her hand to mine. "Rosaline has a lot of nice things to say about you."

Dr. Sullivan beams a smile.

I nod. "Agent Rosaline mentioned she was watching out for you."

The light in Evie's eyes dims, and she drops her gaze to her hands. "I wish she didn't have to, but it's not safe for me anymore. Supers are out to get me."

Nadia gasps, but it was so quiet that only I heard it because I'm concentrating on her every movement and reaction. She crosses her arms and leans back on the couch. "I'm sorry to hear that," Nadia says, speaking up.

Evie bobs her head. "Me too."

NADIA

The more I hear Evie speak, the more I feel she's completely brainwashed. She used the terminology for creatures, only popular with the HPA, and she's paranoid. It's rare for a creature to hunt a particular human who isn't decked in a black uniform, and it's unheard of that multiple people would want Evie dead. She's not a real threat.

"You must be so scared." I force fake sympathy into my voice.

Evie pouts her bottom lip. "Not for long though. I'm not going to spend the rest of my life being terrified."

Evie's words sound familiar. I told myself the same thing when I was banished from the compound. Shifting on the couch, I tuck my bare feet under me, pressing my knees into Hunter. If I look relaxed, I'll seem more believable, and I need Dr. Sullivan to think Evie is somehow getting me to trust the board.

"Well, good for you, I guess," I say. "I know what living in fear is like, and it's not a good feeling."

Dr. Sullivan leans forward. "And what are you afraid of, Emily?"

I glance at Hunter, who quietly stares at his hands. I want to say I'm afraid of losing Hunter, and my family—that I'm terrified of people dying because of me, and I'm afraid of dying, too. But the thoughts stay locked in my mind and instead I say, "You."

Dr. Sullivan's hand flies to her heart, and she looks astonished. "Oh, Emily, I'm so sorry. I'm going to change that."

Hunter lifts an eyebrow but keeps his expression serious. I swing my gaze from him to Evie, and then back to Dr. Sullivan. "How am I supposed to believe you? You're suddenly going to let me go or something after keeping me locked up for two months?"

"Emily, calm down," Hunter says.

I stand up and cross my arms. "I don't want to calm down! You've taken two months of my life."

Stomping to the corner of the room, I slide to the floor, pulling my knees to my chest. I don't know where all this is heading, but Dr. Sullivan isn't fooling me. *Maybe you should play along and see where it takes you.*

Tears burn my eyes, but I hold them back. I refuse to let Dr. Sullivan see me cry. A warm hand touches my shoulder. I peer up and meet Evie's hazel eyes. Both Hunter and Dr. Sullivan watch me from behind Evie, and I ignore them.

Evie leans close and whispers, "Please, give Dr. Sullivan a chance. I know it's hard to believe, but you've been misguided about the HPA."

I laugh. I can't help it. I shouldn't expect Evie to understand. She only glimpsed a tiny part of my world. I should've known it wouldn't have been enough to persuade her. But what I don't get is why she hasn't revealed the truth about Hunter and me. Her keeping my secret is what gives me hope for her. She's not fully convinced by the HPA. If only she knew everything they've done to me—to so many people like me.

It's a huge risk to ask Evie why she's not screaming the truth, but I have to find out. It might be my only chance. I lean in to her and press my lips to her ear and whisper, "Why haven't you said anything?"

She pulls away, and I train my gaze on Dr. Sullivan for a reaction, but she has the same curious expression she did a minute ago. Hunter's forehead crinkles, his worry showing, but it's only worry. It's when his expression turns to panic that I need to start freaking out.

Evie tilts her head to mine. "Because you're my friend and my friends come first. It's not my secret to tell, either. I really do think you're misguided, Nadia, and I hope you'll really think things through and give Dr. Sullivan and the board a chance.

They don't want to kill you." Her voice is so low I have to strain to hear her. "They want you to join us."

I blink a few times and rest my chin on my knees as Evie's words sink in. She's too far gone to convince her they lied to her. She'll have to figure it out for herself, and because of that, I can't be friends with her.

Hunter was right. It was a stupid idea to involve Evie in the first place. I hope she's true to her word. I'll pretend to trust her and be her friend, but there's no real hope that it'll ever be like I imagined. It hurts to think like this, but I want to survive in this world. More than that, I want to live again.

I nod and shift away from Evie to get to my feet. "If what Evie told me was true and you want me to join your cause, you have to prove it, Dr, Sullivan." If Dr. Sullivan intends on playing games with me, I need to test the competition.

Dr. Sullivan smiles. "Of course. I was planning on it. I'm having a new room set up for you as we speak."

My heart drops into my stomach, and I shake my head. "No, not yet. I'm fine where I am for now."

Twisting her lips in a frown, she asks, "You like being locked in a cell?"

I shrug. "No, but it's better than you putting me in isolation somewhere. I want you to start smaller. I want some new clothes, and I want to leave my cell whenever I want."

Dr. Sullivan's eye twitches. "I'll have to run it by the board, but you have to give us something first."

Hunter's gaze shifts between us, and Evie remains on the floor with her back to the wall. I step closer to Dr. Sullivan.

When I'm standing a foot away, I place my hands on my hips and stare her dead in the eyes. "Like what?"

"You said the council didn't hire you to interfere with the transfer the day we caught you. So, who did?" Her eyes narrow as she studies my face like it will somehow give away the answers.

"No one hired me. I owed Dmitri's family a favor. Camille promised it would be an easy job until one of your agents tried to kill me. I was only supposed to be a distraction. Evie wasn't even supposed to be there, but I didn't have a choice. The board moved so quickly." My gaze doesn't waver until Dr. Sullivan breaks it to look at Evie. I take the same moment to look at her as well.

Evie shrugs. "I told you I didn't know anything."

HUNTER

"Good thinking, Nadia. They can't go after a dead girl," Jacqueline says like Nadia can hear her. *"You need to say something, Hunter. I was your partner. Any normal person would want to know more if they lost someone close to them."*

I clear my throat. "Camille was the name of my partner. That thing that killed Rob was not my partner."

"Oh, nice work. I'd totally believe you."

Nadia sucks in her bottom lip. "I'm sorry. It's just the name she gave me."

Dr. Sullivan looks at me with puckered brows. She looks as sad as I hope I look like. "It was hard for all of us."

"Your mom loved me. How sweet."

"Shut up, Jackie," I think.

Dr. Sullivan turns her gaze back to Nadia. "What creature possessed our agent, anyway?"

Nadia strolls toward the door, turning her back on Dr. Sullivan. "This new thing between us works two ways. You still need to prove to me your good intentions." She says it to the door without looking at Dr. Sullivan.

Dr. Sullivan purses her lips. "I'll contact the board as soon as I can."

Nadia peers over her shoulder to me. "Come on, Agent Hunter. I want to go back to my cell. It's been a long morning." She turns to Evie. "I'll see you around, I hope."

I shift my eyes to Dr. Sullivan, and she nods. Crossing the room, I place my hand on Nadia's back but don't restrain her. If Dr. Sullivan wants to play this game, I'm going to take advantage of it as much as I can.

I unlock the door and guide Nadia into the hall, and she smiles at me when the door closes. Holding her head high, she looks confident in her decision, but it doesn't stop the dread from dripping down my back.

"Trust Nadia."

"I do, Jackie. It's everyone else that I don't trust."

Nadia bumps my shoulder. "This is fun, huh?"

I keep my face straight. "It's different." As much as I want to relax and smile with Nadia, I still have to maintain my appearance.

"A good different. I never thought things would change." Her voice strains, and I know she doesn't believe it. Because things haven't changed. Everyone only pretends they have.

TRUST

NADIA

CAMDEN SITS ON the floor against the wall. He hasn't looked at me since I returned from the interrogation room. Hunter left after hovering for only a minute, and I know what Camden's thinking. His eyes speak a thousand words. They're clouded with doubt and anxiety and something else—something more intense, but I can't put my finger on it.

I draw in my sketchbook to pass the time. It's nothing meaningful, but I'm certain the HPA will discuss it in depth. I take the time to draw individual raindrops cascading from a gray thundercloud. Each drop is dual-colored, the top light blue and the bottom midnight blue, and the cloud is lined in yellow and orange even though I don't draw a sun.

I glance at Camden as he stares at the floor and then tear the page from my notebook, crumple it, and throw it at him. His gaze slowly shifts to meet mine, and I offer a small smile. When he doesn't return it, my heart falls to my stomach.

I get up the nerve to speak. "What's your problem? One second you were trying to convince me that fate doesn't exist, and now you won't look at me? I don't get it."

He tips his head back to stare at the ceiling. "I had some time to think about what you said."

"And?"

"I'm trying to give you space. It may not be for the reasons you tried to persuade me with, but I'm doing it because I see the board isn't really the one pushing you away. It's me."

I stand up and cross the room, sliding to the floor next to Camden, close enough that our shoulders touch. He watches me in his peripheral vision, while I blatantly stare at him. I don't want him to think he's done something wrong, or that I'm distancing myself because of him, but I also can't tell him the truth without giving things away.

I pucker my bottom lip out. "I wish there weren't cameras watching our every move so I could explain myself better. The last few days have been complicated, and my past is haunting me. For not doing much, life feels harder than ever."

He reaches out and places his hand on my knee. "If life was always easy, we'd be weak."

"Maybe I'm tired of being strong though." I rest my hand on top of his.

"That's why it's okay to let others be strong for you."

I smile. "Maybe some other time."

The door beeps before cracking open. I can't see who's on the other side from this position on the floor, but I don't need to see to know who it is. Hunter swings the door open and peers around the room before his gaze falls to me on the floor.

I smile. I can't help it. The memory of our kiss rushes hot through my mind, and heat crawls up my neck. "I'm guessing you have some news?"

Hunter nods.

I glance from Hunter to Camden. "Give me a minute."

Hunter frowns while he steps back and closes the door.

Turning to Camden, I lean in close. He presses into me, and I tilt my head to whisper into his ear. "I'm going to be out of the cell more, but you have to trust me that I'm not switching sides, okay?"

He pulls away to look me in the eyes. "I don't like this."

I shrug and push to my feet. "Trust me."

When I cross the room to the door, it opens just when I'm about it reach it. I smile at Hunter again. He guides me into the corridor but doesn't cuff me. I stand a foot away as he locks the cell door.

My heart races when he draws his gaze to mine. I see something resembling happiness for the first time in weeks. He's not stone-faced and serious, like I've grown used to, and his eyes shine in the fluorescent lighting. The corners of his lips curl in a not-quite smile. I stare at them for a moment before he touches my shoulder and nudges me to follow him.

"The board granted you permission to shadow me in the green zone," Hunter says as we enter the viewing area.

I purse my lips. "What does that mean?"

"It means that if you want out of your cell you have to hang out with me."

"Oh."

Hunter chuckles. "Thanks."

I blush. He knows there's no one else in the world I'd rather be with, but I'm surprised by the board's decision. They're really working hard to persuade me, but I'm uneasy about the entire situation. It shouldn't be this simple. The board will never have my interests at heart, and the moment I do something wrong, they'll get rid of me. Even if I chose to be loyal to them, I know where their intentions lie.

He points to a folding chair stationed next to the rolling one at his desk, and I sit down before him. "I didn't mean it like that, Agent Hunter."

He shrugs. "It's cool."

I blow wisps of hair out of my face and lean my elbows on my knees. Staring at the monitor, keeping my face as neutral as I possibly can, I assess how many prisoners are under Hunter's care. I knew there were a few people but didn't realize how many there actually were. My heart aches, watching them pace, sleep, cry, and stare into space. I wonder if the board has gotten anyone to break yet.

I cross and uncross my legs before lifting my foot up and tucking it under me. "So you just sit here and watch us all day?"

"Basically." Hunter leans back in his chair. "I feed you

guys, too."

I play with strands of my hair. "Out of everyone, who's your favorite?"

Hunter side-eyes me, and I smirk. "I don't have one."

"It's me, isn't it? I'm your favorite." I laugh when Hunter blushes. I'm not sure if I've ever seen him blush out of embarrassment, and I'm enjoying this more than I should. It's strange that just a few minutes ago I was depressed, but now that I get to spend alone time with Hunter, even with a camera watching us, it almost feels normal—like none of this has happened, and it's some weird nightmare.

He narrows his eyes at me before grinning. "Don't tell the others. They might get jealous."

The elevator dings and the doors swoosh open. My uplifted mood withers away the moment I lay my eyes on Dr. Sullivan and a boy who looks just like her and Hunter, but with darker eyes. Dr. Sullivan twitches her fingers in a wave when she steps out, and her heels echo as she taps across the tiles to us. The boy locks his gaze with mine, and I'm too nervous to look away.

Heat flushes over my clavicle, and I force my mouth to smile.

The boy glares, but I hold my smirk.

"What's going on?" the boy asks, turning his gaze to Hunter's and then to Dr. Sullivan.

"Just following orders, Mason." Hunter stiffens next to me, his distrust and disappointment in his brother palpable. I wish I could hug Hunter and tell him that Mason might be on his mother's side, but in the end they'll always be brothers and that has to mean something.

"No need to worry, Mason. Emily shares our interests," Dr. Sullivan says.

I smile again even though I'd rather grimace. The only interest I share with Dr. Sullivan is that I love Hunter—and even then, I'm not so sure she feels the same.

Mason looks at me again but doesn't say anything. He turns to his mother and says, "Interesting."

Dr. Sullivan hands Hunter a paper bag before tugging a tote bag off her shoulder and giving it to me. I don't move to open it but just hold it against my chest.

"I thought I'd stop by with some lunch and the clothes you requested, Emily," Dr. Sullivan says. "I hope this is a start to gaining your trust."

I bob my head. "It is. Thanks."

She beams a fake smile. "Glad to hear. I'll be stepping out for a bit with Mason, but I'd like to meet with you later."

I press my lips together. She says it like I have a choice. "Okay."

Hunter taps his finger on the keyboard next to me but doesn't look up from the monitor. "Can I split my double and take a few hours off after lunch then?"

Dr. Sullivan nods. "Of course. I know you're being overworked."

"It's fine, but I promised my aunt I'd put together some new furniture she bought. She needs it tonight for some party she's throwing." Hunter leans back in his chair and laces his fingers behind his head. He doesn't even glance at his brother who's staring right at him.

"Tell Christine I said hello." Dr. Sullivan glances at me once more before grabbing Mason's elbow and then turns on her heels to saunter back to the elevator.

When they disappear, I open the tote and glance inside. Dread seeps into my stomach. I keep my face as expressionless as possible and pull out black pants and a black shirt. I hold up the HPA uniform sans belt and boots and bare my teeth at Hunter in a fake smile.

"Is black my color?" I ask.

His jaw twitches, and he blinks. After a moment, he says, "It'll bring out your eyes."

HUNTER

I study Nadia's serious eyes. I wasn't expecting Dr. Sullivan to give her an HPA uniform. I thought Nadia would get jeans and a T-shirt, something besides the white scrubs, but definitely not a uniform. Nadia's being tested. I'm scared for her to put it on. What if this is how she gets out of here?

"It's never that simple, Hunter. If they ever let Nadia leave the facility, they'd insert some tracker or something under her skin. They wouldn't make the same mistake they did with me. I'm surprised they don't do it now." Jacqueline's pessimism depresses me, but she's right.

Nadia shoves the clothes back in the tote bag and sets it on the ground next to her. She taps her pale fingers on the desk and leans closer to me. "Think they'd be upset if I asked for something with a little more color?" she whispers, but it's loud enough to be heard by anyone watching us. She's testing the board as well.

I shrug instead of answering. I open the paper bag Dr. Sullivan handed me and pull out two sandwiches from the gourmet deli down the street. I eye Nadia as she watches my hands, and her lips twist downward. I hand her one of the sandwiches, and she places it on her lap, but doesn't unwrap it.

"They're really good," I say even though I know Nadia prefers to eat things of the nightmare variety.

She plays with the paper and pulls it down before bringing the sandwich to her nose to sniff it. "Smells delicious."

I laugh. I can't help it. It's like watching someone pretend to like something they find really disgusting and attempt to eat it to please the cook. She takes a small bite and widens her eyes like it's the best thing she's ever had.

I take a bite of my own sandwich and then set it on my desk before turning to Nadia and saying, "Want to help me pass out lunch to the others when it arrives?"

She nods, forcing herself to take another bite. "Should I change then?"

She's making an excuse not to eat, and I don't blame her. "Here, I'll let you into the bathroom."

NADIA

I set my sandwich on the corner of the desk and pick up the tote bag. As I swing it over my shoulder, it knocks my sandwich on the floor. I jump back and cover my mouth. Hunter smirks before reaching down to scoop the scattered lettuce, tomato, meat, cheese, and bread into the paper bag.

It's not that I can't eat, it's just that I don't like to. Nothing compares to how satisfying and delicious a dream is. The only real foods I appreciate and enjoy tasting are desserts.

"I'm so clumsy," I say.

Hunter tosses the bag in the trash. "It's nothing. I can tell you're nervous."

"Very."

I walk behind him as he escorts me to the single stall bathroom. He opens the door and holds it open for me. Hanging the tote bag on a small hook near the door, I glance over my shoulder at him as he watches me.

I arch my brows. "You can't shut the door?"

He presses his lips together. "I can't leave you unsupervised."

"Then get in here and close the door because I'm not giving everyone a free peepshow. You can just stare at the door."

Hunter grins as he shuts the door and leans against it. I rush him, sliding my hands up his chest and around his neck. I breathe in his spicy scent, everything good about him. He kisses my forehead and then my lips, sliding his hands under my shirt to touch my stomach. I relax in his arms, kissing him deeply, pressing into him. He tugs my white cotton shirt over my head completely, trailing his lips trail to my neck and then my shoulder. He brushes them on my collarbone, my skin tingling, my breath quickening, and my heart threatens to crash through my ribcage.

"I love you," Hunter whispers.

A knock on the door sends me reeling backward. Fear slices through me like a blazing sword.

"Hunter? Dr. Sullivan said it was okay to come up here. I'll be at your desk."

Hunter tosses me the tote bag. I turn to face the wall and yank the black shirt over my head as he cracks open the door.

"Hey, Evie. What're you doing here?" Hunter asks. If he didn't answer, the board would get suspicious knowing we both went into the bathroom.

I glance over my shoulder but don't stop changing. I feel her eyes on me for a second before looking away as I shrug out of the white cotton pants and into the black workpants. When I'm dressed, I spin on the balls of my bare feet.

Evie shrugs. "I'm bored. I can't see any of my old friends, and I hate having Rosaline shadowing me, so I figured I'd see what you were doing, Hunter." She bats her eyelashes, and it reminds me of the first time she met Hunter outside of Northern Bell High School. Jealousy sinks in my stomach. I dig my nails into the palms of my hands.

Hunter peers over his shoulder at me, holding his serious expression. I pick up my white scrubs off the floor and shove them in the tote bag and then saunter forward and bump my arm against his as I walk from the bathroom.

Evie's gaze trails from my bare feet to my pale blond hair, and I brush the loose strands from my face. I didn't look at myself in the mirror, and I'm afraid of how scary I'll look. It took a while to get used to Hunter wearing an HPA uniform. I never thought I'd see the day that I'd be in one, even if it's just part of some twisted HPA game.

Hunter clears his throat. "I don't know how entertaining I

can be. Just have to drop those off." He points to a rolling cart of stacked, lidded trays, which someone must've brought in while I was changing. "Then I'm heading out for a few hours."

"Can I come?" Evie asks.

Hunter shifts his feet. "No, sorry. I won't be long though. You can hang out here and watch the monitors if you'd like."

Evie sighs. "Maybe some other time."

Hunter smiles. "Sure."

I glare at the floor. I should be the one making plans with either of them, and instead I have to listen to Evie trying to sneak her way into Hunter's life. She knows we're in love, and she has to know how much this bothers me, so why is she doing it? Why is she tormenting me?

I swallow the lump in my throat. "Hey, Hunter," I say, drawing his attention from Evie. "I'm not feeling so well, so I'm going to pass on the lunch round. Can you please just take me back to my room?"

Hunter's forehead wrinkles as he nods. He doesn't say anything as he touches his hand to my back and guides me into the cement corridor and to the first room where Camden is. Hunter unlocks the door, and I step in.

Strolling toward my desk, I gaze at Camden on his cot. His eyes shoot open when he sees me, and he jumps from the bed, startling me.

He throws his hands in the air. "I knew it!" His deep voice reverberates through my core, and I step back. Strutting closer, he points his finger. I turn on the balls of my feet to move out of the way. My foot catches on my desk chair, my feet slipping out from under me, and pain explodes in my head as I hit it on something sharp. I fall over and smash into the ground, my eyes clouded with purple and black stars, and tears roll over my temples and fall into my hair.

The world closes in on me, and the last face I see is Hunter's.

11

NO LONGER SAFE

HUNTER

"EMILY!" CAMDEN YELLS.

Nadia's eyes roll back, and I rush to stand over her. My heart thuds, anger tinting my vision red. Swiping a tranquilizer from my weaponry belt, I turn on my heels and jam the syringe in Camden's neck. He staggers on his feet before collapsing as the sedative works its way through his system.

"Oh, my God!" Evie yells from behind me, hovering in the doorway without entering the cell.

I ignore Evie and slide my arms around Nadia, scooping her up off the floor. Her arms dangle at her sides, her head lulling back, but she's still breathing. It takes all my willpower to keep my face as expressionless as possible, to stay calm as panic consumes me. Blood paints Nadia's pale blond hair, splashing droplets across the tile. I press her head against my arm to put pressure on the wound.

Bumping Evie out of the way, I grind my teeth and stop. Even though I want to get Nadia to the infirmary as fast as I can, I can't break protocol. I enter in my pass code to lock Camden in the cell, my fingers shaking, now covered in blood.

"Mind helping?" I ask Evie, peering at her worried lined eyes.

Bobbing her head, she swivels on her feet and runs ahead to call for the elevator to take us from the cell block.

"You need to stay calm, Hunter. Tell Phillip to call for Dr. Harvey. I'm sure Nadia will be okay." Even though Jacqueline sounds calm, her fear is as strong as mine, and I'm not sure she believes herself.

The door dings open, and I jog into the lobby. "Call Dr. Harvey. Emily's been injured," I say as I speed past the reception desk. I don't meet Phillip's eyes and head straight for the hallway to the infirmary.

Evie enters first and holds the door open before dashing ahead to hold the other one. "What can I do to help?" she asks, her voice quivering. She looks ready to pass out.

"Get some towels from the cabinet," I say.

Setting Nadia on one of the hospital beds, I grab a white towel from Evie. She pales seeing Nadia's blood and sits on the edge of the next bed over. I cup Nadia's face with my free hand and stare at her closed eyes. She looks so fragile and defeated. It scares me. In this moment with her bleeding in my arms, I'm not sure she has any fight left in her.

NADIA

"Stay with me." Hunter's voice cuts through the darkness, and a pinprick of light glows in the distance. I hover in a void of nothingness, clinging onto the sound of his voice like it's the only thing that'll keep me from disappearing.

The light glows brighter, the world shifting, and I find myself standing amid puffy clouds bathed in pinks, purples, and reds from a setting sun. The warm air wraps around me, smelling like salty sea air, and I spin in a circle.

My heart beats faster as the clouds fog around me. This isn't real. I'm dreaming. It's just like the first and only dream I've ever had when I was stabbed in the shoulder by an agent and fighting to stay alive.

I'm dying. The thought burns through my very core, and I push it away. Camden's haunting, aqua blue eyes shimmer as his image appears in the clouds. I stumble back, fear slicing through me. Not because I'm afraid of him, but because I'm afraid for him. The board is going to kill him. I just know it. They'll blame him if something happens to me.

I peer around the world. "Hunter? Where are you?"

"Is she going to be okay?" Hunter asks but not to me. I know it's about me. I glide through the clouds in search of where the voice comes from, but the pink and purple air presses against me.

"We won't know anything until we can run some tests." It's Dr. Harvey. His low, whispery voice doesn't sound optimistic.

I close my eyes and focus. I have to wake up. *Wake up. Wake up, Nadia. Wake. Up. Now. Now!*

The air shifts, my stomach dropping, and the pink, purple, and orange clouds dissipate as cold wind rushes around me, and I free fall. Blinding light flashes in my eyes. I blink and moan, pain swelling in my head. Bile rises in my throat, and I cough and thrash, trying to catch my breath.

Firm hands grip each of my arms, and I hear Dr. Harvey yell, "Sedate her!"

Ice rushes through my veins a moment later, and I sink back into empty darkness.

HUNTER

My palms sweat as I help Dr. Harvey sedate Nadia. Her screams and panic bury deep in my soul. It kills me that I can't hug her and comfort her like I should. All I can do is stand by and hope Dr. Harvey has enough interest in Nadia to really want to save her.

"If it were anyone else, he'd let them die," Jacqueline says. *"But I see the way he treats her. He sees something different in her. He'll keep her alive."*

I shift on my feet. "Anything else I can do?"

Dr. Harvey shakes his head. "Not right now, but I'll let you know. Why don't you head back to your zone to wait? Emily's in good hands."

I scrunch my brows but don't comment. He's implying that I'm worried, and it makes me nervous. It's getting harder and harder to disguise my emotions. I need to focus more and stop being so careless.

"I'm going to stay here," Evie says, speaking for the first time since Dr. Harvey arrived. "She's my friend, and I want her to know I'm here for her."

Dr. Harvey smiles and touches Evie's shoulder. "I'm sure she already knows."

I turn my back on them, my legs heavy as I force them to work, so I can walk out of here. Stopping at the door, I glance over my shoulder. Dr. Harvey and Evie stand on each side of Nadia's bed and stare down at her.

"You should find Alyssa, Hunter." Jacqueline's voice echoes in my ears as I step through the door. I was planning on seeing her anyway, but now that I have some bad news, I'm afraid to tell her. What if she's had a vision and it's a bad one? What if she tells me Nadia's going to die? What then?

Instead of heading back to my desk, I walk from the building and to my car. "How can I face them? I'm supposed to take care of her," I think.

"She fell. It wasn't anyone's fault."

"If Camden hadn't startled her—"

"You know as well as I do that he's not himself."

I grimace, opening my car door, and think, "Then it's my fault, because I should've moved her to another cell."

Jacqueline doesn't respond. As I reverse from my spot, my prepaid cell phone rings from my center console, and I wait until I'm through the gate to pick it up. It's an unknown number, but I don't even have to guess to know it's Alyssa. She saw I made the decision to find her.

I answer the phone through my stereo. "Agent Hunter."

"You're looking for me?" Alyssa's voice remains calm and doesn't give anything away. I'm not sure she knows or not since it was an accident, and Nadia didn't just decide to fall.

I tap my fingers on the steering wheel. "Yeah, I need to meet you right now. Can you contact Dmitri?"

She sucks in a breath. "Just come to the house. I'll call him when you get here, but he won't be back until tomorrow."

"See you soon." I click off the line and merge onto the highway. I don't know how I'm going to tell Nadia's father, but I better get the courage soon. I need to prepare for what happens next.

NADIA

"The scans show nothing abnormal, so it's safe to say she'll recover without issue."

Dr. Harvey's voice wraps around me and tugs me from the black void. My closed eyelids shine red, and I squeeze them shut. I'm not ready to face reality yet. I want to be nothing for a while longer.

"What a relief," Dr. Sullivan says. "We need her in pristine mental and physical health for the alteration."

The alteration? Panic rises in my chest and squeezes my heart hard enough that I feel myself drifting back into the void. They're planning on experimenting on me. I thought humans were safe from that, but I guess I was wrong. Hunter was, too. I need to get out of here.

I wiggle my toes but don't open my eyes. Dr. Sullivan and Dr. Harvey don't know I'm conscious yet, and I want to keep it that way so I can eavesdrop a little longer. Listening to the pounding in my ears, I count each slow breath I take.

My bed shifts as someone sits on the edge. "Will she be going to the training facility with me?" Evie asks. My stomach tightens with knots at the possibility of being transferred away from here...away from Hunter.

"Eventually. The board won't vote on it until we're all one hundred percent sure she's on our side," Dr. Sullivan says.

Evie's hand brushes my arm, and I hold absolutely still. "And when will you know that?"

"When she willingly gives up information about the council."

I can't stand listening any longer. Moaning, I shift on the bed. I reach up and touch the bandage on my head, and a tear slips from my eye when my fingers feel a bald spot on the underside of my hair. I can't help freaking a bit about my hair, but I force myself to calm down and open my eyes.

I meet Dr. Sullivan's smiling face and shift my eyes to Dr. Harvey and then Evie. Evie touches a tissue to my cheek and then tosses it on the metal tray behind her. Her hazel eyes bore into me. It's like she's trying to discover something I keep locked up in the massive walls I've built to protect me.

Licking my dry lips, I clear my throat. "Where's Camden?" His aqua blue eyes flash in my mind.

"In his cell, Emily," Dr. Harvey says.

I try to sit up on my elbows, but Evie touches my shoulder to keep me down and then raises the top half of my bed with the remote attached to the railing. She smiles at me, and I shift my eyes to Dr. Sullivan. Dr. Sullivan's brown hair hangs loosely over her shoulders. She hugs a clipboard to her chest as she watches my every movement.

"This wasn't his fault. Please, don't hurt him," I say.

Dr. Sullivan tilts her head to the side. "We're not monsters, Emily. We know your fall was an accident. We wouldn't hurt someone you care about."

I suck in my bottom lip to keep my words locked tight in my throat. She's lying through her fake smile. I know that Camden would already be gone if they didn't think I'd close myself off and refuse to help them. And as for the people I care about? The board wants to destroy everyone I love. Dr. Sullivan's crazy if she thinks I don't know that.

I lean my head back on my pillow. "Can I see him then?"

Dr. Sullivan purses her lips. "I suppose so. I'll have Agent Hunter bring him by when he returns. Until then, please get some rest."

I nod and close my eyes. "I'll try."

HUNTER

I put on the leather band and leave my car parked at the park around the corner from Nadia's neighborhood. Alyssa stands on the corner with her hands jammed in the pockets of her trench coat. Her fiery red hair blows over her shoulders and glows with streaks of copper in the pale sunlight. Rocking back on her wedged heel boots, she swings her sweater dress back and forth. Her green eyes shine with tears, and when I stop in front of her, she hugs me.

I pat her back. "Did you see something?"

She pulls away and stares into my eyes. "No. You just look so sad. I'm afraid you have bad news."

I press my lips together. "It's no longer safe for Nadia. There was an accident, and sh—" The words catch in my throat because I don't know how Nadia is. Alyssa grabs my arm and yanks me toward the yellow house at the end of the cul-de-sac. "She was hurt, Alyssa," I say after a moment.

Alyssa opens the front door and motions me into the quaint living room. A red couch and matching leather armchair rest in the center of the room with a coffee table between them. Photograph-like drawings hang in frames on the wall. A packed bookcase leans against the wall by the kitchen door, and a small table with a mirror hanging over it sits near the front door. I set my keys on it and follow Alyssa to sit on the couch.

She picks up the cordless phone from the coffee table and puts in on speaker phone before dialing a number. It rings twice and the line clicks. A mixture of voices, music, and static erupts through the speaker.

"What's wrong?" Dmitri asks. He breathes into the phone, and after a second, the background noise melts away.

I swallow the lump in my throat. "Nadia's been hurt. Camden's been acting weird the last day, and he snapped at Nadia and startled her. She tripped and hit her head pretty hard. I took her to the infirmary, but they made me leave. I don't know her condition. All I know is she's being taken care of by one of the best doctors on staff."

Dmitri sucks in a breath. "I was afraid of something like this occurring."

"You need to get her out, Dmitri. It's not safe. Things are changing faster than I anticipated. The board has some plan that I don't know about, but it makes me uneasy. They're insisting they want Nadia as part of the agency."

"Just hold tight until tomorrow, Hunter," Dmitri says.

My chest tightens. Nadia's had to wait long enough already. Instead of arguing, I say, "I'll try."

Alyssa touches my knee. "Everything going according to plan?" She changes the subject, and I think she's trying to take my mind off things, but it's not working. I can't get Nadia's fearful eyes out of my head.

Dmitri clears his throat. "Everything is falling into place perfectly. Prepare my room for tomorrow, will you? I'm bringing home a special guest."

"Sure, see you then." Alyssa hangs up the phone and turns to me. "Everything will happen as it should."

I don't answer her because even though something happens as it should doesn't mean it's something good. I don't believe things happen for a reason. Not anymore.

"Tell her it's up to us to make things happen how we want them to," Jacqueline says. She's been quiet since I left the facility, and it was almost like she wasn't stuck in my head anymore.

"I'm pretty sure she knows that, Jackie. She's just trying to make me feel better," I think.

Alyssa watches me, and I pull away from my conversation with Jacqueline. "And if it doesn't?" I ask.

"Then we'll figure it out," Alyssa says.

"I hope you're right."

12

NOW OR NEVER

HUNTER

I SIT DOWN at my desk. Before I pick up my phone to call Dr. Harvey, I notice a note under my keyboard. It's scribbled in Dr. Sullivan's messy handwriting, and it takes me a moment to decipher it.

"Why does she want you to bring Camden to the infirmary?" Jacqueline asks.

I shrug even though she can't exactly see me and think, "Did you forget you've been with me this whole time. How should I know?"

"I could never forget, Hunter, and it was just a thought."

I crumple the note and toss it in the wastebasket next to

143

my desk. Pushing to my feet, I head to the corridor and stop in front of Camden's door. He sits on the edge of his cot with his face hidden in his hands, his shoulders shaking.

I don't move. I can't. The last thing I want to do is open the door to the guy who caused Nadia to freak out and accidentally hurt himself. Jealousy runs hot through me, and the fact that Dr. Sullivan told me to take him to see Nadia does nothing for my mood. I need my moment with Nadia first.

"Aren't you going to open the door?"

I shift on my feet. "He's crying," I think to Jacqueline.

"So what? I've seen you cry."

I clench my jaw. "That's different. This guy's crying over my girlfriend."

"Just open the dang door and follow Dr. Sullivan's orders or the board's going to get suspicious."

Lifting my hand, I punch in my pass code. I tug the handcuffs off my weaponry belt before I crack the door open and peer into the room. Camden jerks his head up to look at me and jumps to his feet. His eyes and nose shine red and he looks younger.

I hold up the cuffs. "I have orders to take you to the infirmary."

He hangs his head, raising his arms in defeat. "I'm a dead man, aren't I?"

"Tell him that it wasn't his fault."

Glaring at the floor, I tighten the cuffs on his wrist. "It was an accident. No one is going to hurt you." I grit my teeth as I spit the words out. I shouldn't have to comfort Camden, and if

Jacqueline weren't in my head ready to annoy me, I wouldn't have.

Camden sniffs and blinks a few times. "Is she okay?"

I wish he'd just shut up for a minute so I could walk him to the infirmary without having to play Twenty Questions. "I don't know. I just got back from my afternoon off."

"Oh."

I grip Camden's arm, guiding him out of the cell. He shuffles his feet, and I practically drag him the entire way through the lobby and to the infirmary. Unlocking the door, I push him in front of me and nudge him to the next door where I see Nadia leaning back on a pillow with her eyes closed.

Nadia's eyes flutter open, hearing us enter. She's alone and isn't hooked up to any machines. I'm surprised she's not tied to the bed. She offers a small smile. I can't tell who it's aimed at. Camden picks up his pace, and I let him go so he can jog to Nadia.

He cups her face between his cuffed hands. "I'm so sorry, Emily," he whispers.

I can't stop myself from watching them, keeping my eyes trained on Nadia's reaction.

"Stop torturing yourself and sit down on the chair next to her." Jacqueline's voice lines with sympathy. I wish she wouldn't say anything right now.

I don't respond to her but follow her suggestion and meander to the foot of the bed, plopping down in the chair. She pulls away from Camden and meets my gaze for a second before rubbing her forehead with her hand.

"I should've warned you before I walked into your cell," Nadia says. "And I should've watched where I was going. I have a killer headache, but Dr. Harvey says I'll be okay. Good enough to—" She pauses and takes a breath. "Good enough to be altered or something."

"What?" Camden and I ask at the same time.

Nadia's hand trembles as she tucks her hair behind her ears. She lowers her voice. "I overheard my friend, Evie, talking to Dr. Sullivan. They're planning on transferring us to a training facility to undergo some sort of alteration. I don't know what it means, but I'm scared."

Camden's mouth drops open, and he looks at me. "Shhh, Emily. Don't say another word."

I straighten my shoulders and lean closer, ignoring Camden's glaring eyes. "This is bad."

"It has to do with the tests they ran, right?" Nadia tilts her head to the ceiling.

I nod. "The only time I've ever heard Dr. Sullivan mention altering someone was when she was speaking about people attempting to join the Special Abilities Task Force."

"What the heck is that?" Camden asks. I wish I could have a moment alone with Nadia without him here listening.

I raise an eyebrow and ignore him. "That's not important right now. What's important is that I need to get Nadia out of here tonight."

Nadia covers her mouth, and Camden stares between us. I stiffen as Nadia's name comes out of my mouth. I expect an army of agents to charge in at any second, but nothing happens.

There aren't any cameras in this room. The board is running off good faith that I'll report back to them with anything I hear between Camden and Nadia. I guess they never expected me to turn against them. Too bad for them, though, because I've been against them for months.

"Are you crazy, Hunter?" Jacqueline's voice booms in my ears, and I wince.

I grab Nadia's hands. "We don't have a choice. It's now or never."

NADIA

Blood pounds in my head faster than my heart, and shadows nudge the edge of my vision. I'm conflicted with fear and excitement, and Hunter's words sink deep into me. I'm getting out of here tonight. I don't know how we'll pull it off, and I have a feeling Hunter doesn't know either, but he's trying anyway. What if it gets us killed?

"Nadia?" Camden asks. I draw my eyes away from my shaking hands. "Your name is Nadia?"

I nod. "I can explain everything."

Hunter sighs. "We don't have time. We need to make a plan."

Leaning forward, I touch my fingers to Hunter's lips. "I'm going to make time." I turn toward Camden, who studies my every move and gesture. He's piecing things together that he didn't think about, and a thousand thoughts cloud his narrowed eyes. I force the words to break free from my throat. "Hunter is my boyfriend, Camden."

Camden glowers. "He's what?"

I wince. "I didn't mean for everything to turn out this way."

"You lied to me about everything."

Pulling my hand from Hunter's, I take Camden's instead. "That's not true. I really do care about you, Camden. This whole situation is messed up. I did what I had to do to stay alive and keep my secret safe. The board would kill me if they knew. You know that."

Hunter stands. "I'm going to give you a few minutes."

I gaze at him as he walks to the door but doesn't leave. He's just far enough not to have to listen to everything I say to Camden, and I'm thankful for that. I need to figure out how to make this right without hurting both of them.

Camden leans back and yanks his hand from mine before crossing his arms. "You were only using me."

Tears well in my eyes, and I blink them back. "I swear it wasn't just that. Please, you have to believe me."

"But it's always been him," Camden says, shifting his eyes to Hunter's back.

"I love him."

"What I don't get is how you can be with someone who does this—" He waves his arms around. "Who works for people who want us all dead. That's really messed up. Look at where you are, Em—Nadia. Look at the pain you've been through while your *boyfriend* stands around and does nothing to help you—at least not until he has to do something. He's a monster."

I jerk back, his words stinging as if they hit me, and I suck in a breath. "He's protecting me—us. He's never hurt anyone. If he wasn't here, I'd be worse off."

"Or maybe you wouldn't be in here at all."

Anger sweeps through me, and I glare. Camden has no idea what he's talking about. He doesn't know everything that Hunter has been through—what I have been through. He has a lot of nerve to say these hurtful things to me. "You're wrong. I'm here because I traded my freedom for my father's, knowing they wouldn't kill me."

Camden lowers his brows. "Keep telling yourself that. I still think you're making the wrong choice."

I tilt my head to the side. "Wrong choice?"

"You can never have a normal life with Hunter."

I can't believe what he's saying. I can't believe he has the nerve to say what I can and can't have with Hunter. He's not a seer. He could never guess how my life will turn out. I'll fight for a life with Hunter and who cares if it isn't a normal life? Any life with him is better than none at all.

"And you can never have a normal life with me," I say.

Camden gets to his feet and strolls closer, cupping my face in his hands, his aqua blue eyes staring into my soul. "It'd be better than this. Please, Em—Nadia, give me a chance. I can show you what love should be like. You shouldn't have to live in constant fear or have to sneak around or create fake identities. I love you."

Tears roll down my cheeks. It breaks my heart seeing how desperately Camden wants me to see his side of things, but he can't see my side either. "You don't. You can't."

"You can't tell me how to feel." He shifts to look at Hunter, who stares out the small window in the door. "Your love for him will get you killed."

I laugh. I can't help it. Not because I find it funny, but because that's exactly what will happen to Camden. There's no way around it. I've invaded his mind far too many times, and if I don't make him lose touch with reality, the board will kill him if we don't get out of here. It's best for Camden if he forgets I ever existed when we're free.

I squeeze my eyes shut for a second to find the words I need. "I care for you, but I can't be who you want me to be. I'm not good for you. My mother died after she lost touch of reality because of what my father is—what I am. It'll happen to you, too. I can't let you get hurt or worse because of me."

"And what about Hunter? He's only human, too."

"It's different. Our souls met before we did. We know each other on a different level, and I don't affect him." With the way Camden raises an eyebrow, I know he doesn't believe me. But I don't think I could say anything to defend Hunter that he'd believe at this point. Hunter is his enemy not only because of the black uniform, but because he has me.

"Nadia?" Hunter says, breaking my eyes from Camden. "We're running out of time."

I nod and look at Camden. "I want you to come with me."

"You expect me to trust Hunter to get us out alive?"

"No, I expect you to trust me."

HUNTER

"You're making a mistake," Jacqueline says. *"You're going to get*

yourself—and me—killed."

"Have some faith, Jackie. When have you ever died? I'm pretty sure you're basically immortal," I think. I glance through the window into the hallway once more before walking back toward Nadia. She's paler than normal, and the board would suspect something if it weren't for her head injury.

"I'm just lucky."

Nadia swings her gaze from Camden to me. I sit back in the chair next to the bed. "I think if we plan on leaving tonight, we shouldn't have a problem getting out. You're not in a cell, so it makes things easier, and security won't be alerted to me opening a cell."

"You're right, Hunter, but what about the guards at the gate?"

"I can handle them," I think.

"You're outnumbered."

Sighing, I think, "But I have surprise on my side."

"What about Camden?" Nadia asks.

I draw my attention from Jacqueline mumbling in my mind to Nadia's light gray eyes. She's losing energy fast, the fall taking a toll on her. I press my lips together. "He can't stay here, Nadia."

She frowns. "I'm not leaving without him."

"But if you don't leave, I can't protect you for much longer. What if they decide to transfer you in the morning? You know how fast the board works. If they haven't told me about their alteration plans, I doubt they'll tell me when they decide to take you." I push my hair off my forehead.

"I don't care. I'd have never made it this long without

Camden, and I'm not leaving him behind." Nadia crosses her arms. "That's my final decision."

"I have an idea, Hunter," Jacqueline says. *"You can call security and tell them that you're taking Camden back to Nadia because she's ready to give you information about the council if you allow him to stay with her."*

I inhale a long breath through my nose before releasing it. "Fine. I'll figure it out."

The phone on the wall rings, and Nadia jumps, terror lining her eyes as she holds herself. I pat her leg before getting up and walking to it. Picking it up, I press the receiver to my ear and listen for a second.

"Agent Hunter, speaking," I say.

"Hey, Agent Hunter, it's Phillip. Dr. Sullivan called and wanted me to let you know that she has to cancel the interview with Emily this evening."

"Okay," I say.

Phillip breathes into the phone. "Also, Evangeline Thompson and Agent Rosaline just walked in the door. I'm sending them your way."

I swear in my mind. I was hoping Evie would wait until tomorrow to come back to visit Nadia, and I definitely didn't expect Agent Rosaline to be shadowing her within these walls. There's nothing for her to worry about here. Evie is safe from whatever the board thinks is out to get her.

"Thanks, Phillip." Hanging up the phone, I turn to look at Nadia and Camden. "I have to get you back to your cell. Na— Emily has visitors."

Just as the words escape my mouth, Evie and Agent Rosaline walk through the door. Evie smiles and waves, and Agent Rosaline glares at Nadia and Camden before touching her weaponry belt out of habit. I stand and strut around the bed and grip Camden's shoulder until he stands.

"Nice to see you two again," I say. "I was just about to walk my charge back to his cell."

Evie peers at Agent Rosaline. "Why don't you go with Hunter?"

Agent Rosaline twists her lips to the side. "No, I think I'll stay."

I shrug. "Suit yourself. Emily isn't going anywhere." Yet. I'll be getting Nadia out as soon as the evening shift leaves, and then I can finally be done with this place forever.

13

NEVER GET OUT

NADIA

EVIE SITS ON the edge of the bed and plays with a loose thread on her sleeve. I wish she wouldn't have come back. It's hard to look her in the eyes when I know whose team she decided to fight for. If I had more time, I'd convince her she was brainwashed by the board. Getting involved was too much for her and since the board ripped her away from her normal life, she never had the chance to really think about everything. It's too easy to believe and agree with something familiar, and I'm sure her mother is as convincing as Dr. Sullivan. I wonder what other lies they fed her.

"I was so scared for you earlier." Evie rests her hand on my knee but doesn't look at me. "I thought I'd have to go through the alteration alone. Dr. Sullivan says it's a pretty intense program and that we're cut off from the outside world for a few months to a year."

Agent Rosaline jerks her head up to look at us. "Are you talking about the SATF?"

Evie presses her lips together. "Yeah, but don't tell anyone I told you."

"And they chose you and—" She narrows her eyes at me. "Did you know I was rejected as a candidate? Now they're just letting anybody enter the program. How can they even trust you over me? I've been on their side since I was a kid."

I arch my brows. I didn't expect Agent Rosaline to be so passionate about the whole situation. "Maybe because they sense a little resentment?" I bite my tongue after it's too late to take the words back. I should've just kept my thoughts to myself.

"Excuse me? You can't talk to me that way."

Evie stands up and faces Agent Rosaline, blocking my view of her livid eyes. "I think you should go, Rosaline."

"Gladly." Agent Rosaline turns on her heels and stomps to the door, leaving me alone with Evie.

Evie crosses her eyes and blows out a long breath. She then smiles and sits back on the edge of my bed. I wish she'd leave too, because I don't want her to be around when Hunter comes back. I don't want her to be in the middle when it's time to go. She'll get hurt. Even if her loyalty doesn't lie with me, I'd like her to know that we're not all bad like the board thinks. If she even has a tiny bit of doubt about her place in all this, she'll realize the truth. I need her to realize it.

I fake a yawn. "Thanks for standing up for me. Agent Rosaline's reaction is exactly why I'm not so sure any of this will work out."

Evie thrusts out her arms. Her wide, hazel eyes meet mine. "Are you kidding me? You can't think like that."

I wipe my hand across my forehead. "I'm serious. Agent Rosaline had a point. Why us? Out of all the HPA's talented agents, they want to send two girls who were caught releasing a fugitive to undergo some alteration. It doesn't make sense."

"Because we're special. Don't you want to do something great with your life? You can make a difference. Stop supers from hurting people." Evie bounces as she speaks. She sounds like she's memorized a speech Dr. Sullivan probably said to her to get her to believe all this crap.

I grip her arm and lean in close. "What happened to you, Evie? You've seen things for yourself. How can you think that everyone I know—people who are my friends—would hurt anyone? What about Alyssa?"

"Alyssa's different."

I dig my nails into the palm of my hand. "What about me?"

She laughs. "What about you? Your DNA says you're as human as I am."

Leaning back, I stare at the ceiling. I can't argue with someone who doesn't understand or listen. Her mind is set, and it is what it is. As much as I want to force Evie to see the truth she once accepted so easily, I can't. She's too far gone. She's the only one who can save herself now. I just hope she's strong enough.

HUNTER

"The building should be clearing out any minute," Jacqueline says.

I watch the people in their cells on my monitor. I can't just leave them here locked up. It's not fair. When I'm gone, there will be no one left to fight for them. I stayed with the HPA as long as I have, not only for Nadia, but to save as many innocent people as I could.

"What you're planning is even crazier than taking Camden with you." Jacqueline's voice echoes in my ears.

I squeeze my eyes shut. "Maybe it's the perfect plan," I think.

The more I think about the people in the cells, the more a plan falls into place. It's risky, but a little chaos might just be what we need to keep the focus off us. It'll increase our chances of surviving.

Scooping up my pen, I furiously write my pass code twelve times with a short note. I tear the paper into pieces and stare at them in my hands. This has to work. It'll give people a chance to escape, too. Nadia would want this. I know it. And I won't feel so guilty in the end.

The elevator door dings open, and Agent Rosaline struts out. I shove the pieces of paper into my pocket, a knot settling in my stomach. I thought she'd be gone by now. And if she's here, it must mean that Evie is still with Nadia. This isn't good. This can ruin everything.

"What now, Hunter?"

I force myself to smile. "What's up, Agent Rosaline?"

"What did you just shove in your pocket?"

"Oh, crap!"

The phone on my desk rings, and I fumble to grab it and hold my finger up to Agent Rosaline. The line crackles with background noise, and after a moment, Alyssa's voice echoes through. "You have ten minutes to get Nadia and get out of there! Whatever decision you just made changed everything. I saw you in handcuffs at five past ten." The line cuts off and sweat prickles on the back of my neck.

"Stay calm, Hunter. When I count to three, set the phone down and grab your tranquilizer gun." My heart hammers in my head louder than Jacqueline's voice. *"One. Two. Three."*

NADIA

Silence hangs in the air as Evie waits for me to respond, but the words stay locked up tight in my throat. Footsteps break through the silence, and Dr. Sullivan pushes through the door. Her heels tap the tiles, and each one clicks to the same rhythm of my heartbeat.

What is she doing here? I wasn't expecting to see Dr. Sullivan, and it's like it's my destiny to never see outside of these walls ever again without her breathing down my neck. A fake smile crosses her lips. Something malicious shines in her hazel eyes, causing the hairs on my arms to rise. It's that darkness that makes her eyes different than Hunter's. I don't see any resemblance to him within her anymore.

"I'm glad to see you're awake," Dr. Sullivan says.

Pressing my lips together, I wait for a second to respond. "I wasn't expecting you here tonight. Isn't it kind of late for you?"

Evie shifts on the bed and stands up but doesn't say a word.

Dr. Sullivan pushes her gold-rimmed glasses on her head. "It's never too late to visit my favorite girls. My meeting with the board ended early, and I was hoping to catch you while you were still awake."

Evie glances at me, and I drop my gaze to my trembling hands. "What is it you need?"

"The board wants another scan done as soon as possible to make sure you're really okay. Dr. Harvey will be here soon to complete it."

My heart falls in my stomach. This can't be happening. Hunter's supposed to get me out of here tonight and with Dr. Sullivan here, our plans are ruined. I'll never get out of here now. I'll be forced to do whatever the board wants if I want to survive. I can't handle this. I won't let them take me.

I rub my eyes. "Please, can't it wait until morning? I'm so tired."

"It'll only take about thirty minutes. I think you can manage."

Dr. Sullivan thought wrong. I can't manage. I sit up and swing my legs off the bed. My head pounds and the edges of my vision darken. "No, really, I can't. Just stay away from me."

HUNTER

I punch in my pass code and open Camden's cell door. "Dude, we have to go. Now!"

I leave the door open and run to the next cell and open it. I shove my hand in my pocket, and the pieces of paper scatter everywhere. I swear under my breath.

"Let them open the doors. Go get Nadia. You have eight minutes!"

"My pass code is written on these pieces of paper. Go open all the doors and take the elevator to the ground level. Follow the hall to the right. It'll lead to the lobby. You may have to fight your way out, but you're free."

Turning on my heels, I bump into Camden. I rush past him, and he jogs behind me to the elevator. Agent Rosaline groans from where she's cuffed to my desk. There's only one entrance and exit on this floor, and it's through the elevator to keep it easier to lock down the place when needed.

The ride to the lobby drags on. When the elevator door finally dings open, I peer at the dimly lit, empty lobby and sigh in relief. We might actually make it out of here alive after all. I hold my arm out to keep Camden behind me and then step off the elevator. He stays so close to me that I can hear his heavy breathing near my ear.

"What are you doing, Agent Hunter?" A masculine voice echoes through the lobby.

I jerk my head toward the front door, searching for Dr. Harvey.

"Tell him Nadia wanted to see Camden."

"I'm just taking Camden for one last visit tonight. We won't be long." I shift on my feet, sweat beading on my forehead, my chest tightening. I need Dr. Harvey to believe me. It'll be easier than having to fight him. I don't want to hurt anyone if I don't have to.

"That attitude is going to get us killed. You hurt who you have to. It's nothing personal. We need to survive."

"I'm not like you, Jackie," I think.

"We're more alike than you think."

Dr. Harvey smiles, and I relax a little. "I was heading that way, too. I'm supposed to meet Dr. Sullivan here for some follow up scans to make sure Emily's physical health hasn't changed."

I grind my teeth, and Camden stiffens next to me. "What do I do, Jackie?" I think.

"Get ready to fight."

"My mom?" I've spent the last few months imagining what it would be like to finally reveal the truth to Dr. Sullivan. I even thought about whether or not I could destroy her. But now, I'm not sure I can. It would make me no better than her.

"That woman gave your soul to me fully aware that you most likely wouldn't live. She was planning on experimenting on Dmitri. She wants to experiment on Nadia. She does not deserve your mercy, Hunter."

Stepping forward, I trail behind Dr. Harvey. I eye Camden in my peripheral vision as he straightens his shoulders. We arrive at the door leading to the hallway to the infirmary, and my nerves threaten to freeze me in my tracks.

My feet drag across the tile with each step I take, and I touch my fingers to my tranquilizer gun. I only have one dart left, and I might need it to get out of here. I'll have to use the single syringe to sedate either Dr. Sullivan or Dr. Harvey, and then I'll have to hope the other complies to my demands or else I'm afraid I'll have to fight them.

Dr. Harvey enters in his pass code. The beep of the unlocking door rings in my ears. I take a deep breath and slowly let it out when I see Nadia's terrified eyes as she hovers a few feet from Evie. Dr. Sullivan holds her arm out in a non-threatening manner with her clipboard under the other.

I let Dr. Harvey walk ahead of me and Camden. It's like the world slows, and I freeze. Nadia knocks Evie down and runs toward me. Her light gray eyes shine with tears, and she holds her arms open.

Dr. Sullivan yells something I can't hear. Her clipboard clatters to the ground. Dr. Harvey reaches for something in his coat, and then Camden races forward and jumps on his back. The two collide to the ground, and Nadia glides around them, her feet not touching the floor. Dr. Sullivan screams.

Dr. Sullivan dashes toward the wall where the phone is, and I charge forward and close the distance between us before she has a chance to hit the alarm. Pulling my knife from its sheath, I point the cold metal at Dr. Sullivan's heart. Tears spill from her eyes, and I glower at her.

"I don't understand!" she yells. "I'm your mother!"

"Were. You haven't been my mom since you traded my soul to a sin-eater." My voice comes out low, vicious even. Dr. Sullivan winces as her shirt rips on the blade. I hold my arm steady even though Evie screams. "But you know what? That was the best thing to happen to me. I got to see how the world

really was, and I learned the truth. Creatures aren't the monsters. You and all of these people that believe you—you guys are
the monsters."

163

14

EDGE OF AWAKE

NADIA

MY HEARTBEAT HAMMERS in my ears. My fluid movement gives away my nightmare inflictor side, and there's no turning back. We have to get out of here, and fast, but Hunter faces his mother, and Camden wrestles Dr. Harvey on the floor. Evie stands a few feet away, screaming, and I'm inches away from the door.

"Hunter!" I yell. His dagger sparkles in the fluorescent lighting as his steady arm points at Dr. Sullivan's chest. He doesn't take his eyes off her, but he tilts his head so I know he hears me. "Don't kill her. You're better than her, and I know you'll regret it."

"She'll never stop, Nadia. They'll hunt us for the rest of our lives. This needs to stop here." Dr. Sullivan's eyes shift from the knife to look at me. They're eerily calm. I think she knows Hunter might not have it in him to kill her.

I glide forward. "Hunter, please. There has to be another way."

Evie stops screaming, and the room falls silent. Camden managed to sedate Dr. Harvey with a tranquilizer, and the doctor lies face down on the ground. Camden strolls up next to me and puts his hand on my shoulder.

Hunter shifts his feet. "Like what? Look what this woman did to Evie. She turned her against you. And what she did to your father...to Camden. Look what she's done to you, to me, to us. You really think I should let her go?"

"He's right, Nadia," Camden says.

Evie sobs and steps closer to me. "You think I'm against you?"

I narrow my eyes. "I think you don't know what to believe and right now, you believe the evil in the world is outside this room when it's standing in front of you."

Evie presses her lips together before saying, "Evil is everywhere."

Dr. Harvey moans from behind us, and Camden leaves me to stand over him. Hunter's arm doesn't relax so I take a few more steps forward and touch his shoulder. He shifts closer to me, and I reach out and pull a small syringe from Dr. Sullivan's lab coat pocket.

I draw my gaze to Dr. Sullivan. "It's a shame I'll never

know you as my boyfriend's mother. I hope you remember I let you go and that I'm not after humanity. I hope you realize Hunter isn't the enemy either. You think you're saving the world by protecting humans, but you're wrong. We're protecting the world because we're protecting the innocent."

I jab the needle into Dr. Sullivan's arm. She glares at me without a word until her eyes close, and her body falls to the tiles. I turn to look at Evie, standing with her arms crossed over her chest, tears streaking her cheeks, and she looks so conflicted.

I hold out my hand. "Come with us, Evie."

She shakes her head. "I can't. I can't give up my life like that."

I frown. "But you are giving up your life by staying here. You might think you're free, but you're not. The only way to do that is to come with us."

"I'm sorry."

Hunter grabs my hand. "We have two minutes to get out of here."

I don't say anything more as I turn away from Evie and glide next to Hunter with Camden on my heels. We exit the infirmary into the lobby. The dim lights leave shadows everywhere, and the front door stands only a few feet away.

"Is this a trick?" A voice asks.

I shift my eyes from the door to a group of humans and creatures standing near the elevator door without moving. I glance from Hunter to Camden and then back to the people. "Hunter's with us."

Hunter jogs to the door, putting his hand on the handle

and stares out. "When you get to the parking lot, veer right and follow the perimeter of it to the front gate. I'll take care of the guards. Don't stop for anything and don't run in a straight line. They have tranquilizer guns."

Nobody moves until I glide forward and touch Hunter's shoulder. "You ready?"

He nods. "Don't leave my side."

I glance over my shoulder at Camden. "You can come with us and fight or help the others escape."

Strolling forward, he Camden holds up a stolen tranquilizer. "You know I'm always with you."

Hunter pulls the door open, and cool night air blows my hair from my face. I suck in a deep breath since it's been so long since I've been outside and take Hunter's hand. I can't believe we're finally leaving this place. I can't believe we're finally free.

An alarm rips through the silence, making my heart falter. All the hope I had a second ago disappears when the world kicks into action. Dashing forward, I race next to Hunter, and we run for our lives.

HUNTER

"Go!" Jacqueline's voice echoes in my ears.

I yank Nadia with me, and she grips my hand like I'm the only thing keeping her moving. We race toward the parking lot. If we can make it to my car, we'll be free. Nadia will be safe behind metal and glass, and Camden and I can knock out the two guards at the gate. Cold air whips around my face and sweat freezes on my forehead. My lungs burn with each breath I take, but I can't stop. All our lives are in danger.

A gunshot rings out. I push Nadia with my shoulder, and we duck next to the side of a red Porsche. Another pop echoes in the night, and a tranquilizer dart smashes against the car door. Nadia gasps. Swiveling on my boots, I watch as Agent Jake, a guy I only know by brief greetings, runs in our direction.

I get to my feet and yank my knife from its sheath. Jake's gun only holds two darts at a time, and he won't stop to reload the gun. It's in our training not to stop for anything while facing a threat.

"Get to my car," I yell at Nadia. "I'll hold him off. If I'm not there in two minutes, leave without me. Camden can take the guys at the gate."

She stands up next to me. "I'm not leaving you."

Before I have a chance to argue with Nadia, Camden charges forward and runs straight for Agent Jake. "Get her out of here!" Camden yells, colliding with the agent.

I yank Nadia's hand, but she doesn't budge. My gaze flicks between Camden and the agent, and then to Nadia. Tears flow down her cheeks and leaving streaks on her pale skin.

"We have to go or we'll die," I say.

"She won't leave him, Hunter," Jacqueline says in my mind.

Clenching my jaw, I take a breath. Nadia's going to hate me if I make her go, but we can't stay. Another pop sounds out. I wrap my arms around her waist, lift her over my shoulder, and dash toward my car. She screams and hits my back, but I don't stop. Camden chose to fight. He chose to do it for Nadia. I have to make sure she gets out alive.

NADIA

"No!" I scream, pounding my fist into Hunter's back, but he doesn't put me down. Tears blur my vision, my heart shattering into a million pieces as I watch the boy, who has helped keep me alive the last two months, collide with the black-haired agent.

The agent drops to the ground, swinging his arm out, and knocks it behind Camden's knees. Camden falls to the pavement, fighting hard, thrashing, but it's no use with how the agent straddles him and points his knife at his chest. Sobs rake through me, stealing my breath away. Camden struggles to knock the agent off him, and I realize at any second, Alyssa's vision will come true.

Another shot rings through the air, and a dart whizzes past us and smashes against a blue truck. I jerk in Hunter's arms, but he tightens his grip. Everything freezes as my gaze falls upon Camden jabbing a syringe into the agent's neck.

My heart beats in overdrive. "Camden injected the agent with a tranquilizer. We have to wait for him!"

Hunter drops me to my feet and opens the back door of his car. Spinning to look back at Camden, I gasp, dark shadows clouding my vision. My heart sinks into my stomach, the hope a had a second ago now ripped away. I scream, the noise burning from my throat to pierce the air. The agent jabs his knife into Camden's chest, sending Camden crumpling under his weight. Not even a second later, the agent falls on top of Camden as the sedative steals his consciousness like he stole Camden's life.

"Cam!" I scream, rushing toward him.

Hunter snatches my arm and drags me to his car, pushing me onto the backseat. He slams the door shut, sealing me off from the world. My lungs burn as I lose control of myself, heaving painful sobs into my hands. I can't believe Alyssa's vision came true. Camden died because he loved me. Even after all the lies and secrets, he sacrificed his life so I could live. So I could be free.

"We can't leave him here, Hunter. Please, stop. You have to stop." My chest clenches, and I gasp for breath. "Hunter!"

"Nadia..." His voice comes out low and defeated. It cuts through my soul. Without having to say it, I know he's not turning back. "Going back will get us both killed. I'm sorry. I'm so sorry. I—"

Anger swells in my entire being, numbing the heart-wrenching grief rolling through me. "Maybe that's our fate! Maybe we're destined for death! Look at us, Hunter. Everywhere we go, people die. People give up their lives so we can keep going. It isn't fair. Jacqueline died because of us and now Camden. I can't deal with this if our love will constantly have people dying around us. It's not worth it to me. I can't live with that thought."

Hunter stares at me in his rearview mirror, and something shifts in his eyes. The hazel color lightens to lavender and then back to hazel. "Nadia, please. None of this was our fault. I was going to fight that agent, and Camden chose to do it instead. And Jacqueline...she's alive."

My head aches as much as much as my heart. I inhale a few slow breaths to keep from getting sick. I blink a few times as

Hunter's eyes shift color again, and a memory of Jacqueline with Hunter trapped in her head consumes me. "She's—" My hands tremble in my lap. "She's inside your mind, isn't she?"

Before Hunter can answer, he slams the brake pedal, and I smash into the front seat. An agent with long blond hair tied back in a ponytail saunters to Hunter's door. Hunter flings it open, knocking her back.

Digging my nails into the palms of my hands, I force my grief and despair to stay locked away. I need to prepare myself to fight.

I have to do it for Camden.

HUNTER

Agent Lucy falls to the ground. Jumping out, I leave Nadia in the backseat, restraining restrain the agent under me while I reach for my tranquilizer gun. I only have one dart left, and if I can tranquilize Agent Lucy before Agent Sebastian realizes what's happening, I'll already be back in the car, and if he's smart, he won't stand in my way.

I touch my finger to the trigger, but before I pull it, a pop rings in my ears, and my shoulder stings. I swear under my breath and yank the dart out, but it's too late. My vision already blurs.

"Let me take control of your body!"

"Okay, but we don't have long," I say out loud.

Agent Lucy frowns and then my ears pop, and I'm numb all over. I blink, but nothing happens. I watch as Jacqueline uses my arms to touch the agent's face. Agent Lucy's eyes roll back, and then suddenly I'm blind to the outside world as I watch her disturbing actions flicker through my mind. I watch her kill six creatures and burn down two houses that belong to creatures. I feel the pain and torment of all her victims, and her evil squeezes my soul before a light blinds me, and then I feel relief.

I wonder if this is how it feels to die.

NADIA

Flying from the backseat, I rush to Hunter as he slumps over the blond agent. She doesn't move under him, and my eyes dart up to the man training his tranquilizer gun on me. I grab Hunter's leg and pull him as hard as I can, while still being protected by the car door.

The agent laughs and steps closer. I jerk my arm out and tug Hunter's knife from its sheath, pointing it at the agent. He grins but doesn't back off. I'm going to have to fight him while keeping Hunter alive and keeping the agent from tranquilizing me. *You're going to fail.*

I push the somber thought from my mind. "Stay back, and I won't hurt you. I just want to leave."

The agent pulls the trigger of his tranquilizer gun. I drop to my knees as it flies over my head. He lowers his gun to his side, and my heart hammers against my ribcage. He reaches for his knife next, and I realize he's out of darts. I may have a fighting chance.

Standing up, I glide around the door. The agent's eyes widen for a second, probably at how fast I can move. I've been playing human for so long that I have to concentrate on allowing myself the freedom to be myself.

"This is your last warning," I say. "I don't want to kill

you."

He doesn't back off.

I press my lips together and grip the knife in my hand, steeling myself as the agent closes the distance. I hold up my knife. Instead of jabbing it at him, I throw it at his head as hard as I can. The heavy metal handle strikes him in the middle of his forehead.

Stumbling back in surprise, he rubs his head. I take the small distraction to drop to my knees next to Hunter and pull his tranquilizer gun out from under him. A strong hand grips my shoulder and flips me over, and I aim the tranquilizer gun at the agent and pull the trigger.

The agent raises his dagger and thrusts it down at me. Jerking my legs up, I kick him in the stomach. His blade clatters to the ground, the sound slicing through my soul, and I watch as the tranquilizer takes effect, and he passes out.

I tug on Hunter's heavy, unmoving body. "You can do this, Nadia. You have to do this." I strain as I lift him and manage to get his shoulders onto the floor of the backseat. Rushing around to the other side, I open the back door and yank him the rest of the way in using every tiny bit of inhumanly strength I have from my nightmare inflictor side.

I get behind the wheel, driving forward, and crash through the boom barrier to head to the street. As I accelerate, the tires squeal when I don't brake at the next corner and turn left onto a four-lane road. My knuckles whiten as I grip the wheel, and I don't stop. I speed down the empty street and run every stop sign I pass.

"What happened?" Hunter's voice wraps me in love, hope, and relief, just hearing that he's okay.

"I saved you," I say.

Laughing, he sits up on the backseat. "I was supposed to save you."

Tears burn my eyes as the events of the last hour sink in—Evie refusing to leave the facility with us, Camden giving his life so I could escape, finding out Jacqueline is alive, and nearly losing Hunter to the agents. Everything rests heavy on my soul, threatening to shatter me into a million pieces.

Hunter leans between the seats and touches my shoulder. "Pull over. I'll drive."

I shake my head. "I'm not stopping until we're home." Tears spill from my eyes, and I blink to clear my vision as Hunter points out the signs to the highway.

"We're okay, Nadia. We're safe now," he says.

I suck in a breath. "Then why doesn't it feel that way? Why does it feel like this isn't over yet?"

I can't stop the foreboding feeling from gripping my insides. I'm alive and away from the dangers of the facility, but I still don't feel safe. I don't feel free. I only feel like the worst is yet to come, and I'm not ready for it.

15

GOOD RIDDANCE

HUNTER

I THROW MY cell phone out the window. "Get off at the next exit. I think we should ditch my car."

"You want to go on foot?" Nadia cuts across two lanes and exits the highway.

"No, but they know what to look for. No doubt someone is tracking us now." I lean my elbows on my knees. "If we can get to a payphone, you can call for help."

Nadia pulls into a gas station, leaving the engine on, and I follow her out of the car. I search our surroundings, but the place is deserted at this hour. Nadia pops in the change I hand her, and she dials a number.

"Cian?" she asks. I'm surprised she didn't call Alyssa. "It's me, Nadia. I need help and fast. I'm at a gas station off Poinsettia Street." She presses the receiver to her ear and shifts her gaze to me. "No, I'm not alone. How long do you think?"

I sweep my gaze around our surroundings again and stiffen when a white van stops at the stop light, but it doesn't belong to the HPA. It's just a minivan. A glowing ATM sign draws my attention to the store, and I rub my chin.

"If you use it, they'll be here within minutes," Jacqueline says.

"And we'll be gone by then," I think.

"Okay, thanks, Cian. Will you call my father and Alyssa and tell them where I'm heading?" She nods even though Cian can't see her through the phone. "Thanks again." Nadia hangs up the phone.

"Where are we going?"

"Twenty minutes north of here. A friend of Cian's will pick us up and take us to a warehouse near the river. He said my father won't be home until the morning, and we can get things sorted out then." She wrings her hands together.

I glance through the window of the convenience store. "I'm going to grab one of those souvenir shirts and withdraw as much cash as I can. We'll have to hurry because I'm sure they're watching my banking activity."

She nods and tucks her hair behind her ears. "I'll wait in the car."

I force myself to walk away, because I'm nervous about leaving Nadia alone outside. She gets in the car and locks the doors. Running inside, I grab a brown shirt from the small rolling rack with the words, *This Dude Loves Bacon* screen printed on the front of it with a bacon smiley face. I toss a twenty on the counter from my wallet and then slide my debit card into the ATM and pull out the maximum limit. With what I have on me and what I withdrew, I only have fifteen hundred dollars. I wish I could get more, but without being near a bank at a decent hour, all the money I've earned over the last six months is no longer mine.

Folding the wad of cash, I run from the convenience store and hop in the front seat the moment Nadia unlocks the door. She reverses into the street and hits the accelerator, squealing the tires. She speeds down the road and merges back on the highway, and I expect an HPA van to pull up behind us, but none ever do.

Nadia exits the highway and pulls into a parking lot of a grocery store. I change shirts, unclick my weaponry belt and leave it on the seat, and say goodbye to my BMW wagon. I get out at the same time as Nadia. She rushes to my side and grabs my hand.

"Over there." She points her finger at a small-framed woman leaning against a four door sedan. The woman's shoulder length hair is dyed pink, and she wears a studded belt with her black jeans and low-cut top.

Nadia pants next to me, still shaking, and I do my best to comfort her by squeezing her hand. When we close in on the woman, she hops in the car and starts the engine. She doesn't say a word as I hop in the back, and Nadia slides onto the front seat. I peer out the window at my BMW one last time.

"Say goodbye to your old life, Hunter."

"It's not goodbye, Jackie. It's good riddance."

NADIA

I don't say anything for a long time as Isla, the fairy Cian sent to help me, drives us toward the city. My heart weighs heavy with grief, and I can't get Camden off my mind. I replay the memory of him being stabbed in the chest over and over in my head. Tears spill on my cheeks, my whole body shaking. I hold back my sobs the best I can, and then Hunter rests his hands on my shoulders, setting me off.

"This is almost over." He rests his chin on my seat, his warm breath tickling my ear. "Can you believe we survived?"

I breathe deeply, heaving. "Do you think the others made it out okay?"

"I hope so." Hunter brushes his lips on my ear, and I shiver.

Isla taps her fingers on the steering wheel. "So it's true?" Her musical voice cuts through the air, and I shift in my seat to stare at her. "You two were imprisoned by the HPA and managed to escape?"

Hunter clears his throat. "Something like that. It wasn't easy. We lost someone on the way out, but there may be others. I let out fourteen other people."

Isla's eyes widen. "Cian didn't mention that."

My chest tightens. It's because I didn't tell him. I was so worried about being followed that I didn't think about those creatures who were on my cell block. They're going to need help. "Do you have a phone? They're still out there and need help."

Isla nods and touches her center console. I open it and pull out a small, old flip phone, and when I go to open it, the phone buzzes in my hand. I press it to my ear and listen for a second before I say, "This is Isla's phone."

"Nadia!" Alyssa's voice pierces my ear and tears spill onto my cheek. "I was so scared that Hunter didn't get you out in time."

"Me too. But, Lys, I need to call Cian. There are others that need help," I say.

She sucks in a breath. "I already told him." Her voice comes low, stabbing at my heart. "But I should tell you, only half of them made it."

I cover my face with my hands. That's eight people dead because of the HPA. Eight people I should've tried harder to save. Guilt and grief course through my mind, and I lean my aching head on the cool window. "I want to destroy them, Alyssa. The HPA needs to pay."

"I know, Nadia, but we need to focus on the things at hand right now. Dmitri is on his way back. He'll tell you everything you need to know. I can't say anything else though because I can't risk changing the outcome of our future." The line cuts in and out.

I push all my overwhelming emotions away. "Okay, Lys. I trust you." I have nothing else to say that won't induce gut-wrenching sobs, so I turn in my seat and look at Hunter. I want to tell Alyssa everything that happened but not over the phone. I hope I can see her soon. I've missed my best friend.

HUNTER

I wish I could pull Nadia to the backseat, so I could wrap my arms around her and hug her. She's been through so much in the last few days—weeks, really. I'm not sure how much longer she can keep it together. She looks like she'll break any second, and I'm afraid it'll be impossible to put back her pieces the way they're supposed to be.

"How are you holding up?" Jacqueline asks.

I shrug even though the gesture is lost on her. I don't know how to answer her question. I don't know how I feel apart from what I feel for Nadia. Glancing at my reflection in the window, I don't respond to Jacqueline.

Nadia's light gray eyes shine with the pain and anguish I wish I could take from her. She holds out an old cell phone, and I press it to my ear and say, "What's up?"

"Nadia sounds bad, Hunter," Alyssa says.

I sigh. "She's been through a lot."

"I'm heading to the warehouse now because I don't think she should have to wait until morning to see me. But, Hunter, listen to me carefully. Do not tell anyone about yourself until Dmitri arrives, all right? As far as they know, you were picked up because the HPA suspected you had ties to the supernatural community."

"Okay, got it."

"See you soon."

The line cuts off, and I flip the phone closed and drop it into the open center console. Leaning back on the seat, I rub my eyes with the palms of my hands. Exhaustion trickles into my mind, and I fight to keep alert. I can't let my guard down until I know we're somewhere safe.

"Hunter, you never answered my question..."

I squeeze my eyes shut and think, "That's because I don't know, Jackie. The last time I was really involved in this world was when I was trapped in your mind."

"Don't be nervous."

"Oh, okay, I'll just turn off my nerves then. Great advice."

Jacqueline sighs. *"I won't let anything happen to you."*

I bite back a laugh so Nadia and Isla don't hear and think I've lost my mind. "You can't just go around killing people on my behalf."

"It's not on your behalf."

I tap my fingers on my knees. "I guess things never really change, huh?"

"You're wrong. Look where we are now."

The car comes to a halt, and I jerk my head up to look out the window. Just ahead of us looms a red brick warehouse with boarded windows and a single bare bulb illuminating a set of blue painted, metal double doors. A tall chain-link fence with barbed wire surrounds us, and past the building, the city towers in the distance. The full moon hangs high in the sky, the stars now faded pin-pricks of light disguised by the light pollution from the city.

I jump from the car when Nadia does, and my boots sink into a mixture of slush and mud. Spring is coming soon, and I hope with it comes a new beginning for me. I want nothing more than to have a fresh start with Nadia away from all this.

"Lys!" Nadia yells, gliding away from.

Shoving my frozen hands in my pockets, I watch Nadia's white hair blow behind her as she clings onto her best friend. Alyssa smiles at me over Nadia's shoulder, her eyes shining in the harsh lighting, and she motions for me to come closer.

"Act like you belong here."

"I do belong here," I think.

I stroll away from the car and walk toward Nadia. She pulls away from Alyssa and turns to me. For the first time in a very long time, she smiles a genuine smile. I hold open my arms, begging her to fall into them. She presses her face to my chest, sinking into me, and I brush my fingers through her hair and trail my hands to her lower back. I hold her close and kiss her like I've never kissed her before. Her lips brush mine, warm and salty with tears, and my shoulders shake as everything finally sinks in. I never thought I'd see the day I'd be away from the HPA and I could be with Nadia. But, I'm also grieving. I can't help it.

The HPA forced me to give up my family. I'll never see my Aunt Christine again or Mason. I can't ever hope to reconnect with my dad either. They'll always be memories from a past I hope to forget.

Nadia pulls away from me and wipes tears from her eyes. "I never thought I'd be so happy and sad all at once. I want to laugh and cry." She smiles through her tears. "I feel like I've been away from you for so long even though you were always near me."

"I hate to interrupt, but don't forget I'm here."

Nadia's eyes widen. "Jacqueline..." She covers her mouth for a second and then says. "You don't know how relieved I am you're alive."

It's strange having Nadia talk to me like I'm Jacqueline.

"Tell her I won't be in here for long."

I twist my lips to the side and brush Nadia's hair from her face. "It's like old times, but better, huh?"

"Oh, shut up, Hunter."

Alyssa steps up next to us and touches my shoulder. "It won't be for much longer. I don't see a face, but I had a vision about a girl, and it felt like Jacqueline. I thought she was haunting me, but now it all makes sense. I didn't know because Jacqueline can't make decisions."

"See?"

"She's way better at concealing herself than she was at concealing me," I say, ignoring Jacqueline.

Alyssa looks at Nadia and then me. "Let's keep Jacqueline a secret for now. Life's complicated enough."

"She's worried about changing the future."

Boots crunch and Isla clears her throat, pulling me from my thoughts with Jacqueline. "I have a few spare rooms you can stay in as long as you want."

I draw my gaze to the warehouse. "Thanks again. I owe you one."

NADIA

Alyssa hugs me one more time. "Are you sure you're going to be okay? I really don't mind if you need to inflict a nightmare on me."

Pulling away, I shake my throbbing head. Isla checked my stitches and said they were done exceptionally well, but I'm still in quite a bit of pain. I know inflicting a nightmare will help, but I swore I'd never do it to Alyssa again and I'm not breaking my promise. "I can wait another day."

She grimaces but doesn't argue. "I'll be across the hall. Come get me if you need anything." She looks past me at Hunter. "Same goes for you."

Hunter nods and links his fingers behind his head, his eyelids, heavy almost half shut. He looks ready to pass out. It's been so long since I discovered I can visit Hunter's dream world that I can't wait to be alone with him. Well, as alone as I can be.

Shutting the door, I turn to Hunter. He smiles at me, patting the spot next to him. I ease onto the bed, slow and calculated, aware of each movement, and then I snuggle into his chest. It'll take a lot of time before I can feel like my old self, and I'm not sure if I want to now. I need to be aware of my every movement. It's how I'm going to survive in this world. I hate the HPA, but being within their prison prepared me for what happens next.

Hunter's heartbeat drums against my cheek, and his chest rises and falls with each slow breath. I trail my fingers up his bare stomach and to his chest, and then I touch his cheek before leaning up to kiss him.

He stares into my eyes. "I'm here if you need to talk."

I smile. "I don't want to think about anything right now. I just want to be with you."

His lips brush against my forehead, and he closes his eyes.

Within a minute, hunger burns in my stomach. I find my fingers trailing up Hunter's face to his temples. The hunger that burns within me is more than my need to visit his dream. My soul craves to be with Hunter. It desires to escape this world to be in one that is in our control. My soul wants nothing more than to forget everything horrible that happened today.

Opening my eyes, I stand in the middle of a never-ending field of brightly colored tulips. Each row of flowers blooms in a different color. I reach down and pick a fuchsia one. The crystalline sky stretches unending in a blue like I've never seen before, and in the distance emerald green mountains with snowy white peaks decorate the horizon.

I spin on the balls of my feet before strolling into the next row of sunny yellow tulips. A warm breeze tickles my neck, and I smile while tilting my head to the sky. Hunter's dream is magnificent and enchanting, and I sense no fear or pain in this heavenly place—only love, happiness, and adoration.

"You like it?" Hunter asks from behind me.

"I didn't think you were capable of imagining a place like this, Hunter. Why do I always get the rundown cities?" A familiar, feminine voice trickles around me.

Peering over my shoulder, I catch sight of Hunter and Jacqueline sitting on a long, green painted, wooden bench. I can't believe my eyes. It's really Jacqueline. She's in her own body, and her dark, curly hair hangs wildly around her head. Her lavender eyes glow against the golden hue of her skin, and she beams a bright smile at me.

I glide over to them. "You're real!" I squeeze Jacqueline's

arm, shaking her once.

She arches her eyebrows. "Not really, but here I am. Almost like I'm good as new. I'm going to miss creating my old body once I'm out of Hunter's head."

I frown but then quickly force myself to smile. "I hope it's soon."

Hunter and Jacqueline both say, "Me too." They glare at each other, and I laugh and sling an arm around each of them.

"Maybe we should all just stay in this dream world forever." I kiss Hunter's cheek.

"No way. I'm not going to be the third wheel," Jacqueline says. "And don't forget about Alyssa. She'd be pretty pissed if we abandon her."

I laugh. Everything feels so normal. It's almost as if today never happened—that the last two months didn't happen. Camden's face flashes through my mind, and I suck in my bottom lip. He'll be the constant reminder of how I'll never have a normal life. He told me so himself.

Jacqueline grabs my hand. "You can't be sad in this beautiful place, Nadia."

A tear slips onto my cheek, and I glance between Hunter and Jacqueline. "I'm trying not to be. It's just so hard to forget no matter how much I want to."

Hunter slides his arm around my waist, and Jacqueline doesn't let go of my hand. They walk next to me as we cross through the fields to a crystal clear lake. Jacqueline dips her bare foot into it, and Hunter lifts me into his arms.

He kisses my cheek, and I watch Jacqueline wade deeper

into the water. "Then I'll make you forget," he says, kissing me again. "In this dream, it's only us and nothing can hurt us."

I nod. If only I could spend the rest of my life hidden in a dream.

16

US AGAINST THE WORLD

NADIA

HUNTER'S CHEST RISES and falls as he sleeps next to me. I pulled myself from his dream a few minutes ago and was greeted by golden rays of sunshine drifting through the crack in the boarded window.

Rolling off the bed, I pad out into the hall. From the outside, the warehouse looks abandoned and rundown, but within its walls is a remodeled fortress for creatures in need of a temporary place to stay. Watercolor paintings of the ocean hang on the tan walls, and the wood floors gleam in the recessed lighting. It reminds me of a luxury apartment complex. I imagine I'd stay somewhere like this if I were to decide to go to college. *You haven't even finished high school.*

I push the thought away. I haven't thought about my future in so long, it's hard to have hope that I'll actually have one. I was almost positive I'd die at the termination facility, and now that I'm free, I'm not sure what my future has in store for me.

I stroll down two flights of stairs instead of taking the elevator and discover a modern kitchen with stainless steel appliances, marble countertops, an eight-burner stove, and a glass table situated in the corner near the first window I've seen without a board hung up over it.

Laughter echoes from the other side of a swinging door. Shuffling across the gleaming tiled floor, I crack the door open. The door leads into an open living area and dining room. Tucked in the corner of the living area is a foyer with a chandelier, and my heart pauses when I gaze at my father smiling at Isla.

My father's inky black hair drapes over his neck longer than the last time I saw him, and he has it styled back with hair product. He wears a gray suit with a deep sapphire tie, and a silver watch sparkles in the lamplight when he waves his arm in the direction of the door.

"Dad?" I ask as I step into the living area.

He draws his gaze from Isla to me. Before I have a chance to move, he's already hugging me. He kisses my forehead and looks down at me. Tears spill onto my cheeks, and his shoulders shake as he fails to hold back his own tears.

"Oh, Nadi," he whispers as he pets my hair. "You don't know how relieved I am to see you. I didn't believe Cian when he told me. I was preparing to get you out of there in a few days. I'm sorry I wasn't the one to help you. I've failed you."

I sniffle. "You didn't fail me. Your plan would've been better, but Hunter said we couldn't wait. Dr. Sullivan was going to transfer me to some place to be experimented on."

"All that matters is that you got out and you're safe."

I suck in my top lip. "Not everyone made it. Camden died, Dad."

He grimaces. "I'm sorry, Nadi. Alyssa mentioned he was fond of you."

"He died because of me."

He cups my face, his obsidian eyes boring into my soul. "Don't think like that. Camden died because the HPA killed him. It wasn't because of you."

I wipe my eyes and blink the lingering tears away. No matter how much I know it's the truth, I will always feel guilty. I'll always think about the what-ifs and if Camden was right about me and Hunter. *He wasn't, though.*

"I guess," I say.

"Dmitri?" I turn to look at Isla standing behind me. "Would you like me to bring our guest in?" Her nose crinkles as a thought sweeps through her mind. I'm gathering that she's not exactly pleased with whoever my father brought with him.

My father stiffens and peers down at me. "I need you to go wait in your room for a few minutes. Can you send down Hunter? I need to talk to him alone."

I twist my lips to the side. "What's going on?"

Isla shifts on her feet next to us, and she and my father lock eyes. My father touches my shoulder. "I don't want to worry you. Just give me a few minutes to talk to Hunter. Then I'll tell you what's going on. Please, just send him down, okay?"

I open my mouth to argue but then just turn on the balls of my feet and glide back into the kitchen instead. Why does my father want to talk to Hunter? I'm annoyed he wants to tell him some top secret information before me. He'll never stop treating me like his fragile little girl. But I'm not fragile. I survived the termination facility. I deserve to know what has my father on edge.

I stomp up the stairs with my head bowed, my hands clenched at my sides, and I slam into a solid chest. Hunter grabs my shoulders and pulls me to him before I lose my balance and trip down the stairs.

He smiles, and I melt into his arms and breathe in his scent. Tilting my head up, I kiss him. His hands brush my hair back and run over my shoulders and down my arms before sliding to my lower back.

After a minute, he pulls away. "I was just coming to look for you."

I pucker my bottom lip. He brushes his lips to mine again, kissing away my pout, and I smile against his mouth. "Too bad my father wants to see you or I'd suggest we hide in our room all day."

He chuckles. "I wish. If Jacqueline wasn't screaming in my ear that I better learn to push her into the void, I'd consider ditching your dad."

My eyebrows knit together. "Something's going on,

Hunter. He won't tell me what, but he trusts you."

He nods. "I think I know what it is."

I stare at him for a long moment, but he doesn't elaborate. "You're not going to tell me what this is about?"

"It's better if you wait for Dmitri just in case I'm wrong."

I huff and shrug out of his arms, walking a few feet away.

"Nadia, wait," Hunter calls.

I glare at him. If this is how Hunter and my father think they're going to treat me, then they're going to be sorely disappointed. "You're supposed to be on my side."

He steps closer, but I hold my hand up and touch my fingers to Alyssa's door. His shoulders lower before he brushes his messy hair out of his face. "I am on your side. It's us against the world, you know."

"Then why doesn't it feel like it?"

HUNTER

Nadia enters Alyssa's room and leaves me standing in the hallway. I don't know what has come over her, but I just want to make things right. If I thought she'd let me in to talk, I would knock on Alyssa's door, but Nadia's shut me out for now.

"Don't take it personally, Hunter. You two have been through a lot. Nadia's been away from everything so long, she only wants to take control of her life again. Isn't that what you did when I freed you?" Jacqueline asks.

I turn and stride toward the stairs and think, "You're right. It's why I moved in with Aunt Christine."

"After you meet with Dmitri, maybe you should sit down and talk to Nadia. You have a lot of catching up to do. All of you, real-

ly."

I reach the bottom stair and enter a gleaming, stainless steel and marble kitchen large enough to counter one in a restaurant. Voices trickle in through a swinging door. Pushing it open, I step into a large room with a leather sectional couch, wall-to-wall bookcases, a formal dining room with a black table and high-back chairs, and an entertainment center with a flat screen TV mounted on the wall above it.

I shift my eyes from the floor to Dmitri, and he glides to me and swings an arm over my shoulders in a half hug. I pat his back as he smiles at me, but shadows line his obsidian eyes and I sense something's wrong.

"Thank you for taking care of Nadia," he says.

"I don't need any thanks. I love her." I watch Isla exit the warehouse from over Dmitri's shoulder.

He presses his lips together. "I can see that. You must know, life isn't going to be easy, but I'm going to do my best to see that my daughter can live how she wants."

"I'd like that for all of us." Running my fingers through my hair, I lean on my heels. Dmitri didn't want to see me to tell me what he wants for Nadia, but it's nice that he is. I don't know what I'd have done if he didn't accept me so easily. I'd never want Nadia to have to choose.

The door bangs open, and we both turn in its direction. Bright sunlight haloes two figures. I blink colorful stars from my vision, watching Isla close the door. My mouth drops open as I recognize the other figure. It takes me rubbing my hand over my face to get me to compose myself.

"I don't believe it," Jacqueline says.

"Alyssa did say Dmitri was going to change the council," I think.

"By kidnapping council members?"

My jaw tightens. "Looks like it."

Isla tugs Mr. Soto by his elbow and pushes him toward the sectional. He falls onto it and winces when Dmitri glides to him and hovers over the ancient man. I didn't think it was possible, but Mr. Soto's wrinkles appear deeper, the folds of his skin ashy. Dark bags hang under his sunken eyes, and white hair streaks his long beard.

"I don't understand why you're doing this, Dmitri," Mr. Soto says.

Dmitri holds his hand up and cuts Mr. Soto off. "Don't talk, Javier."

"I'm the head of the council. I demand you let me go."

I shuffle closer and stand next to Dmitri. "Some leader you are."

Dmitri touches my shoulder, and Mr. Soto furrows his brows. They cover half his eyes, and he looks ready to tackle me. Isla laughs from the door. I straighten my shoulders, then glare down at the old man, and he glowers right back at me.

"And who are you?" Mr. Soto asks.

"Don't tell him," Jacqueline says.

I roll my shoulders.

"Hunter's here to help me make some changes in our world."

"He's a child, Dmitri, and human. What can he offer?

What changes?" Mr. Soto shifts on the sectional, and Dmitri crosses his arms.

I raise an eyebrow and say, "You don't know what I'm capable of doing, Mr. Soto. Who says I can't rip your soul from your body right now if I wanted? Unlike you, I'm ready to fight for innocent people. What are you doing? Still hiding out in your compound?"

"I'm not redeeming Mr. Soto, Hunter."

"He doesn't know that, Jackie," I think. "Let me have my moment."

Mr. Soto narrows his eyes until they're tiny slits set in his wrinkled face. "You don't scare me."

Dmitri squeezes my shoulder, and I glance at him in my peripheral vision. No one speaks. The heavy air presses in on me. I wish Dmitri would've told me the reason why he wanted to see me so I could've prepared myself better.

The door to the kitchen swings open, and my gaze falls upon Alyssa and Nadia. Alyssa steps forward, and Mr. Soto clutches his chest when Nadia glides closer and steps in front of me. She leans over, staring Mr. Soto in the eyes, and smiles.

Mr. Soto pales. "You're alive."

Nadia straightens her shoulders. "You should have more faith in me, Mr. Soto. Hunter and I saved seven other people from the termination facility last night, and they won't be the last ones either."

Dmitri clears his throat. "She's right, Javier, and that's why you're here. I want you to step down from the council. I'm not the only one who thinks so either. Your ways are not the ways of the future. The HPA grows stronger every day and hiding isn't the answer."

Mr. Soto scoffs. "I built that council!"

"And you'll be the reason it gets destroyed," Alyssa says, interrupting.

"I won't do it. I know what's right for our community. This isn't the first time humans have tried to eradicate us. It'll blow over soon enough."

I laugh. I can't help it. "Only when there are no more creatures in the world."

Dmitri reaches into his pocket and pulls out a small talisman. "This is your last chance to agree to step down, Javier."

He shakes his head. "You'll have to kill me before I give up control of the Creature Council."

Dmitri glances at me. "No, I have a better plan in mind. You see, Hunter knows how to work the HPA, his mother is a board member, and I think they'd be willing to make a trade with him. They'll grant him and Nadia amnesty for turning you over. Alyssa saw it. Either way, you're not leading our world down the path of destruction."

My head pounds as Dmitri's words sink in. If what he says is true, Nadia and I could have a life together without worrying about the board or the council. We'd be free from all of this. We could find normalcy.

"Seems like karma that in the end you'll get what I always wanted," Jacqueline says.

"Don't worry, Jackie. I'll figure out how to help you, too," I think.

NADIA

My heart races as I glance between my father, Hunter, Mr. Soto, and Alyssa. Isla stands quietly by the door, and after a moment, she crosses the room and heads into the kitchen without a word.

Mr. Soto jumps to his feet and points his finger at Hunter. "*Llamo en el poder de mis antepasados.*"

A cold breeze brushes my hair, and fingers of icy dread slide down my spine. I've never seen Mr. Soto invoke his powers, but just from the shift in the air, I know this shaman is more powerful than he looks.

My father jerks his arm forward and presses a small talisman with a tiny spike to Mr. Soto's chest. Mr. Soto's eyes widen. He falls back on the couch and stares blankly at the ceiling. Hunter steps back. I wrap my arms around him, and he kisses my forehead.

My father turns to us. "I'm sorry you had to witness that. I wanted to tell you my plan sooner, Hunter, but I had to guarantee I'd get Mr. Soto here. And Nadia, I wanted you to wait upstairs."

I press my lips together. "What for? This involves me, too."

Alyssa grabs Hunter's arm and pulls him away from me and toward the kitchen. I don't bring my eyes back to my father until they're out of sight. Shifting on my feet, I tuck my white hair behind my ear.

"Because I wanted to make sure Hunter is really willing to do it. He'll have to face the people he betrayed, and it could get ugly." My father lowers his gaze. "You know how fast things can change."

"Even if he doesn't do it, I will," I say. "If I have to face Dr. Sullivan and an army of agents for the chance to be free from all this, I'm willing to try."

He shakes his head. "No, I want you to stay here."

"I'm not letting Hunter meet with the board alone."

He sighs. "Haven't you been through enough?"

"Hasn't he?" I turn away from my father and stride toward the kitchen. "I'm helping Hunter with this, Dad. You can't stop me."

17

NOT EVERYONE IS A SHEEP

HUNTER

NADIA GLIDES INTO the kitchen and pulls me from the table. I scoop up a muffin as she nearly drags me up the stairs and back to our room, leaving Alyssa and Isla in the kitchen. She shuts and locks the door behind us and tugs at her hair as she stares at the ceiling.

"We need to talk," she says.

I don't know what I was expecting, but it definitely wasn't those four scary little words. Nadia's white hair veils half her face, her eyebrows pinching together over her hardened gaze. She flops back on the bed and motions me forward. I force my legs to move until I'm sitting next to her with her hand cupped between mine.

"You're upset," I say.

"That's not helpful, Hunter. This is the part where you tell her that you're not going to try to protect her, and you think she's the strongest person you know," Jacqueline says.

"Shut up, Jackie," I say out loud.

Nadia stares into my eyes. "What's she saying?"

"That I'm not being helpful." I twist my lips to the side.

Nadia pushes her hair back. "Well, she's right. I've been imprisoned in a tiny room for two months. Now it feels like I'm going to end up being imprisoned here. My father wants you to go on some crazy mission to give Mr. Soto to the board, and he expects me to sit back and watch. He's crazy."

"He's trying to protect you." Running my finger over her cheek, I lean in to kiss her, but she pulls back.

She touches my neck, her fingers gliding under my jawline. "Well, I don't need it. You do. I want to protect you for once, Hunter. You committed treason against the board. What he wants you to do is dangerous."

I exhale a long breath through my nose. It's going to take a lot of convincing for the board to even hear me out, and it'll be dangerous just attempting to call them. I'm not exactly sure what I'll say, but it has to be good. It has to be good enough to guarantee Nadia's and my freedoms—Jacqueline's too.

"That's why you two need to sit down with the others. They'll help you." Jacqueline's voice echoes around me, and I ignore her.

"But wouldn't it be worth it?" I ask.

"Not if you're dead. We barely made it out of the termination facility alive and Cam—" She pauses and blinks fresh tears from her eyes. "Many people didn't."

Pulling her onto my lap, I hug her from behind, resting my chin on her shoulder. She melts into me, and I hold her for a long moment as she pulls herself together. She twists in my arms and wraps her legs around my waist and hugs me. Her heart beats against mine, her breathing warm on the nape of my neck, and I imagine what life would be like without all of this hanging over our heads.

I rest my forehead against hers. "It's okay to talk about Camden, Nadia. It's okay to tell me everything you're going through. From this point on, no more secrets. I think two months of not being able to talk to each other was long enough."

She kisses me and then says, "I feel so guilty about everything. If I had just told him I was unavailable from the start, I think he'd still be alive. I feel terrible for putting you through it, too. I wasn't thinking straight."

I frown into her lips. "You don't know that anything would be different. You're impossible not to love. And don't worry about me. I'll admit I was jealous, and it sucked watching him comfort you when it should've been me, but you were thinking about staying alive and keeping up with your Emily persona."

She sucks in her top lip, and I can't resist kissing her again. I never want to take my hands off her. The wrongness of the world doesn't feel so terrible when we're together, and it's because we're right for each other despite everything that has been against us all these months.

"Maybe we should just hide here forever. Being locked in this room together wouldn't be so bad." Nadia shifts off my lap to sit next to me. "If only my father wouldn't be crazy enough to try to exchange Mr. Soto himself."

I play with the ends of her long white hair. "I feel a little bad for Mr. Soto." I don't know why I say it out loud, but I couldn't push the thought away. We're basically bartering his life for our freedom.

She crinkles her nose. "Mr. Soto isn't some innocent man we're dealing with. People die all the time because of how he runs things, and the other council members just let him. If he didn't think people would have a problem with it, he'd be the sole voice and authority of the supernatural community."

"So why do the council members put up with him?" I ask.

She shrugs. "That's something to ask my father about."

"The other council members know, Hunter. They're the ones who set Mr. Soto up to be taken here. I can feel it. Doesn't it make sense? Maybe they want to see change, too." Jacqueline has a good point. It's probably the same reason no one has come busting down the warehouse to save Mr. Soto.

I tap my fingers on Nadia's knees. "Jacqueline thinks it's because the council members are on our side."

She stares at my hand on her knee. "Possibly. What I do know is if that's true, they're going to owe us."

Standing up, I grab her hands and pull her to her feet. "Don't forget this will be the last time we ever help them. After everything is over, I want us to live a normal life. I don't want to fight anymore if I don't have to."

"What about changing the world?"

"Yeah, Hunter. What about changing everything?"

I cup Nadia's face and look into her eyes. "If it works out how it should, we will have changed the world. The council will be given the push it needs to fight back. People will have a better chance against the HPA." I lean down and kiss her before pulling away. "We probably already started changing it—I'm sure everyone has heard about us in the HPA, and now that they know one person doesn't see creatures as bad, more people will follow behind. You'll see. Not everyone is a sheep."

NADIA

Hunter trails behind me as we head back to the kitchen. I'm feeling less lost and scared now that I've had a chance to talk everything through with him. I know in my heart this is the right decision. Mr. Soto would do the same if the situation was reversed. That man has been cruel to me since I was little for no reason. He's not an innocent being. He's powerful, intelligent, and I'm sure he'll fight his way out of the HPA. Maybe then he'll learn what life is like for everyone else in the world.

My father, Alyssa, and Isla stare at a map at the table. The three of them look up at me when Hunter's boots squeak on the floor. Alyssa smiles. Her green eyes shine in the sunlight beaming in through the window.

We've made a decision," I say.

Alyssa winks at us. I'm sure she already knows what we're planning.

Hunter rests his arm across my shoulders. "Nadia and I will contact the HPA to negotiate an exchange, and we'll do it together."

My father rubs his hand across his forehead. "I don't like this. Maybe I should negotiate instead."

Alyssa shakes her head. "It has to be them, Dmitri. Hunter's mother wouldn't really want to see her son die."

Hunter clears his throat. "We all know that's not true, but she's more likely to hear me out."

I squeeze his hand.

Isla taps her nails on the glass table. "I still don't believe this. I never understood how your dad could be so confident and put together when you were gone, Nadia." She glances at my father. "I just didn't expect it to be because of him." She points at Hunter. "How did you do it? How did you keep Nadia alive all this time?"

Hunter gazes at me. "It was all her. She convinced the board she was completely human and told them she hated the council. They liked that about her."

"I thought they ran tests on people? Wouldn't it have shown in her blood?" Isla stares at me like I'm some miracle here to give the answers to how to survive in life when I don't know anything.

My father touches Isla's shoulder. "Blood tests won't show Nadia's nightmare inflictor side unless they take blood while she's in a dream. Nadia's a human chimera with two sets of DNA. Her nightmare inflictor's side and her human half."

My mouth falls open. "How do you know this?"

"Veronica Sanders did the tests for me before we realized you inherited my ability. She was convinced you were completely human. But then one night, right after your eighth birthday, you managed to break into Javier's apartment and gave him a real scare. Veronica then tested you again the next time you needed to inflict a nightmare, and sure enough, your DNA matched mine."

Alyssa gasps and then laughs. "It makes sense! No wonder Mr. Soto has always been awful to you."

I laugh because out of everything my father said, the one thing Alyssa really thought about was Mr. Soto. I don't remember ever invading Mr. Soto's mind, but I guess it's a reason to dislike me. "I wish you'd told me sooner. Then I'd have understood why Mr. Soto hated me so much."

My father moves away from the table, and Hunter drops his arm from me so my father can hug me. "There are a lot of things I wish I'd done differently. That was one of the lowest points in my life. I was grief-stricken and having my hope for you being human and leading a normal life was crushed. I never wanted this curse for you." His eyes line with tears.

I bury my face in his chest. I used to think I was cursed—that I was destined to be alone in this world, invading people's dreams, and being feared for the monster within me. I never knew my father felt the same way. He's always been so confident and assuring. I thought he was okay with being who he was.

"It's not a curse, Dad. It's hard, and it can suck sometimes, but I don't think I'm cursed anymore. Curses mean that bad things will happen, but—" I peer at Hunter and smile. "A lot of good has come from my nightmare inflictor side."

"I fell in love with Nadia in a dream world, Dmitri. Even what you would think of as her dark side is still beautiful and good to me."

My father smiles. It's a gesture I've never seen come easily to him. I never thought about it before this very moment, but I wonder if it's because he hates his dark side like I used to hate mine. He wasn't as lucky as me. He lost my mother. A tear rolls down my cheek as sadness washes through me.

"I'm just glad that after everything, you still have a chance at normalcy, Nadia. You get a chance to experience life as it should be." My father kisses my head before pulling away.

"Only if everything goes according to plan," Isla says, pulling me away from my thoughts and back to reality.

A lot is riding on my father's plan. I just hope it works as it should. I need it to work. Not just for myself, but for everyone I love.

HUNTER

I look over Nadia's shoulder at the map of the city. Dmitri circles a spot near the river and points at it. "The exchange must take place here. You'll have the river to protect you both if the HPA tries anything stupid, and—" He runs his finger to the closest bridge. "I can watch from here with back up if you need it. The important thing is that if anything happens, jump into the river. The water nymphs will protect you."

Knots tighten in my stomach. I don't know if I'll get the HPA to agree to meet at the river on our terms. They're aware of what they refer to as the water monsters in the river. After an agent tried crossing that specific bridge a few years ago and ended up drowning in the river, the HPA won't even let agents go near it.

"I'll see what I can do," I say.

"It has to be there. If the board doesn't agree, then we won't go through with it," Dmitri says.

I nod. "Okay, so what do we do now?"

Alyssa presses her hands on the table, moving the map. "You need to call your brother first. He'll listen long enough to hear you out. He'll force your mother to listen."

I frown. "I'm not exactly on great terms with Mason."

Nadia touches my hand. "But he doesn't want to see you dead."

"She's right, Hunter. Your brother has faith that in the end you guys will all be together. He thinks you can overcome your differences," Jacqueline says. It's the first time in a while that she has said anything.

"I'm afraid he'll find out that it's impossible," I think.

"No, Hunter, it is possible. Your brother might not know it yet, but he wants the same thing you do. He wants things to change."

If only I could make it happen.

18

READY FOR ANYTHING

HUNTER

I SIT NEXT to Alyssa in the front seat of her Corolla and glance at Nadia in the visor mirror. She leans her head back and gazes out the window. Dmitri and Isla stayed behind at the warehouse with Mr. Soto, and it's up to us to arrange a meeting with the HPA to hopefully exchange Mr. Soto for our freedom.

"You have three minutes to convince Mason and then you need to hang up. The HPA is tracking his phone to try to locate you if you call," Alyssa says.

I push my hair out of my face. "What should I say?"

She taps her fingers. "He's your brother. You know him best."

"Start with the truth. Tell him about how you met Nadia and why you did what you did," Jacqueline says.

"I don't know if he'll understand," I think.

"He might surprise you."

Alyssa pulls into a gas station with a convenience store, and I hop out before she can even put the car in park. Running to the payphone, I pop in some change and dial Mason's number. My hands shake as my nerves get the best of me, and I lean my back on the wall to watch the parking lot.

"This is Mason," my brother says.

"I don't have long, Mason, but it's me," I say.

He sucks in a breath, creating static in the phone. "Dude, Hunter, you have to turn yourself in. Mom says if you do, they won't punish you."

I laugh. The sound comes forced and cold and echoes through the air. "That's bull. She's lying to you. She has agents out trying to kill me now. I almost died last night."

He's quiet for a second and then says, "So why are you calling me? You know I can't do anything."

"I need you to get Mom to convince the board I'm not trying to destroy them. I want five minutes to talk to her over the phone, but I need you to prepare her. I have something to offer that she won't be able to refuse." I twist the phone cord.

"You released your entire cell block of prisoners, Hunter."

"You have to understand, Mase. I didn't do it for the prisoners. I did it for my girlfriend. Mom was going to send her to be a part of SATF. I had to get her out of there."

"The Emily girl everyone is talking about? You gave up

everything for a girl? What about me? I'm your brother. You dragged me into the middle of something I don't want to be involved in." His voice rises over the line.

Alyssa honks her horn.

"Her name's Nadia. And, please understand. I love her, and I owe her my life. She saved me," I say.

"Saved you?"

"Nadia risked her life to take my soul back to my body after the sin-eater incident you so easily forgave Mom for, even though she didn't deserve it. Nadia went against the council to do it and lost their protection."

"Oh."

I think I'm getting through to him. I take a quick breath and ask, "So will you help me? All I need you to do is to tell Mom I want to make a deal, but only tell her a minute before six. It's when I'll call your phone. I don't want to give the HPA time to track me. If you mess up or tell her sooner, I'm dead."

He sighs. "Okay, fine. I'll do it."

"If you decide to go against me, I'll know, Mason," I say. I don't want to threaten him, but my brother needs to know how important it is that he doesn't let me down.

"You can trust me, Hunter. I'll surprise her with dinner at home and tell her then. Be careful, bro."

I hang up the phone and jog to Alyssa's car, slamming the door. She reverses from the spot and exits the lot. She speeds down the street and onto the highway and heads in the opposite direction of the warehouse.

My brows furrow. "Where are we going?"

"The Haven," Nadia says from the backseat.

"Tell them they're crazy," Jacqueline says, finally saying something since I hung up with my brother.

I shift in the seat and glance between Alyssa and Nadia. "Why? That sounds dangerous."

Nadia's eyes water. "Because Cian told me I could tell Liv about her brother myself. We won't be there long."

NADIA

Cian hops from his stool when Alyssa, Hunter, and I stroll into the hallway that leads to The Haven. He pushes up the sleeves of his purple dress shirt, and I notice his slacks have been tailored to his short stature for once. He greets me with a smile and pulls his blue-framed glasses from his shirt pocket and puts them on.

Grabbing my hand, Cian kisses my knuckles. "Nadia, dear, I don't believe my eyes. First you free Dmitri and now here you are, a free person as well. A lot of people want to talk to you, you know. There are rumors about adding a spot to the council for you."

I smirk, a genuine smile hard to find. "My father's more deserving. I'd never take a position in a million years, even if they begged me. I'm so over everything. I just want to move on."

He nods, twisting his lips to the side. "That's a shame. You'd make a great leader."

I grimace. "No, not really. I did things because I had to, and I had a lot of help." I look behind me at Hunter. "I'd have never made it without Hunter."

Cian looks past me at Hunter, and Alyssa steps in front of him and smiles at Cian. Cian raises his eyebrows and then takes a step back, crossing his arms. "Does Dmitri know?"

"Know what?" I ask.

He presses his lips together for a long moment and finally says, "That your boyfriend is an agent."

My eyes widen. How would Cian know? "What? How could you tell? Hunter's not an agent...at least not anymore."

Cian shifts on his feet. "He's wearing half a uniform. I can spot them from a mile away."

"Dmitri knows, Cian, and Hunter's been helping us for months, but please, don't say anything. It's important. Dmitri will come to you when he's ready to talk."

Hurt clouds Cian's eyes. I guess my father's never kept him out of the loop before. I'm sure he knows about the plans in regards to the council, since he's the one who sent Isla to get me, but he might not know the extent of my father's plan or how crucial Hunter is to everything. People are reluctant to put their faith in those they perceive as enemies.

"You got it, doll face." Cian glances at Hunter once more before touching the door handle. "Liv's waiting in the VIP lounge. I closed it so you'll have some privacy."

I touch his shoulder. "Thanks, Cian. For everything."

Sliding my arm around Hunter's waist, I guide him into the club. Alyssa saunters on his other side, and we move through the crowded dance floor without giving anyone a second glance. Hunter rests his arm on my shoulders and kisses my head. I offer him a small smile. His hazel eyes flash lavender, and Jacqueline's presence probably helps disguise Hunter from any soul manipulators in the room. I wonder how she's taking all this.

Alyssa points to a black painted door in the corner, half hidden behind a group of people standing around a table, sipping drinks from glass goblets. We stroll around the crowd to the VIP lounge. Alyssa stops in front of it and turns to face me. She leans over and presses her lips to my ear and whispers, "I'm going to stay out here. Liv doesn't need us all in there."

I press my quivering lips together. I want to beg Alyssa to come with us, because I need the support too, but she's already made up her mind.

The last time I saw Liv was when she and Mr. Augustine, Northern Bell's librarian and a family friend, broke into the termination facility to try to rescue my father, Camden, and a young girl named Ella. Unfortunately, their plan failed because Hunter showed up unexpectedly and was forced to fight a shifter named Blaine because Blaine wouldn't hear him out. Meeting Liv and having her be one of the only people to attempt to help me when the council denied me was the reason I knew I could trust her brother. She was the reason I shared my secrets with Camden in the first place.

My heart hurts just thinking about him. I've kept thoughts of Camden away all day, and now that I'm here about to face his sister, I don't know what to say. How do you tell someone their loved one died? Nothing about this situation is right.

"I'm here for you," Hunter whispers into my hair. "You'll get through this."

But I'm afraid I won't. Reliving Camden's death all over again is enough to break me into a million pieces. Liv will hate me when she finds out it's my fault her brother died. And I deserve her hatred. I deserve to have a shadow hanging over me for the rest of my life.

I take a breath, and Alyssa opens the door and then moves out of the way. Hunter steps in first, and I close the door behind us. A heavy silence presses around me when the noisiness of the club cuts off.

Liv sits at a black leather booth with a glass of red elixir in front of her and smiles when she sees me. She stands up, opening her arms, but I don't move. I can't. My legs stop working, frozen in place. I can't bear to tell her what happened to Camden. Tears automatically spill from my eyes. Through my blurry vision, I watch her smiling face twist into a frown. Her electric blue eyes widen as things piece together in her mind. Her hand flies to her chest, and my heart aches watching her heart shatter before my eyes.

Hunter nudges me, and I glide forward and grab Liv's hands, holding them between mine. "I'm so, so sorry, Liv. I couldn't save him. It's all my fault."

She sniffles, clearing her throat. "What happened?" Her voice comes hoarse, and she clutches the table for support.

My throat burns as the words try to hide. I force my mouth open, but only shuddering sobs rip from me. I can't do it. I can't tell her.

Hunter squeezes my shoulder. "Your brother died saving us. He fought an agent so we could get to a vehicle."

Liv wipes her eyes with the palms of her hands. "That sounds like something he'd do," she says with a smile through her tears. "Always saving people. That's how he ended up there, you know. He saved his best friend."

I swallow the tears in my throat. "I wouldn't be alive without him, Liv. I cared about him a lot."

She nods. "I have a feeling he cared about you, too."

Hunter shifts on his feet. "More than you know." He doesn't say it in a jealous way, but like he's stating a fact about Camden.

Liv turns her eyes to Hunter and tilts her head to the side. She reaches up and touches his face as recognition settles in. "I know you."

I touch her shoulder. "Hunter has always been on our side."

She narrows her eyes. "You're the reason Blake died, and we couldn't save Camden and Dmitri."

Hunter takes a step back, and I step in between them. It was a bad idea to bring Hunter here. Liv's not as easily convinced as I was hoping. Her watery, icy blue eyes bore into mine, and I hold her gaze. "Don't you dare blame Hunter for that night, Liv. You know Blake was unpredictable and volatile. If he had let Hunter explain to him you all were on the same side, none of us would've been in this mess, and I wouldn't have lost two months of my life."

"And Camden would still be alive," she whispers.

Wrapping my arms around her, I hold her as she cries into my shoulder. "I wish I could go back and change things. I wish it were me instead of Camden. I'll live with the guilt of his death on my conscience forever, but nothing can change."

She shudders as she sucks in a breath and relaxes in my arms. "I'm sorry. None of this is any of our faults. The HPA is the one we should blame. They did this. They put us in this situation."

"The HPA wronged us all," Hunter says.

Liv pulls away from me and looks over my shoulder. "You're right, Hunter. I'm glad to see you realize that."

HUNTER

"We should give them a minute," Jacqueline says.

I nod, agreeing with both Liv and Jacqueline, and step back to the door. I crack it open, and Alyssa peeks in and moves out of the way so I can close it behind me.

"I see Liv decided not to kill you," Alyssa says.

I furrow my brows. "Kill me?"

"Don't worry. Nadia wouldn't have let it happen."

I sigh. "I guess that's something."

Alyssa leans against me. "Liv needed to see you and to learn for herself that you're on our side. She has a voice with the enchantresses. She'll convince them to team up with Dmitri in reforming the council. It's important for all the governing bodies to stay together in this mess."

"They should ask you to be on the council," I say.

Alyssa laughs. "And give up doing whatever the heck I want?"

I shrug. "You'd make a good leader."

She bumps me with her shoulder. "Thanks."

"Looks like the council will have a hard time filling Mr. Soto's seat," Jacqueline says. Her voice comes quiet against the loud music, and I focus on listening to her.

"Do you blame them?" I ask Jacqueline in my mind.

The VIP door opens, pulling my thoughts from Jacqueline, and I look into Nadia's gray eyes. They're free of tears, and she looks stronger than ever. In this moment, I know she's strong enough to help me get through the next few days.

"She finally sees a future with you," Jacqueline comments.

"Are you ready?" Alyssa asks.

"Yeah," Nadia and I say at the same time. I kiss her forehead, and she leans into me. I think we're more ready to face the future now than we've ever been. I think we're ready for anything.

19

TOGETHER MAKES US STRONGER

HUNTER

"DID YOU GET that, Hunter?" Dmitri asks.

I point at the X on the map. "Stand here and don't step more than five feet forward until Nadia arrives with Mr. Soto."

"And then what?" Dmitri studies my face like he's trying to read what's going on in my head.

"The moment Nadia is on the O, you both step back into the river." Jacqueline's voice echoes in my ears, reminding me of what happens next.

I need to concentrate, but all I can focus on is the ticking of the wall clock as the seconds pass by and the time moves closer to six. I imagine Dr. Sullivan will be angry and threaten me, and I'm worried she won't want to make a deal.

"That's your mom's favorite thing to do. She competes with the devil in deal making."

Dmitri shakes my shoulder. "Hunter, focus. What do you do next?"

Clearing my throat, I say, "Wait for Nadia and then jump into the river."

"Good. I think you're as prepared as you're going to be," he says, pressing his lips together.

I tap my fingers on the map. "I hope it's enough."

Nadia comes up next to me and rests her head on my shoulder. "We'll get through this."

"Did Alyssa see that?" I ask.

Nadia frowns. "No, but we don't need her to tell us that everything is going to work out. I can feel it. For once I'm not afraid, and we don't have to hide what we mean to each other. Standing together makes us stronger."

"But are we strong enough?"

"We don't have a choice. We have to be."

NADIA

Doubt clouds Hunter's eyes. I wish I could convince him we'll succeed, but I don't have any reassuring words, because it's hard not to doubt myself. My faith in Hunter is what keeps my voice steady and allows me to act like we're going to make a difference. *You will make a difference. Things are already changing because of you.*

"I'll watch the both of you every step of the way. If things go wrong, I'll be ready," Dmitri says. "I wouldn't put you two in this situation if I thought you'd fail. That's why I'm asking you to do this. I believe you are the only ones who won't fail."

I stare into Hunter's hazel eyes. He holds my gaze, his tightly knit eyebrows relaxing, and then he leans down and kisses my cheek. I smile and shift my gaze to my father. He watches us but doesn't say anything. He's already accepted Hunter into our lives and trusts him enough to put the fate of our world in his hands. In our hands.

I pull away from Hunter and hug my father. "I can't wait for this all to be over."

"Me too, Nadi. We have a lot of catching up to do," my father says.

The door swings open, and my mouth drops open when Mr. Augustine steps in. He was my mother's best friend growing up. The last time I saw him was the day I saved my father. He looked after me and Alyssa when my father couldn't.

His bald head gleams with sweat, dripping onto his mauve dress shirt. He grins when he sees me and opens his arms, and I rush to him and hug him, surprised to see him here in the warehouse. I was pretty certain he swore off the supernatural world altogether after tagging along on the rescue mission that failed to save my father the first time.

Alyssa comes into the kitchen after Mr. Augustine and smiles at me from behind him. She plays with her red braid but doesn't say anything. She just watches Mr. Augustine hug me and then strolls to stand next to Hunter.

"Alyssa told me you were free." Mr. Augustine squeezes my shoulders and laughs. "I had to come see you for myself. Did you know I was planning on breaking into that dreary facility on my own to get you out? But—" He points at my father. "This guy didn't think I had it in me."

I raise my eyebrows and smirk. "Well, I think you could've done it."

Mr. Augustine pulls a lavender handkerchief from his back pocket and wipes his head. "Or at least given them a good fight." He smiles and hugs me again before strolling to the kitchen table and plopping down on a chair. "The HPA wouldn't have known what hit them."

My father chuckles. "You're right about that." He removes the map from the table and rolls it up, tying a rubber band around it. Gliding toward the stairs, he glances at us. "After you're done catching up, Sandy, I'd like to speak with you upstairs."

Mr. Augustine gets back to his feet. "Now's fine. I only have a few minutes before I need to get home."

"We need to head out soon, too," Alyssa says.

I hug Mr. Augustine one more time. "Thanks for being here for me," I say.

"No thanks needed," Mr. Augustine says.

He walks across the kitchen and follows my father upstairs. I turn to Hunter, watching him stare at the tiled floor without lifting his head to meet my gaze. He's lost deep in his thoughts. I hope he can pull himself out of them long enough to call his mother.

I slide my arms around him, and he finally draws his attention to me. "I can make the phone call if you want. Dr. Sullivan might talk to me.”

He shakes his head. “I don't want to put you through that.”

I touch his cheek. “You wouldn't be putting me through anything.”

Standing on my tiptoes, I brush my lips against his until his shoulders relax, and he kisses me back. It's short and sweet but full of love and hope and promise, and when he pulls away, he's smiling.

“You two ready?” Alyssa asks.

I nod. “Let's get this over with.”

HUNTER

“You need to say as much as possible in a short amount of time,” Jacqueline says.

I sigh, staring out the windshield. “I know that, Jackie.”

“Want to practice with me?” Her anxiety swirls in my mind and makes me anxious.

“No. I want you to shut up and stop blasting me with your emotions.” Rubbing my eyes, I tilt my head back. “And trust me. I have this handled.”

“I do trust you, Hunter.”

I don't respond. Instead, I swivel in my seat to look back at Nadia. She's been silent since we left the warehouse, now staring out the window, lost in thought. I wish I could be in her head to hear her thoughts, but only for a moment.

“You're worried,” I say to Nadia.

Alyssa merges onto the highway without saying a word.

Nadia pulls strands of her hair. “It's just hard.”

I reach back and touch her knee. "I know."

"Are you worried?"

I nod. "Yeah. I'm afraid I'll mess up."

Grabbing my hand, she brings it to her lips to kiss my knuckles. "You won't. That's the only thing I'm not worried about."

We stare at each other for a few minutes. Alyssa pulls into an empty parking lot in front of a small strip mall, idling in the parking spot. I scan the stucco building for a payphone but don't see one.

Alyssa reaches into her purse and pulls out a flip phone. It's old, the numbers faded, but the screen lights up green when she presses the power button. "It's safer for us if we keep moving. I'm going to circle the neighborhood, and when the call is over, I want you to toss the phone out the window. If I tell you to hang up, do it, okay?"

I nod. "So why here?"

"It's one of the only areas nearby populated by all humans." Alyssa reverses and drives from the parking lot, staying at the low speed limit. I wait until she makes a right at the street behind the strip mall to start dialing Mason's number.

It's a minute to six. He should be with my mom already with her already expecting my call. I just hope he convinced her to listen to what I have to say.

The phone rings once before clicking, and I hear breathing echoing through the line. "Mom?" I ask.

After a second she says, "Oh, Hunter. I can't believe you're calling. You know there's nothing I can do to help you. You committed treason."

I swallow the knot in my throat. "I couldn't let you hurt Nadia."

"You're just like your father. Always thinking with your heart and not your head," she says. Her words lace with disappointment, but I don't take offense. I believe my dad is the better of my two parents, even if he isn't around.

I shift in my seat. "I don't have time to talk about my decisions. I've called you because I want to make a deal with the board."

Dr. Sullivan laughs, the sound of her voice like scraping pieces of metal together. "A deal? You expect me to make a deal after you released your entire cell block and got two of my agents killed?"

"Yes, exactly. And I didn't kill anyone. You can thank the sin-eater, Jacqueline, for that."

Dr. Sullivan gasps. Jacqueline sighs in my mind, and I ignore her and press the phone harder to my ear. I need to focus.

"What happened to you, Hunter? I don't understand. You've been working with supers after everything they've done to you—to us? How do you live with yourself?" I'm taken by surprise by Dr. Sullivan's words. Her voice hums low not sounding like the ice-cold doctor I've grown used to.

"Hunter, get to the deal," Jacqueline says.

I push my anger back. I want to scream into the phone that none of this had to do with creatures and that my mom was the one who put me into the situation in the first place. I want to tell her I live with myself just fine, and I'm better than ever. For once, I'm in control of my life.

"How do you? At least I don't imprison and kill innocent people."

"Hunter!" Dr. Sullivan's voice echoes in my ear.

"Oh, quit it, Dr. Sullivan. I don't have time for this. I called to make a deal. If you don't want to hear me out, then fine. You'll never see me again."

"Hear him out, Mom." Mason's muffled voice echoes through the line. "Haven't you messed up our family enough already?"

Dr. Sullivan clears her throat. "I'm listening."

"I have something you and the board are desperate for, and I'd like to trade it for amnesty. You will call off the searches and forget we exist. You'll let us live the rest of our lives without fear. If you break our deal, I won't let you off so easily." I peer at Nadia in the visor mirror, and she nods her head.

"You'll tell us where the Creature Council is?" Dr. Sullivan asks.

"I'll do one better. Nadia wasn't lying when she said she didn't like the council. If you give us what we want, we'll give you a council member."

"You have a council member?" Dr. Sullivan's voice raises a notch higher, and I can sense all the thoughts running through her mind through the line. "And you're willing to give them to us?"

"That's what I said."

She breathes into the phone. "I'll call an emergency meeting with the board. I'm sure we can work something out,

Hunter."

"I'll call you later then. You tell the board that everything has to be on my terms or there won't be a deal," I say.

"Okay, Hunter."

Alyssa taps my knee. "Hang up the phone."

I hang up without hesitating. When Alyssa turns left at the next street, I chuck the phone out the window, and it clatters on the sidewalk. Alyssa punches the accelerator, driving fast toward the highway. Within a few minutes, we're miles from the neighborhood. The knots in my stomach loosen, and I release a relieved breath.

It's done. Dr. Sullivan will make it happen. The moment I mentioned I'd trade a council member for our freedom, I knew she'd agree to the deal.

Nadia leans forward, resting her hands on my shoulder. "You did great. I know it wasn't easy confronting her like that." She stretches her seatbelt and kisses my neck just below my ear. I suck in a breath, and she does it again and giggles.

I shift and smirk at her. "This was the easy part."

Alyssa weaves between lanes. "Yeah, now it's just making sure the HPA keeps their word."

"Ask her how," Jacqueline says, speaking up for the first time since I yelled at her. I know she's dying to be included in the conversation. Being around Nadia and Alyssa again in the outside world reminds her of what she's missing living in my mind.

"Dmitri has a plan for that, too, right?" I ask.

"It's a mixture of threatening and trust. Your mom doesn't

really want to see you dead, but she doesn't want to die either. If she or the board betrays you, she'll lose her freedom. She'll know what it's like to live in constant fear. Dmitri has a lot of connections. She wouldn't last a day outside of her precious facility walls." Alyssa glances at me in her peripheral vision.

"Why not just kill her then?" I ask. "Kill them all?"

Nadia rests her chin on my shoulders. "We aren't monsters, Hunter. My father always says the death of our enemies is a last resort. If we go around killing everyone, it makes us no different from them, and they'll grow in numbers and force. The board members will be replaced, and then what?"

I puff air through my lips. "I just wish we could make them see."

"It's not the board that needs to see. It's everyone working for them," Jacqueline says.

"You're right," I think. "I guess not killing them all is a start."

"You're not a murderer, Hunter. I hope you never have to be."

20

THE CHANCE TO LIVE

NADIA

"YOU LOOK TIRED," I say, rubbing Hunter's shoulder as he leans on his elbows and studies the map my father marked up with his plan.

He yawns, looking at me. "And you look hungry." He brushes my white hair with his fingers. Most of my color has drained away because of my head injury, my anxiety, my inability to sit still—all the little things are taking a toll on me. "You're turning into my beautiful nightmare inflictor."

I smirk. "You have to be a little bit crazy to love my monster side."

"I love all of you."

I lean in and kiss him. He combs his fingers in my hair, pulling me closer. He tastes of the chocolate cake Alyssa baked to settle her nerves, and I slide my tongue into his mouth and kiss him deeply, like his kiss is the only thing I desire right now.

A cough interrupts us, and I reluctantly pull away and meet my father's gaze. He stares at us with raised eyebrows. I swear his cheeks look rosy. I've never seen my father blush.

Cringing, I offer a smile that looks more like I'm baring my teeth. "I thought you were out."

My father crosses his arms. "I just got back."

Hunter pushes his chair back, and it squeaks across the tiles. "I'm going to find Alyssa. I need to make the call."

I grab his hand. "I'll come with you."

As we turn to head toward the stairs, my father says, "Nadi, wait."

Hunter squeezes my hand and kisses my cheek but doesn't wait to go up the stairs. I spin on the balls of my feet and place my hands on my hips. My father looks ready to lecture me, and I prepare to argue that I've wasted two months, and I'm only trying to catch up on my life.

"You need to invade a dream," my father says, surprising me. I'm shocked I'm not going to get The Talk about Hunter. Maybe he knows I don't need it. "I know of a local volunteer. Let me take you."

I pout my bottom lip. "I'm supposed to go with Hunter and Alyssa for the HPA call."

He motions me to come closer to him, and then he wraps his arm around my shoulders. "They can handle it. What you need is to get your strength back. You need to be ready for what is to come."

"I am ready," I argue.

"Nadi," my father says.

I sigh. "Okay, fine. Give me five minutes." My heart falls into my stomach thinking about invading another dream. I've grown used to Camden's dreams, and now I'm terrified of invading a mind and not seeing him there. It's the same feeling I had after Hunter returned to his body. It's just hard to get used to the unfamiliar. It's hard to move on. *Camden would want you to be happy.*

A tear slips from my eye, and before I can turn away, my father touches my chin and peers down at me. His eyebrows lower as he presses his lips into a thin line and studies my face. And then he hugs me. His sinewy arms squeeze me against his hard chest, and I breathe in his familiar scent of warm cologne.

"You can talk to me about anything," he says as he kisses my head. "Let me help you."

I sniffle back my sobs. "How do you get over losing someone? I feel like Camden's death was my fault."

My father pulls away and stares at me with tears in his eyes. "You never get over them. You just learn to live without them. It's painful and empty, and sometimes downright unbearable, but there are also good things in life to take your mind off the heartache." He swipes his hand across his eyes.

"What good have you found?" I ask. I know he's thinking about my mother. My words cut open a fresh wound on his heart because he blames himself for my mother's death, even though it was an agent who killed her.

He smiles through his sadness. "Watching you grow up is one thing. Helping people in need is another. I surround myself with a lot of people, and they help ease the pain."

I hug him again. Maybe he's right. The grief I feel over Camden is tolerable as long as I'm not alone with my thoughts. If I can get through the next nightmare, I'll get through more, and then I can find some normalcy again. Camden would want that. He thought he could give it to me, and maybe he could've, but normal doesn't have the same definition for everyone. Constantly invading Camden's dreams was not my normal—he was the exception. I wish I had more time with him, but I know deep down it would've never worked. A life with me would've been an inevitable death for him regardless. There was no changing his mind. It's why he gave me the chance to live. I can't waste it.

Footsteps clomp on the stairs. Stepping away from my father, I turn toward Alyssa and Hunter. Alyssa's eyes glass over, and she's seen me make a decision—maybe both the decisions I've made in the last few minutes—to find my normalcy and my decision to accept Camden's choice to save me even if I don't like it.

I tuck my hair behind my ears. "You two will have to go without me."

Hunter's brows furrow. "Okay." He doesn't argue, but he's not happy about it. His jaw tightens, and he clenches his fingers at his side. His hazel eyes shift to lavender and back, and then he turns to Alyssa. "Ready?"

Alyssa bobs her head and pulls her car keys from her pocket. She turns to me. "We'll be fine. You two stay safe, okay?" Linking her arm with Hunter's, she practically drags him from the kitchen.

"Don't wait up." I wave at them as they leave, and the door swings shut behind them. Crossing my arms, I turn to my father. "So, where are we going?"

"Just down the river. We can go by foot. Think you can keep up with me?" he asks.

I smirk. "I should be the one asking that question."

He laughs and slings his arm over my shoulder. We both glide through the living area and out of the warehouse. Alyssa's headlights flash over us when she makes a U-turn and heads toward the front gate.

The brilliant moon casts a pale stream of light on the half frozen river, and the city glows in the distance. The chilly air wraps around me. My father guides me to a small walking path that runs as far as I can see alongside the river. I look over the guardrail. A section of ice near the shore splits as a water nymph gazes at us from below. Her mesmerizing face is covered in silver and blue scales, and if I didn't know any better, I'd have missed her completely.

"I'm not looking forward to the ice bath," I say as I turn away and glide ahead of my father.

"It'll be for just a few minutes."

Pressing lips together, I hug my arms against me. "Doesn't mean I have to like it."

He chuckles and grabs my shoulder to slow me down. "I'll

make it up to you. I promise."

"It's not necessary. I'd do it a thousand times if it means I could be free."

"You will be free. We'll make it happen."

HUNTER

Alyssa speeds in the opposite direction of the city and cuts across two lanes before exiting the highway. She slows down at an intersection and turns right without completely stopping for the signal.

She swears under her breath. "The board made a decision. They're going to agree to the exchange, but they want something else, too."

A pit forms in my stomach. "What is it?"

"You mentioned Jacqueline being alive to your mom. The board wants her, too." Alyssa glances at me before looking at the road again. "You changed things when you mentioned her. I didn't know how bad until now."

I shift in my seat. "Think we should back out? There's absolutely no way to give her over even if I wanted to."

"You wouldn't give me up, Hunter?" Jacqueline asks, her voice soft, almost a whisper in my ears.

I shake my head and think, "Don't sound so surprised."

Alyssa frowns. "No, we have to try. I don't know what'll happen when you deny them. Maybe they'll still be interested."

I twist my lips to the side. If they don't agree to our terms, then we won't have a deal, and Nadia and I won't get our freedom. We're worse off than other people in the real world because the HPA knows exactly who we are and can put their unlimited resources to finding us. We'd have to live somewhere like the compound, and Nadia doesn't want to live like that. I don't want that either.

"What do you think they'll do?" I ask.

She shakes her head. "You know them better than I do. Let's just call and find out." She digs into the center console and pulls out another old flip phone.

I lift an eyebrow, wondering if Alyssa has some collection of ancient phones lying around, but don't ask. She grabs my hand before I have a chance to dial and just holds it for a second.

"What are you doing?" I ask.

"I just had a vision. They're ready to track Mason's phone. You need to call someone else instead."

I frown and think for a minute. The only other number I have memorized is Dr. Sullivan's, and I'd think they'd track her phone, too.

"Call Dr. Harvey, Hunter," Jacqueline says.

"I don't know his number," I say out loud.

"Well, I do. I've had a lot of time on my hands the last two months. I've memorized the HPA's entire directory just from the times you've used it."

NADIA

My father stops in front of a grand condominium complex overlooking the freezing river. The size of each unit alone screams luxury. I've never been in a condo larger than my quaint little house. A wrought iron fence surrounds the community, but my father punches in an access code at a gate leading to a set of stairs that take us into the complex.

We step onto a private street, freshly salted and free of snow. Each unit is identical with light tan, stucco walls with red brick accents, large windows, a garage, and a short set of stairs to the front door.

My father takes my hand, and we climb the steps of the first home. A tall, narrow window without a curtain shows off an entryway with a black metal chandelier and white marble floors. A glass and metal table sits against a short wall, cluttered with framed family photos, a bowl for keys, and a few candles.

Warm air hits my face when my father opens the door. I follow him into the home and look around. A grand piano rests upon a cream and black area rug, and a leopard-print chaise lounge and leather recliner is positioned in front of a small fireplace. Built-in book shelves display an array of books, figurines, and photos, and across from a large window a flat screen television hangs on an ivory wall.

We pass a formal dining room with a bulky wooden table with fabric-covered chairs. It's set with fine china and candle centerpieces and looks like no one ever actually eats in the room.

"This way," my father says.

He pulls me down a short hallway and past an open kitchen with gleaming stainless steel appliances, frosted glass fronted cabinetry, a large island with a built-in sink, and an eating corner with large glass windows showing off a snowy deck and the brightly lit city skyline.

We come to a set of carpeted stairs. I keep close behind my

father as he soundlessly glides up. I sense a sleeping couple in the bedroom at the end of the dark hallway, and my stomach burns with such intensity that I clutch the wall to steady myself.

Gliding ahead of my father, I crack the door open. Two figures sleep under an abstract, white, gray, and black duvet in a four post trestlewood bed. A matching headboard and night tables take up most of the wall behind them. Maroon walls and tan carpet bring warmth to the room, and white shuttered windows allow in a sliver of moonlight.

Without saying a word, I cross the room and press my fingers to the temples of a man with short brown hair and neatly trimmed facial hair. The world shifts, and within seconds, I stand amid his dream world.

The air shifts again, and I turn and face my father. He peers around the snow covered park before bringing his eyes to me. It's been years since we've entered a dream together, since I was little and he was teaching me what to do, and I don't know how I feel about it now.

"We don't have a lot of time," he says. His black hair blows in an icy breeze, a dark contrast to the frozen, snowy world.

I nod and press my feet to the ground. The snow melts and the brown grass under my boots blackens as my presence kicks the nightmare into action.

The dark clouds churn overhead, and laughter echoes in the distance. My father tilts his head in the direction of the noise, motioning for me to follow behind him. In our wake, we leave a trail of death and decay, the brilliant, glittering snow melting and turning into black, muddy mush.

The dreamer ice skates on a frozen lake on the outskirts of the park. A blond woman, who I recognize as his significant other, twirls around him, and they look so happy with beaming smiles and squinty eyes. They both have red noses, but neither looks like they care that they're freezing.

"Can you believe we're getting married tomorrow?" the woman asks.

The dreamer pulls her to him and kisses her. Stepping onto the frozen lake, I crack the ice below me, sending steaming, black dream essence wafting around me. I don't fall through the ice as it breaks and keep moving closer to the couple. I suck in the dream dust, inhaling deeply, and energy courses through me.

My father steps onto the ice next to me, shaking the unstable ground. The couple freezes and pulls away from each other. Fear pours from the dreamer in cold waves of deliciousness. I smile as his worst nightmare takes hold of his dream world, ruining it. He grabs onto the woman, and she screams, losing balance, and falls through the ice.

"Melissa, no!"

I glide forward and grab her hand. She explodes in my arms, and I inhale her tantalizing peppermint dream essence. The dreamer yells as tears escape his eyes and freeze on his cheeks. He lies on his stomach and reaches through the broken ice, but it's too late.

My father stomps the ice again. The dreamer rolls and slowly drags himself toward the edge of the frozen lake before he falls through the ice himself. The gray sky splits, and the air fogs with dream dust. I glide behind the dreamer as he struggles to save himself, his fear hot and intense, as loud cracks echo through the air and the ice crumbles around him.

"Help!" he screams. "Help us, please!"

He shimmies to the edge of the lake, struggling to find sold ground. Sneaking up behind him, I bend down and grab his ankles, flipping him over and through the ice. His screams cut off as the nightmare shatters around us. I take in as much as I can before I pull away from the dreamer's mind.

"Let's go," my father says.

I follow him from the home without a word. I feel alive and myself again. I feel strong and invincible. I just hope it's enough to survive another day. I hope it's enough to get through the deal with the board.

HUNTER

My heartbeat pounds in my ears as I dial Dr. Harvey's phone number. It rings twice before the line clicks, and heavy breathing erupts through the speaker. Alyssa touches my knee but keeps her eyes on the road ahead, navigating through the neighborhood.

"Tell the board they're crazy if they think they can get away with tracking my call. If they try it again, the deal is off," I say.

"Let me take my phone to Dr. Sullivan." His breathing quickens, his footsteps echoing through the line. The sound stops, and he's silent for a moment. "Before I hand over the phone, I just wanted to thank you for not killing me."

Shifting in my seat, I stare out the side window. "We're not monsters, Dr. Harvey. The board twisted your view of the world."

"I'm starting to see that," he whispers. Through the line, I hear a quick knock and then low voices over Dr. Harvey's breathing.

"Did you hear that, Hunter? Someone is questioning the board's ideals."

I smile to myself and think, "Think it'll make a difference?"

"It might."

"Dr. Sullivan speaking."

I shake my head, focusing on listening to the background voices past Dr. Sullivan's cold voice. "Don't think I don't know the board well enough not to know what to expect?"

She laughs, a hard, forced sound, and then says, "I told them not to underestimate you."

"Maybe next time they'll listen. I'm one step ahead of you, Dr. Sullivan, which brings me to our deal. I expect you're going to ask for more than the council member, and the answer is no. You can't have Jackie. It's the council member for mine and Nadia's freedom or nothing."

I listen to the hushed, exasperated conversation through the line. The board sounds appalled and nervous that I knew what they were planning. Alyssa smirks, and then her eyes turn glassy. She grips my knee and frowns, and my chest tightens.

Before Alyssa can open her mouth to tell me what she saw, Dr. Sullivan's voice rings through the line and she says, "We'll only give you your freedom. Now, don't you underestimate us, Hunter. We'll find Nadia soon enough unless you give us someone else worth our time."

I grind my teeth. "The council member for Nadia's freedom then. I'll take my chances against the board."

"I'll help you kill them all." Jacqueline's anger seeps through me, and red shadows wash over my vision.

"No," Dr. Sullivan says.

Alyssa swerves to the side of the road and puts the car into park. She snatches the phone from my hand and presses it to her own ear. She listens for a second, the silence between us thick and angry toward the board.

Her eyes shine as she brings her gaze to mine, and then she says, "How about a seer then? I have a valuable ability that could be very useful to you."

I wish I could hear Dr. Sullivan's reaction.

Grabbing Alyssa's arm, I try to snatch the phone away from her, but she opens her door and jumps out.

"You're curious," Alyssa says. Her voice echoes into the night. "I wouldn't bother discussing it. You have one minute to accept my offer, which I know you will. We'll meet tomorrow at noon at Riverview Park. You can bring one agent and one vehicle. I'll know if you try to fool me. If your board tries anything funny, the deal's off, and you can expect a real war on your doorstep."

21

NOT GOING DOWN WITHOUT A FIGHT

HUNTER

I TOUCH ALYSSA'S shoulder before she goes in her room. She narrows her eyes, and in the low lighting, she looks fierce and confident. It's the same way Nadia is within a nightmare.

"You haven't said a word since you hung up on Dr. Sullivan," I say, shifting on my feet when she glances down the hallway.

Standing on her tiptoes, she whispers, "You should know better than to think I'm going to let the HPA take me. Don't tell anyone about my part of the conversation. Not even Nadia."

I lean against the wall and cross my arms. "You have a plan, right? You need to tell me so we can prepare."

She opens her door and turns away from me, though she peers over her shoulder. "No, actually I don't. But as soon as I think of something, I'll tell you. But seriously, don't tell anyone what I did. I don't want them to worry. I can take care of myself."

"Are you sure?"

Alyssa shuts the door without answering. Flinging my door open, I slam it behind me. I plop on the bed and turn on my back to stare at the ceiling. Alyssa was crazy for offering herself to the HPA, even if she doesn't plan to follow through with it. They know about her now, and they'll want her. I can already think of a million reasons why. One being they believe it'll leave us at a disadvantage, which it will, and secondly, they'll try to use her against us. Even if Alyssa's visions are only predictions, the HPA already has the upper hand, and we can't have the shift in power lean more toward them.

"I'm sure everything will be fine. Alyssa knows what she's doing even if she doesn't have a plan," Jacqueline says.

I rub my eyes and yawn. "But why would she do this in the first place?"

"She got the board to agree, didn't she? Maybe they wouldn't have otherwise."

"We could've thought of another way. You know Nadia's going to freak. She's going to be angry I didn't try harder to stop Alyssa."

"Nadia will understand. She would've done the same thing for Alyssa if the roles were reversed. That's what best friends do. They always want to save each other."

NADIA

The warehouse is quiet when we enter the living area. Alyssa's car was parked out front, but I only sense one person awake. Isla sits at the kitchen table, hovering over a steaming cup of tea, and she smiles at my father when he enters.

My father touches Isla's shoulder, and she yawns. "It's late. You should get some sleep."

Isla stretches her arms up. "I stayed up to tell you that the HPA agreed to a deal. Alyssa said noon tomorrow."

Noon? That's only ten hours away. Dread runs its cold fingers up my back and squeezes my heart. I can't believe it's happening so fast. What if things go wrong?

"Good. We can go over our plan one more time early in the morning," my father says.

Isla tilts her head up to gaze at him. "I also need to make a run to the city to pick up a few people from The Haven. Cian says they're running out of rooms there, but people keep coming since word of Mr. Soto's disappearance was announced. Want to join me?"

My father looks at me, and I wave my hand. "Go. It's fine. Just be safe. I'll go talk to Hunter."

"He's sleeping," Isla says.

I shrug and cross the kitchen to the stairs. "He doesn't have to be awake for me to talk to him."

HUNTER

Jacqueline sits next to me on a lounge chair. We stare at the turquoise ocean and crystalline sky blending into each other on the horizon the longer I stare at it. Running my fingers through the warm, white sand, I tilt my face toward the beaming sun overhead.

"I'd like to go somewhere like this one day." Jacqueline lifts up her giant sunglasses, her lavender eyes bluer with the water reflecting in them. "I could use a real vacation."

I laugh. "Me too. I've only seen the ocean once, and it was raining. Nothing like this."

The air shifts, and I feel Nadia's presence. Sitting up, I turn around and watch as my beautiful nightmare inflictor shimmers into view. Her bare feet kick up the sand, each graceful step swaying her short white sundress around her thighs. A white lily tucks behind her ear, and her glittering, white hair blows behind her.

Smiling, I jog to meet her, hooking my hands to her waist to lift her off the ground, bringing her to meet my lips. Her cool hands slide down my shoulders until she rests them on my back. "I'll never get used to your dreams." Her light gray eyes catch the blue of the sky.

Nadia waves to Jacqueline, grinning. Trailing my lips from her jaw to her neck, I kiss her neck and carry her back to my lounge chair. She laughs as I plop down with her on my lap. Resting her back against my chest, she links our fingers together.

I kiss her temple and say, "It's been a long day. We could all relax a little."

Jacqueline sits up. "Or a lot." Getting up, she strolls down the beach without another word. For being constantly present in my mind, she still knows how to give me space.

Nadia watches Jacqueline disappear down the beach and then shifts on my lap to face me. She searches my eyes for a moment and leans closer to kiss me, pressing against me. I run my fingers through her hair, playing with the soft strands. I brush my lips on her chin and slowly move to her jaw and then to her neck. Her breathing quickens, matching mine. Love and desire wash over me in a wave from her to me. It's what I love about Nadia visiting my dreams. I know her like no other, and we can sense and feel each other's emotions as if they were our own.

"I can't wait to really be alone with you," I say. While not as prominent, I can still feel Jacqueline's presence as if it is a shadow over me.

"Isla said noon." Nadia puckers her bottom lip, her desire shifting to worry, and I kiss her again.

"We just need to get it over with." I want to tell her so badly about the board only wanting to grant me my freedom, but Alyssa's plea swirls through my mind. Nadia's stressed enough as it is, but the guilt hits me hard when I look at her.

She lowers her brows. "What's wrong?"

I press my lips together. "Just nervous."

"It's something else. I can sense it. You can't hide things from me in the dream world," she says.

Shifting my gaze to the ocean behind her, I sigh. "I want to tell you, but I can't."

She climbs off my lap and stands up, crossing her arms. "Why not?"

"You have to trust me, Nadia, please. Let's just enjoy the

dream. Who knows if we'll get the chance to share another again?" I get to my feet and pull her to me, kissing her hair before moving to her temple and then to her lips.

She frowns as I kiss her for a moment and then laughs against my mouth. "You're right. There's enough to worry about in the morning."

NADIA

I can't shake the sinking feeling in my stomach. As much as I want to enjoy this beautiful paradise Hunter created, it's hard to ignore the sharp edge of reality pressing against the dream world, threatening to shatter it at any moment to wake us up.

Pulling away from Hunter, I gaze into his amazing hazel eyes. They stare at me so intently it feels like they're looking past me and into my soul. He smiles and grabs my hand, pulling me toward the water.

Ocean mist sprays his bare shoulders, waves crashing at our knees. He scoops me into his arms and jogs deeper into the water. I float on my back and let the waves drift me wherever they want. Maybe if Hunter and I float here long enough, we'll just drift away in the dream world and never have to face reality again.

Dreams aren't forever, I think to myself.

Hunter shakes his wet curls, splashing saltwater in my face. I laugh and kick water at him, letting him chase me a few feet. He pulls me into his arms again, and I kiss his salty lips, a hint of sweet chocolate tickling my tongue, but not enough to set off my nightmare inflictor side. My monster half couldn't destroy this dream even if it wanted to because Hunter's in control.

"Hunter!" Jacqueline calls the shore.

He pulls away from me, and we both turn our eyes to her.

"Someone's knocking on the door to the room," she says.

Just as the words escape Jacqueline's mouth, the sky above us cracks as the noise of the outside world threatens to wake Hunter. Kissing him one more time, I wave to Jacqueline before I pull from his dream.

I sit upright on the bed and stare at the door, a knock echoing through the room. I get to my feet and glide across the carpet, cracking the door open to see Alyssa. Her red hair spills over her shoulders, and she covers her mouth with her hand as she yawns.

I step into the hall and close the door. "What's up?"

She looks at my closed door. "I was going to wait until morning to tell you this, but I couldn't sleep."

I can feel it in my bones that Alyssa's going to tell me what Hunter wouldn't, and by the way her eyes line with worry and her forehead creases, it's something bad about tomorrow. I step closer to her door and motion for her to go back into her room. I sit on the bed, and she plops down next to me, leaning her head on my shoulder.

"It's bad, isn't it?" I ask.

She shrugs. "Not for you."

"What does that mean?"

Alyssa's hands tremble in her lap. "Well, the HPA decided that one council member wasn't a good enough trade to make a deal with us, and they asked for Jacqueline, but Hunter told them no."

"So, it's not happening?" My heart sinks, thinking about having to be on the run from the HPA.

"It is, but I might've done something stupid."

I hold my breath and wait for her to finish.

"I offered myself instead."

"You what?" Shadows edge my vision, my heart pounding in overdrive. Alyssa's crazy if she thinks I'm going to trade her freedom for mine. I'd rather be on the run and afraid the rest of my life than lose my best friend. "You're not really planning on going through with it, right?"

She shakes her head. "No, but I'll do what I have to."

I rub my hand over my eyes. "You don't have to do anything. This is my fight and my freedom. I don't want you going with us at all."

"You're going to tell Dmitri," she says.

"Yeah. I'm serious, Lys. I'll figure it out. I'm not going down without a fight."

HUNTER

Opening the door, I step into the hallway. Nadia nearly runs into my chest while grabbing the fabric of my T-shirt to squeeze it between her fingers. She gives me a good shake. "Did you really think I was going to let Alyssa anywhere near the exchange point tomorrow?"

I raise my hands. "I had nothing to do with this."

She puffs air through her lips. "Maybe we should call everything off. My father can bring in a small army to take care of whoever shows up tomorrow."

"I thought the point was not to kill anyone," I say. "Show

them we're not monsters."

"Or kill who you have to," Jacqueline adds, even though Nadia can't hear her.

She glares at me. "Well, maybe I want to be a monster now."

Jacqueline laughs in my mind. *"You should let her."* I imagine rolling my eyes in my mind and ignore Jacqueline.

I kiss Nadia's forehead because, even when she's angry, I can't help myself. She sighs, pressing her lips into a thin line. Hugging her, I squeeze the trembles from her shoulders, and she buries her face into my chest. I pull her back with me in the direction of the room, but she resists.

"It's not quite morning yet," I whisper into her hair.

"I need to talk to my father," she says, cupping my chin. "You're welcome to come, but only if you're on my side. I'm not getting Alyssa involved."

"Told you Nadia would do anything to save her best friend," Jacqueline says. *"Want to make a bet that Alyssa will get involved anyway?"*

"I'm not taking the bet because you're probably right," I think.

"Hunter? Did you hear me?" Nadia asks, drawing my attention to her.

I nod. "Yeah, sorry. I think Alyssa getting involved is bad, too, but I also think we might need her help. It's not safe if your offer of freedom isn't on the table. The HPA is tricky. I'm sure they're already planning on backing out on their word."

Alyssa's door cracks open, and she peeks her head out. "Listen to Hunter, Nadia."

Nadia twists to look at Alyssa and lifts her hand. "No. I don't want to hear it, Lys. We have seven hours to figure this out, and you getting involved is not how I imagine it happening."

Storming away, Nadia disappears down the stairs. I shrug when Alyssa looks at me, and then she strolls after Nadia. Leaning against the wall, I rub my eyes. Everything is falling apart before we've even done anything.

"It'll all fall together, Hunter. We'll make it happen."

"How can you be so sure, Jackie?" My voice echoes around me, and I snap my mouth shut.

"Because we have to. It can't go down any other way."

NADIA

"We have a problem," I say when I enter the living area. My father sits on the couch with the map rolled open next to him. He jerks his head up to look at me, worry creasing his pale forehead, and then shifts his eyes past me.

"It's not a problem," Alyssa says coming up behind me.

"You offered yourself to the HPA without a plan!" My voice echoes through the room, and I glower at Alyssa. I bet this is how she felt when I refused to change my mind about going with Jacqueline to return Hunter to his body. She was sure I'd die, like I'm sure the HPA will get their hands on her. Alyssa is as stubborn as me, so I know it'll be nearly impossible to change her mind.

My father gets up and stands between us. "Alyssa, is this true?"

"Sort of," she says. "I wasn't planning on actually going through with it."

My father touches my shoulder as I open my mouth, and I snap it shut. Crossing my arms, I glide to the couch and sit down.

"What I don't understand is why you did it. I know you had to have a good reason." My father shifts on his feet and motions for Alyssa to sit on the other side of the couch. He perches between us and rests a hand on each of our knees.

"Of course I did. They wouldn't grant Nadia her freedom otherwise. Without that, they'll hunt her down. I saw it." Alyssa eyes water when she looks at me.

I lean my elbows on my knees and blow strands of pale blond hair from my face. "You know as well as I do that your visions aren't set in stone. You've seen me die before, and it didn't happen."

"Nadi, you also know some things don't change," my father says.

"They're not planning to kill you." Alyssa crosses and uncrosses her legs. "They'll make you wish they did, though."

I shudder at the thought. "What are we going to do then? What's the plan?"

My father rubs his chin for a moment. "I have an idea. It'll be risky, but I think it just might work."

22

— ✦ —

EXPECT THE WORST

— ✦ —

HUNTER

"I WANT YOU to promise me if you feel like you need help in any way, you'll give me permission to take control, and I'll keep us alive." Jacqueline's voice echoes in my ears.

I stare at Nadia as she paces the living area. She circles the sectional and walks along the bookshelves, and then peeks in the kitchen, before walking to the front window and peering through a crack in the board.

"I'll let you take control if any of us needs help," I think.

I hate that I need a backup plan for staying alive—I hate more that it involves letting Jacqueline take control so she can basically kill anyone she needs to. She does it without thinking twice, but not without reason. I've never seen her kill anyone just for fun. It makes it a tad bit better...but only a little. I wish she didn't have to kill at all, but it's better than me becoming a killer.

"I'll do my best, Hunter."

"I'm counting on it, Jackie."

A knock sounds on the front door, causing Nadia to freeze in place. I don't think we were expecting any more visitors than the four creatures hanging out in the kitchen while Isla throws together an early lunch.

I couldn't eat anything even if I wanted to. My stomach twists in knots of nervousness, and all I want to do is get this over with. I want this to be the last time I have to face the board—and my mom—again.

Nadia peeks through the peephole and unlocks the deadbolt, opening the door. A familiar black-haired girl with icy blue eyes stands on the threshold. She carries a small package in her hand and steps into the room when Nadia moves out of the way.

The woman wears a knee-length, faux fur jacket over a gray dress with tights and knee-high black boots. Pulling her unbuttoned jacket off all the way, she hangs it on one of the empty hooks near the door. She shifts her gaze to me and freezes.

Nadia steps up next to her. "I'm surprised to see you away from the compound, Ana." Nadia greets the council member with a serious expression.

"While I'm a part of the council, my loyalty lies with the sisterhood, Nadia, and they wanted to give this to the hum—"

Ana studies my face. "I'm guessing him."

Nadia waves me over, and I reluctantly stand and stride over. "Hunter, meet Ana, she's on the council."

"I know," I say and then regret my words.

Nadia's eyes widen at the same time as Ana's, and the enchantress pales. The enchantress offers her hand, and I shake it.

Tilting her head to the side, she says, "Tell me how you know who I am."

Jacqueline swears in my mind. My throat burns, my mouth automatically opening against my will. It's like something's come over me under the enchantress's gaze, like she could pull with truth from me without my permission. Her hot power courses over me as I try to resist, and sweat beads on my neck.

"I've met y—"

Nadia grips the enchantress' shoulder. "Stop it now!"

Shaking my head, I snap my mouth shut, the sizzling power draining away. "What's wrong with you? I would've told you if you'd just asked."

Dmitri glides into the room through the kitchen and glances between the three of us, raising his eyebrows. I step away from Ana and turn toward the wall to keep my cool.

"I see you've met Hunter," Dmitri says to Ana. "He's the reason your council exiled my daughter and also the reason she and I are still alive. He's doing the exchange with Nadia because his mother is on the HPA board."

"What?" Ana says. "Why didn't you tell the council sooner?"

"I wasn't planning on telling you at all. Hunter's none of

your concern." Dmitri shifts his gaze to the package in her hands. "I see you come bearing gifts."

She hands the package to Dmitri, who hands it to Nadia. "The sisterhood would like you and Hunter to have this charm. It's not much, but it'll protect Hunter from creatures in our world, which I now see he'll really need. Never take it off."

Nadia unwraps the box and pulls out a leather necklace with what looks like a vile filled with red liquid. She tosses it to me, and I hold it up to the light before sliding it over my head. "What is it?"

"A few drops of very powerful blood."

Ana smiles when I frown, but I don't take the necklace off even though it's the strangest gift I've ever been given. It's scary to think what the HPA would do if they found out that power runs in the blood of enchantresses. They'd probably try to capture every last one of them.

"Well, thanks, I guess," I say.

Nadia grins, and Dmitri pulls Ana aside and whispers in her ear. She nods before looking over to me, and then she waves at Nadia and heads to the door without another word.

Gliding up to me, Nadia picks up the small vile from my neck, holding it between her fingers. She laughs "You'll get used to receiving strange gifts."

Dmitri clears his throat, drawing our gazes to him. "I made it clear to Ana that she is to tell no one about your connection to the HPA."

I shrug. "I don't really care."

"You should, Hunter," Jacqueline says.

Dmitri presses his lips into a line before saying. "You still have family involved with them. Certain, more malevolent, creatures might see them as an opportunity to test your loyalty. It's just better to pretend to be a nobody."

I brush my hair from my forehead. It's funny. Just months ago I wanted to be somebody, to make a difference, and now, I'm supposed to be no one.

"Think of yourself as a superhero. They pretend to be a nobody when they're actually a somebody."

I grind my teeth to keep from laughing at Jacqueline's comments. She's really turned into my conscience these last few months. It'll be strange when she's gone, but I'll be glad when I'm alone with my own thoughts.

"I'm kind of a nobody right now anyway," I say to Dmitri.

Nadia kisses my cheek. "You're amazing and brave and confident, Hunter. Don't forget you're about to face people that most of the community fears. You're someone special to me."

I smile, and she kisses my cheek. Dmitri clears his throat to remind us he's still standing there, even though I could never forget his tall, gangly frame casting a shadow over me. Nadia steps back, and I shove my hands into my pockets.

Dmitri touches Nadia's shoulder. "Go tell Alyssa she has five minutes. I'll meet you out front with Mr. Soto."

Nadia nods. Gliding away, and I watch her go. My chest tightens, realizing how close it's getting to noon. What if I'm not ready? What if the HPA throws something unexpected at us?

"We have a few tricks of our own, too, Hunter." Jacqueline's a lot calmer than I am, and it helps me relax a bit.

I turn back to Dmitri staring down at me. His eyebrows knit together for a second before he composes himself. "Are you ready?"

I roll my shoulders. "Yeah, I've got everything covered. You can trust me. I won't let anything happen to Nadia or Alyssa."

Dmitri nods. "Take care of yourself, too. You're not only doing this for Nadia."

I bob my head. "I know, and I will."

Dmitri glides away, and I step out front, the cold air hitting me in the face. I suck in an icy breath and slowly let it out. It helps keep me focused on the three most important things I need to do today—keep Nadia and Alyssa alive, keep Jacqueline and myself alive, and get the HPA out of my life for good.

NADIA

"If things go wrong, I want you to know how much I love you and that I'd do anything for you," I say.

Hunter tucks my hair behind my ear and then kisses my forehead. "You say that like you're telling me goodbye."

I blink tears from my eyes. "You never know."

"This isn't goodbye, but I love you more than anything. I will fight for you with everything I have, and I will win," Hunter says.

And I believe him.

I believe him with everything in me. Things are going to work out how they're supposed to because we're going to make them. I knew I'd always have to fight for how I want to live my life and that I'd have to fight for the people I love. It's all I know now and all I will ever know. My life is worth it.

Standing on my tiptoes, I cup Hunter's face, kissing him like I've never kissed him before. I kiss him like it's the last thing I'll ever do and with all the love I have for him. His fingers trail over my waist and to my lower back. I jump up into his arms to wrap my legs around him. My back hits the side of the warehouse, and he smiles into my lips. I don't want the moment to end, but the front door squeaks open. Hunter sets me down on my feet, and I meet Alyssa's uncertain eyes. It's the first time I've seen her without the confident attitude she always possesses.

Pulling away from Hunter, I meet my best friend's emerald gaze. "Please tell me you didn't see all of us dying."

She shakes her head. "No, but since the board knows I exist, they haven't made a clear decision. I have no idea what to expect."

I frown. "I guess we expect the worst and fight like heck for the best."

HUNTER

Nadia hugs me once more before following Alyssa to a white Honda with dark tinted windows. Dmitri stands next to the driver's side door, and when Alyssa opens the back door, I glimpse Mr. Soto in the backseat.

I wave at Dmitri and stroll toward the gate. I'm walking four blocks along the river while Nadia will drive and park at a house with a backyard that has a gate leading to the park where I'll be meeting Dr. Sullivan. Slush lines the empty river walkway, and the air feels a few degrees warmer than it did yester-day. Spring is a few weeks away, and I can't wait to put this winter behind me.

The outer edges of the river remain iced over, but the center flows as the ice melts away. I shiver, thinking about how cold it's going to be when I have to go in it. I'm relying on some mythical water creature I've only heard stories about from the board, but Dmitri swears will get us to safety without having to worry about the HPA following us.

My boots kick the snow, and I shove my hands into my jacket pockets. It's a lot farther than it looked on the map, and I'm afraid I'll freeze to death before I even make it there. The sky overhead stenches in a clear, endless blue, and pale winter light reflects off the snow, reminding me of Nadia's white, shimmering hair when she enters my dreams.

Jacqueline sighs in my mind. *"Stay focused, Hunter."*

"I am focused," I think.

"You're thinking about Nadia."

"Well, she keeps me focused."

"How about you try to think about surviving instead."

"I'm thinking about that, too. How about you keep your anxiety under control and have more confidence. That'll help me more than the bickering." I hum to myself as I think to Jacqueline in my mind. If anything, she's the one distracting me.

"Good point. Sorry. I just hate not being in control in these kinds of situations."

"Have some faith in me, Jackie. I don't want to die, so I'm

pretty sure that's enough motivation to keep you alive, too." I glance over my shoulder and then turn back to the path in front of me. It's almost like everyone knows what's going to happen. They're staying locked away inside. It's what I'd do if I could.

"You're right. This area is heavily populated with creatures. The water nymphs protect them. I'm sure Dmitri sent a warning out. Only the brave or careless would risk being seen right now."

I sigh in my mind. "You don't have to respond to everything I think about."

"Oh, don't worry, Hunter. I don't."

Shaking my head, I blink my eyes to concentrate on my surroundings. The last thing I need to worry about is what Jacqueline hears going on in my mind. I should try harder to block her from hearing my personal thoughts, but it just gives me a headache. It's easier to concentrate when I act like she's not there.

A small green sign with bold white letters declares that Riverview Park is up ahead. I'm ten minutes early, and I'm expecting Dr. Sullivan to be nearby. I prepare to walk into a park with a hundred HPA agents pointing tranquilizer guns at me, ready to take me out as quietly as they can.

Swallowing the lump in my throat, I dig my fingernails into my palms to stop my hands from shaking. The only weapon I have is a small kitchen knife since most creatures don't need weapons. I wish I'd have kept my weaponry belt.

I step from the snowy walkway and lurk behind a dead tree and peer around the eerily quiet park. The park equipment is covered in melting snow, and the parking lot hasn't been cleared in a while. A small sign is taped on the park hours sign with faded ink that says the park is closed for winter. My heart drums in my ears as I glance around at nothing. No one is here. I'm alone, and a heavy pit forms in my stomach. It feels like I walked into a trap.

I'm about to turn on my heels to jog in the direction I came from when a rush of calm washes over me. Jacqueline does her best to keep me from freaking out, but it's hard to get rid of the feeling of dread closing around me.

"Do you hear that?" Jacqueline asks.

Moving toward the tree, I peer around the trunk. Footsteps crunch through the snow. I watch as Dr. Sullivan strolls from the direction of the street. She wears a heavy, burgundy winter coat, buttoned to her neck with boots instead of her usual high heels. Her brown hair is pulled into a fierce bun, and she's not wearing her glasses.

"I don't like this, Hunter," Jacqueline says in my mind.

I straighten my shoulders and back, forcing myself to stroll out from behind the tree. Agent Rosaline stands by Dr. Sullivan's side with her hands trained on both her knife and her tranquilizer gun.

I lick my dry lips and meet my mom's gaze. "We told you that you could only bring one agent."

Dr. Sullivan grins. "I did, Hunter. Evangeline isn't an agent yet."

I shift my boots but don't move forward. "So why is she here?"

Evie steps out from behind Dr. Sullivan and waves tentatively at me. Her chin-length, dark brown hair is mussed in the back, her golden skin paler than usual. She blinks her glassy eyes like she's holding back her tears. Leaning on her heels, she tips her head toward the ground and doesn't meet my eyes again.

"I needed someone here that you wouldn't want to kill. I'm not coming near you, Hunter. I've lost my trust in you."

I narrow my eyes. "You never had mine."

23

ΛNYTHING IS POSSIBLE

NADIA

"WE'RE GOING TO get through this," Alyssa says.

"Think if we say that enough, it'll come true?" I ask.

She smirks. "It never hurts."

After turning off the car engine, I unbuckle my seatbelt. My hands tremble, my teeth chattering, and it takes all my strength to pull myself together and calm down. I have to do this for Hunter. He's at Riverview Park by now and expects me to show up. It's five minutes until noon, and it'll take a few minutes to get Mr. Soto from the backseat.

Alyssa climbs out, and I reluctantly follow her and open the back door. Mr. Soto glares at his hands but can't talk or argue. His shaman magic has been corked by an elf enchanted charm and with the tack stuck in him, he can't hurt us.

I tug on Mr. Soto's arm, but he doesn't budge from the backseat. He's a lot heavier than he looks, and I can't command him to leave either. Alyssa jogs to my side, and together, we pull Mr. Soto from the car. He sits on the ground, acting like a toddler throwing a tantrum, but I don't blame him. I'd resist any way I could if I were in his position. Popping the trunk, I pull out a tarp and lay it on the ground next to Mr. Soto. Alyssa helps me drag him on, and he glares daggers at me with his eyes.

I grab his bearded chin and stare into his angry eyes. "You had your chance. All you had to do was agree to step down from your position on the council. You were doing a horrible job, and it's not my fault the other members agreed with my father."

He growls like a frightened animal. Stepping back, I grip onto a corner of the tarp with Alyssa holding the other side. With help from the slush, we manage to drag Mr. Soto toward the walking path that will take us to the back of the park, closest to the river.

Low voices echo in front of us, and I motion for Alyssa to stop. Gliding to the corner of a retaining wall, I crouch down to look around the corner. Hunter hovers ten feet away, near a bare tree, and about thirty feet from him stands Dr. Sullivan, Agent Rosaline, and Evie.

I can't believe Evie is here. I dash back to Alyssa and lean close to her and whisper, "Evie's here. What do we do?"

Alyssa grabs my shoulders and looks me dead in the eyes.

"She chose her side, Nadia. We can't change the plan. I don't have time to go through all the options."

"But her being here can change things," I say.

Alyssa's eyes glaze over, and she shakes her head. "You're right. They do. Today is going to cement Evie's decision to believe in the HPA. She's lost to us now."

Tears blur my vision, and I swipe my hand over my cheeks. I regret the day I told Evie about our world. Her life would be much different now. She would still be attending Northern Bell High School, living with her dad, and none the wiser to creatures and the HPA. I took everything from her, and the guilt of ruining her life presses on me. *The HPA would've gotten to her eventually. They always do.*

I push the thought away. It might be true that Evie's life was already in the hands of the HPA with her mother working as one of their doctors, but she could've had time to enjoy a normal life.

"Maybe someday she'll see the truth." I steel myself and force the tears away.

Alyssa hugs me. "Only if she decides she wants to. People do change. Anything is possible."

I hold onto her words. It helps me remember that destiny isn't in charge. While I've felt that fate always played a role in my life, maybe I've been wrong all along. Things do change, and I'm in control of my life and what happens to me.

And today, whether the deal goes smoothly or not, I'm not letting the HPA influence my life and my decisions. I'm not afraid of them anymore.

HUNTER

Whispering echoes through the air behind me. Without having to look, I know Nadia's here with Alyssa and Mr. Soto. I don't take my eyes off Dr. Sullivan, waiting for her to make the next move. If she thinks she's in control, she won't be expecting that we're not here to exchange Alyssa for Nadia's freedom. We're here to make a point that we won't be messed with anymore.

"Are you ready to make the exchange?" Dr. Sullivan says. "I have agents waiting for my call not far from here, so time is limited."

"Why is she telling you this? She could easily have us swarmed," Jacqueline says.

I ignore Jacqueline's questions even though I'm thinking the same thing. "How do I know you're not going to send them here once the exchange is made?"

Dr. Sullivan places her hands on her hips. "You might not believe me, but I really don't want to see you dead, Hunter. You're my son. While I don't agree with your decisions, I do love you. And since you got your brother involved in this mess, I swore to him I'd do everything in my power to see you can live your life how you want to."

I frown. There's something in her voice I haven't heard in a long time. Warmth? Love? I can't put my finger on it, but I believe what she's saying. It's hard not to. I lower my gaze to the cold ground for a second before bringing my eyes up again. "Then why can't you just let us go and pretend like we don't exist?"

Her eyes soften, and she twists her lips down. "You know

why, Hunter. I work for the greater good. I have humanity to think about. These supers you seem to think are so good kill and murder innocent people every day. They torment and body snatch and cause so much pain."

It takes a lot in me to not roll my eyes at her. "What do you think you're doing to all the innocent people locked away in your facilities?"

Dr. Sullivan glowers at me before looking to Agent Rosaline and Evie. "They're not people, Hunter. They're monsters."

"There's no point in arguing. Let's just get this over with."

I nod, and Dr. Sullivan takes it as me agreeing with her, and I don't correct her otherwise. Releasing a breath, I straighten my shoulders and look behind me. I glimpse Nadia crouching next to the wall, waiting for my signal.

"Well, Mom, I guess you think I'm in love with a monster, but just know that Nadia's the one who saved me and brought me back to my body. Do I need to remind you how I lost it in the first place?"

Dr. Sullivan's face pales, and she shifts on her feet. She's finally seeing that her actions and decisions to give my soul to Jacqueline is the reason I'm against the HPA. I keep my expression serious even though I want to smile. Dr. Sullivan's eyes shadow as her own guilt grabs hold of her. She's going to have to live with the knowledge that it was her actions that led to us being in this position today. She's the reason I'll never be her son again.

Dr. Sullivan's hand flies to her mouth. "I'm sorry, Hunter. I'm really sorry. I regret ever making that deal in the first place."

"I don't regret it," Jacqueline says, and I ignore her.

"Not me. It was the best thing that ever happened to me," I say.

Agent Rosaline shifts and taps Dr. Sullivan's shoulder, and the two of them share a look before Dr. Sullivan nods and composes herself. "I guess there's no changing the past." She glances at her watch. "Now if we could complete the exchange, I'll call off the agents, and you'll be free of the HPA."

"If you betray me, your board will regret it."

Dr. Sullivan shifts. "You don't need to threaten me. You have my word."

"Give Nadia the signal, Hunter," Jacqueline says.

I raise my hand up and wait.

NADIA

Hunter raises his arm and waves his hand, signaling me to bring Alyssa and Mr. Soto to him.

Alyssa crouches down next to me, and I hesitate. "Dr. Sullivan really is going to keep her word if the exchange goes through. I saw it."

I eye her in my peripheral vision. "It doesn't matter. You're not going with her."

"I wouldn't blame you if you asked me to though. They won't hurt me," Alyssa says.

Shifting, I meet her green eyes. "You're ridiculous for even mentioning it."

She smiles. "I knew you wouldn't ask me, but I had to give you the choice anyway."

"Thanks, Lys, but it was never a choice I needed to begin

with. You can still choose to leave though. Hunter and I can handle this on our own."

She shakes her head. "I only have one thing to do, and I promise I'll leave once it's done."

My heart sinks into my stomach, wishing my father wouldn't have let her get involved. He could've locked her in a room until this was all over, and I'd know she was safe and alive even if I wasn't.

"You better," I say. Fear covers me in a cold blanket as I push to my feet and force my legs to work.

Peering over the river, I watch the thin ice near the shore crack and break off. The pieces of ice float on the current and disappear. The top of the water nymph's blue, scaly head peeks out, and I smile at her before trudging through the snow to grab onto the corner of the tarp Mr. Soto still lies on.

The sound of the tarp scraping against snow, mud, and concrete echoes through the air, and it's the only thing I hear apart from my heart beating in my ears. Hunter watches me for a quick moment, his hazel eyes sparkling in the pale sunlight overhead, and that one look gives me the courage to step out from the trees to face Dr. Sullivan again.

Alyssa helps drag Mr. Soto, and we stop next to Hunter. I stand straight, leaning into him. Alyssa hovers over Mr. Soto with her hands on her hips, her fiery red hair blowing behind her. She looks so brave and confident, I wish I could siphon some of it away from her to use on myself. I never knew how she could face her fears without flinching. Even the one time I invaded her mind and inflicted a nightmare on her, her dream persona still managed to look me in the eye.

Dr. Sullivan bares her teeth at me with one of her fake smiles, but I don't react. I keep my lips pressed together and my head high as I look her in the eyes. Strands of her brown hair fall from her bun and blow behind her, and I only look at her even though Evie shifts next to her, hoping to catch my gaze. I refuse to let my guard down for Evie. Not now. Not when the people I love, who chose to stay by my side, need me the most.

Hunter's cool fingers touch the top of my hand, and I twine my fingers through his. We stand ready to take on whatever the world has to throw at us. We're ready to face Dr. Sullivan together, and we're prepared to fight for what we want.

Dr. Sullivan's eyes shift to Alyssa. "I assume you're the seer? What a noble thing of you to offer your freedom for—"

Alyssa holds her hand up. "You can save your speech for someone else. I already know what you're going to say, and it's not going to make up for the fact that I have to live the rest of my life with the people who brought nothing but pain to the people I care about."

Dr. Sullivan locks her fingers together and drops her gaze to Mr. Soto lying on the tarp. She steps forward, but Agent Rosaline moves to cut her off. Evie stays completely still. If it weren't for her breath fogging the air, I'd have thought she had frozen to death.

"The council member." Dr. Sullivan's voice barely sound over a whisper. I keep my amusement locked deep inside. She looks like she's seen something she wasn't sure existed. A dozen thoughts run through her blinking eyes, and she shifts her feet again as if she can't wait to get her hands on Mr. Soto.

Clearing my throat, I force the words to come from my mouth. "His name is Javier Soto, and he's the only remaining founder of the Creature Council."

Dr. Sullivan takes another step closer. "What is he?"

I shrug. "We told you we'd give him to you. We didn't agree to tell you anything about him."

Dr. Sullivan frowns. "Fair enough. I'm sure we'll get it out of him."

I squeeze Hunter's hand. "So, do we have a deal? You'll grant us amnesty, and the HPA will let us live wherever we want without interference?"

She nods. "You'll never hear from us again. You both are free."

HUNTER

Dr. Sullivan glances behind her at Evie wringing her hands together and back to Mr. Soto lying on the tarp. His magic was bound, and there's nothing he can do. He's helpless for what might be the first time in his life.

"Go get the council member and the seer, Evangeline," Dr. Sullivan says.

Evie sucks in her bottom lip without moving. "I don't think I'm strong enough to drag him all the way here."

Dr. Sullivan clicks her tongue. "Make the seer help you. How do you expect to join the SATF if you can't follow simple instructions?"

Evie pushes her hair from her face and clenches her fingers into fists. Wind blows in her face, and her eyes water, and she clomps through the slush and mud in our direction. Her teeth chatter, her wide hazel eyes glancing from Nadia to me, and then to Alyssa. She stops five feet away from us.

Nadia drops my hand and glides over to Evie. Evie stumbles back but catches herself before she falls, and Nadia lifts her hands in a non-threatening way. Nadia stares at Evie with warmth in her indigo eyes.

Reaching out, Nadia touches Evie's shoulder. "I wish things could be different, Evie. I really thought we could be good friends. I forgive you for choosing them and wish you the best in life. I want you to remember me as the girl from Northern Bell and not the monster the HPA swears I am, okay?"

Evie blinks her eyes but doesn't say anything. Pulling away from Nadia, she turns to Alyssa. It's been months since Alyssa and Evie have been face to face, and I wonder if Evie feels any differently toward Alyssa—maybe she feels guilty, if anything, but I'll never know.

"Get ready, Hunter," Jacqueline says, speaking up for the first time since Nadia stepped out with Alyssa and Mr. Soto. *"Things are going to get ugly real fast."*

"I'm ready, Jackie," I think.

Evie shifts on her feet, letting Nadia hug Alyssa once more before she moves to the opposite side of the tarp, ten feet away from me. Her pale blond hair catches a breeze, blowing behind her. Her indigo eyes narrow as she twists her lips into a smile.

"Come, on, Alyssa. Pull that end of the tarp," Evie says.

Alyssa reaches down and grabs a corner of the tarp and helps Evie drag Mr. Soto. My heart pounds in my ears, the muscles in my shoulders tightening as I watch Alyssa close the distance to Dr. Sullivan.

The wind stops, a heavy silence falling around us.

Alyssa drops her corner of the tarp.

After a second, the world kicks into motion. Alyssa reaches down and pulls the small charm from Mr. Soto. Agent Rosaline raises her gun, Dr. Sullivan's eyes widen, and Evie screams.

24

———— ❧ ————

WASN'T SUPPOSED TO END LIKE THIS

———— ❧ ————

NADIA

MR. SOTO JUMPS to his feet. Evie screams again, making me cringe, the screeching sound echoing in my ears. It takes everything in me not to run to her and tell her that it's okay. I'm not even sure it is, though. Mr. Soto spins in a circle, fear and anger marring his face, ready to kill us all.

"Back off!" he bellows, thrusting his hands at Evie.

His power knocks her off her feet, and she flies through the air, skidding across the snowy pavement. My heart hammers against my ribcage, each beat threatening to break it through. Evie doesn't move, lying still in the snow. I'm not sure if she's alive.

Agent Rosaline lifts her tranquilizer gun and aims it at Mr.

Soto. Dr. Sullivan steps back a few feet but doesn't run away. She's relying on her agent to save her, but I doubt a little tranquilizer dart is enough to save them now.

"*Llamo en el poder de mis antepasados,*" Mr. Soto shouts.

Power courses through the air to Mr. Soto as he calls upon his shaman ancestors to gather more power to fight off the agent. The air lowers in temperature, clouds covering the sun. It feels like I'm a part of a living nightmare, except this time I'm not the one in control.

Agent Rosaline pulls the trigger, but her hand jerks and the dart flies straight into Alyssa's shoulder. Alyssa's emerald green eyes widen as she wobbles on her feet. She wasn't fast enough, and now she can't run like she was supposed to.

"Lys!" I scream.

Mr. Soto jerks his head toward me, deeming me a lesser threat, and turns back to Agent Rosaline. I glide through the snow and grab onto Alyssa's jacket. She falls to her knees, the sedative taking effect fast. I can't leave her in the middle of everything. She'll get hurt or worse.

Sliding my hands under Alyssa's arms, I drag her back. Agent Rosaline shoots another dart at Mr. Soto, and he pushes power in her direction, knocking her off her feet. I walk backwards and shift my eyes from Mr. Soto to Dr. Sullivan and Agent Rosaline.

"Ten more feet," I say out loud. "You can do this."

"Nadia!" Hunter yells. I jerk my gaze in his direction. "Go with her!"

I shake my head. "I'm not leaving you. Mr. Soto will kill

you."

Alyssa moans in my arms. I tug her limp body to the river's edge. Her red hair sticks to her face, her skin paler than usual. Touching her cool cheek, I push her hair out of her face. This might be the last time I ever see Alyssa again, and I'm afraid to let her go.

"Nadia," she whispers as her eyes flutter open. "You have to stop Mr. Soto."

"But what about the HPA?" I ask.

"They're not the ones you need to worry about now. Mr. Soto is going to try to kill you." Alyssa closes her eyes, and I gently push her into the icy water of the river. Shimmering, blue scaly hands break through the thin ice and lock onto Alyssa's shoulders and pull her under. Alyssa disappears in the dark depths of the river, and my heart squeezes in my chest as her words echo through me. There's no way I'll ever stop Mr. Soto. He's one of the most powerful creatures I know. If he wants me dead, I'll be dead.

There's nothing I can do to stop it.

HUNTER

"You can't make her go, Hunter," Jacqueline says, her words echoing through me. I watch Nadia slide Alyssa into the river and she disappears with the current. I hope Dmitri was right about the water keeping us safe instead of drowning us.

"I wish she would, though," I think.

I creep along the outer edge of the park. I need to circle to the top to stop Dr. Sullivan from making a run for it. Evie lies motionless in the snow, and I'm tempted to walk by her body without stopping, but I know Nadia would want me to.

Bending over, I press my cold fingers to her neck, feeling her pulse drum against my fingers. I release a breath and drag her limp body behind the nearest tree. Mr. Soto's power only knocked her out. Maybe he won't kill anyone after all. He might just want to get out of here.

A pop echoes through the air as Agent Rosaline shoots her tranquilizer gun. Mr. Soto flicks his hand, sending the gun clattering a few feet away in the snow. Agent Rosaline reaches for her knife and stands in front of Dr. Sullivan. She's willing to die to save my mom, and I have no idea why. Dr. Sullivan has done nothing for Agent Rosaline. If I were her, I'd be protecting myself.

"Not everyone hates Dr. Sullivan. Agent Rosaline shares her beliefs. She thinks Dr. Sullivan will save humanity."

I shake Jacqueline's voice away and draw my gaze from Agent Rosaline to Dr. Sullivan. Dr. Sullivan reaches into her coat pocket and pulls out her cell phone. Digging my nails into the palms of my hands, I charge from the trees in my mom's direction. I can't let her call the HPA. Nadia's still here, and they'll come and kill us all. It wasn't supposed to be like this. I was supposed to follow Nadia and Alyssa to the river, but I couldn't. Some tiny part of me doesn't really want Dr. Sullivan to die. I need to show her we're not all monsters.

"Mom, no!" I yell.

She covers her face as I collide with her. Falling back together, I land on top of her. Her cell phone drops from her fingers and skids a foot away. When her hazel eyes meet mine, I no longer see the icy, cold-hearted woman I've grown used to these last few months. She's weak and scared and defeated. She knows I'm the one in charge now and doesn't have the same hold on me like she used to.

I grit my teeth, holding her hands down. "I don't want to hurt you, but I can't let you make that call."

"That monster will kill me," she says, tears dripping down her temples. "Can't you see? Look whose side you're fighting on."

"I'm not fighting on anyone's side. I'm fighting for me."

A thud echoes through the air, drawing my attention away from Dr. Sullivan. Agent Rosaline crashes into a block wall and crumples to the ground. Dr. Sullivan cries out, struggling under me. I shift to look behind me as Mr. Soto brings his threatening gaze to me.

He raises his hands, out for my blood, and I cover my head with my hands, lying over Dr. Sullivan. She cries in my ear, stopping me from hearing anything.

"Hunter, let me have control!" Jacqueline screams.

I blink my eyes, my head pounding, but I can't focus to form a thought. All I can do is wait for Mr. Soto's power to rip me apart.

NADIA

"No!" My voice echoes over the wind, screaming through the air. I glide forward so fast I'm practically flying. "Don't hurt him!"

I launch myself at Mr. Soto's back, the air knocking from my lungs as I collide with the old shaman. He lands in the snow face first, and I wrap my hands around his neck and squeeze. He thrashes under me, trying to knock me off. I lift my knee and crush one of his flailing arms under my weight. He doesn't scream or yell, but continues to chant in the language of his ancestors.

Mr. Soto jerks his free arm out and reaches back and grabs my wrist. His nails bite into my skin. Tears burst from my eyes as pain swells in my arm. I yank my arm away before he snaps my wrist. The movement causes me to lose my balance as my weight shifts to my knee pinning down his other arm.

He pushes up with one arm, strong and agile for his age, and he knocks me off him. I land hard on my hip, grinding my teeth to keep from screaming. Rolling out of his reach, I scramble to my feet.

"Dmitri is going to regret kidnapping me." Mr. Soto flings his arm out at me, forcing me to drop to my knees.

Panting, I push back to my feet. "He won't because it was the right decision to make."

"Javier! Let her go!" My heart rises into my throat at the sound of my father's voice. "It's me you want."

Mr. Soto thrusts his hand at my father, sending him flying into a tree before he drops to the ground.

I scream and ram into Mr. Soto with my shoulder, but he swivels and pushes me away. Waving his hand at my father again, he lifts my father's body from the ground and tosses him into the icy river. Tears well in my eyes as he sinks underwater, and a water nymph takes him. I'm left to defend myself and Hunter.

"Your father's bravery is why I liked him, but killing him won't do anything. He won't suffer in death."

I don't know why I find comfort in his words. Death shadows over me knowing Mr. Soto plans on making my father suffer in life by killing me. But the last thing I want is to see my father die. I don't want anyone to die.

Getting to my feet, I glance at Hunter still protectively covering his mother. If I could just get to him, maybe we could run to the river.

Mr. Soto tilts his head to the sky, chanting in a deep voice so low I can't make out what he's saying. The freezing wind whips around me, and my hair veils my face, obscuring my view. Power hits me hard in the chest, stealing my breath, and I fly off my feet in the opposite direction of the river. Twisting in the air, I land on my side instead of my back and blink through the glittering blue stars peppering my vision.

I crawl toward the nearest tree and duck behind it. Mr. Soto sends another burst of power toward me, jolting the tree. The trunk cracks and branches rain around me, scratching my face and hands as they scatter across the slush.

Gulping a few deep breaths, I push away the pain in my side and force myself to get up. I don't know how much longer I can keep evading him. I need to get to the river. *You can't leave Hunter...*

I don't want to die either.

The tree shakes and splits as Mr. Soto continues to unleash his power on it, the branches blackening and smoking. Fiery ash falls around me, and my coat smolders and catches fire. I scoop up a handful of snow to put the flames out but don't move from the tree. It's the only thing protecting me from Mr. Soto. I need to rest for a moment or I don't think I'll make it more than a few feet.

The crack of power deafens me, and I cover my ears as it hits the tree. I'm trapped, and I can't fight back. I can't do anything to save myself.

Mr. Soto's power will consume me.

HUNTER

Nadia's screams echo through the air, cutting through the pounding in my head. I roll off Dr. Sullivan, and she clings to me, stopping me from turning to look at Nadia.

Nadia's cries rip through the air again, and I yank Dr. Sullivan to her feet. "Get off me. I have to go."

"You saved my life. I knew you still loved me." Dr. Sullivan hugs me, and I shrug from her arms. Her eyes widen. "Let me call the board. They'll help us. I swear on my life I won't let them hurt you."

"Give me control, Hunter. Do it now!"

I push Jacqueline's voice away.

Dr. Sullivan searches the ground for her lost cell phone, and I jog the few feet where I threw it and kick the snow off it. Dr. Sullivan smiles, but instead of picking it up, I stomp on the cell phone and smash it.

I point at Dr. Sullivan. "I'm not going back. Go hide behind that tree before Mr. Soto comes back to kill you."

I turn and search for Nadia.

Mr. Soto raises his arms to the sky, tilting his head back.

The air around him shifts and moves with a power so strong it's tangible. It reminds me of what it looks like when you peer at something as heat rises in front of it.

He jerks his arms at a tree, and it cracks and splinters. The sound rings in my ears, but I don't cover them. Nadia screams and stumbles away from the tree as it clatters to the ground, sending slush spraying out from under it.

Yelling, Mr. Soto thrusts his arms toward Nadia. She drops to her knees, her voice silencing and her eyes roll back. Her unconscious figure lands face first in the snow. It melts around her, steam radiating from her skin. Red rage shadows my vision, and my feet pound the ground as I charge Mr. Soto.

Yanking the small kitchen knife from my belt, I hold it out and rush him. He turns on the balls off his feet, shooting power at me, but I swivel to the side and keep running at him.

"Give me control, now!"

"No!" I yell.

I collide with Mr. Soto and sink the knife into his stomach. He yells and punches my shoulder, but I move with his motion and swing my arm up and smash my fist into his jaw. He trips over a snow covered curb, and I pull the knife from his gut and then ram it in again, cutting off his chanting.

"Please, don't kill me," he begs, his eyes widening. He coughs and spits blood into the snow.

I narrow my eyes but don't say anything.

"You're not a murderer, Hunter. Stop. You don't really want to do this."

"Shut up, Jackie! He doesn't deserve to live." My voice

echoes in my mind.

"Let me do it, please."

Anger rolls through me, and I lock my fingers around Mr. Soto's throat. His beard scratches the side of my index finger, and my hand squishes his deeply wrinkled skin. "He doesn't deserve to be redeemed," I think. "He deserves to die as the monster he is."

"I'm not thinking about him, Hunter. I'm thinking about you. I'm trying to save you. Please, just give me control. Let me do this."

Tears burn my eyes and glance away from Mr. Soto's pleading face to look at Nadia curled up, steaming in the melted snow. She's paler than I've ever seen her in real life and looks like she did when she got caught in the nightmare catcher Jacqueline had accidentally set during our time at the compound. Her light gray eyes stare at nothing, a haunting look that cuts to my soul. A ray of sunlight breaks through the clouds across her face, reddening her cheek under its warm light.

My breathing comes fast and heavy, panic overtaking my fury. My anger dissipates as grief grips at me and threatens to consume me. I was supposed to fight for Nadia. I was supposed to be the one who gave my life for her. It wasn't supposed to end like this.

"Fine, Jackie. Take control. You can keep my body for now, too."

25

FINALLY MADE A DIFFERENCE

HUNTER

PAIN BURSTS IN my shoulder. I yell out, but then a second later, the world shifts, and I lose control of my body. My soul aches, and I groan as Mr. Soto's monstrosities pass through my mind.

His life flashes through me, scene after scene, and I watch as a young version of Mr. Soto towers over a guy a few years younger than me. He chants and calls upon his power and then forces it into the guy until the guy's body can't take it anymore, killing him.

Next I watch as Mr. Soto walks through a small village with a torch, setting everything around him on fire. People scream and run, and his haunting laughter echoes around me.

The world shifts again, and I watch as Mr. Soto stands in front of a woman, not much older than my mom. She touches his shoulder, looking at him lovingly, like he's the one person in the world she cares about. Within seconds, her warm eyes shift to fear, and Mr. Soto glances over his shoulder as an HPA agent runs toward him. He grabs the woman, and just when I think he's going to pull her away to protect her, he holds her in front of him as a shield. The agent stabs her through the heart, and Mr. Soto drops her and leaves her alone, dying on the ground.

The last scene shimmers in front of me from moments ago. Mr. Soto gathers all his power and blasts it at Nadia. She screams and falls to the ground, and anger blurs everything around me. The world shifts, my vision restoring, and Jacqueline jumps and swivels to look at Agent Rosaline.

Gripping a knife in her hand, Agent Rosaline holds it up at us. "How could you do this, Hunter?" She shifts on her feet and looks ready to collapse. "Look at what kind of monsters you protect."

"Agent Rosaline, get over here now. We've lost already," Dr. Sullivan says.

Jacqueline shifts our gaze over to her before returning it back to Agent Rosaline.

"Not all creatures are monsters," I say. My voice echoes in my mind, and confusion wraps around me before I remember I gave Jacqueline control of my body.

Agent Rosaline clenches the knife tighter. "You've lost sight of what we stand for, Dr. Sullivan. Hunter isn't your son. He's the enemy."

"Please, Rosaline," Dr. Sullivan says, her voice low like she's talking to a frightened animal. "I need you to help me with Evie. She's alive, but her leg is fractured. I can't do it alone."

"Not until I finish this. I lost my partner, my position as an agent, everything I worked so hard for because of the fear and pain he caused me." Agent Rosaline turns her eyes toward us. "I was wrong about you. You not only protect the monsters, you're one of them."

Jacqueline steps forward and raises my hand out. "Put the knife down, Agent Rosaline, and I won't hurt you." It's disturbing that it's my voice I'm hearing, but I know I didn't say the words.

Agent Rosaline screams and launches at us. Jacqueline knocks the knife from her grip, and the agent collides with Jacqueline. The world spins as we fall to the ground.

Jacqueline doesn't fight off Agent Rosaline but instead just lies still beneath her. I internally wince when Agent Rosaline punches my face even though I don't feel the pain. She raises her fist again, and Jacqueline turns my head sideways and takes a punch to my jaw.

"Jackie, fight back," I say. *"You have to do something."*

"No, Hunter," she thinks. "Not yet."

"Then when?"

"When she kills you."

Fear and anger swirl around me. I was willing to give my body to Jacqueline because I didn't want to deal with life right now, but it didn't mean I wanted to deal with death either. I concentrate on taking back control of my body, but I hit what feels like a solid wall when I try.

"You can't do this, Jackie!"

Sadness and guilt nudges at me. They're not my emotions but Jacqueline's. "I'm sorry, Hunter. I truly am. It's the only way to get my own body."

"No!"

My ears pop. The world shifts, and I expect to open my eyes, but I'm no longer lying on the ground. I'm standing above Agent Rosaline as she wraps her hands around my throat and squeezes the life from me. I spin in a circle, weightless in my translucent form, and I notice a blue string tethering me to my body. I'm not dead, yet, but must've projected myself out in an attempt to regain control.

"Jackie!" I yell. *"I swear I'm going to kill you!"* But it's no use. Agent Rosaline will kill my body before I even have a chance.

"You can't do anything. Why don't you go wait by Nadia? She needs you now more than ever." Jacqueline's voice echoes through our tether.

I frown. *"What do you mean? Nadia's dead."*

"No, Hunter, Nadia's alive, but she's barely hanging on."

NADIA

"Hello?" I call. "Can anyone hear me?"

I glide a few feet into the darkness and then a pinprick of light grows around me and swallows me. Stand in familiar rainbow mist, soft and cool against my hot skin, I run my fingers through the shimmering colors.

I could never get used to dreaming on my own, but here I am, trapped in my own head. Floating forward, I squint to try to see through the rainbow colors surrounding me.

"Nadia?" Hunter's voice wraps around me clear as day.

"Is it really you?"

Hunter shimmers into view. All my fear and heartache melts away when I look into his hazel eyes. "I thought I lost you." He hugs me against him and kisses my forehead before brushing his lips against my nose and then meeting my lips. He feels so alive and real, even in my own mind, and I let his love soak into me.

"I couldn't let you die," I say.

He frowns, his eyes clouding. I study his face and bring his hands to my cheek and lean my face against them. His love for me shifts into heartache and grief, but it's not for me. It's something else.

He opens his mouth to say something, but the words don't come out, and he gazes at the shimmering, rainbow ground.

My brows knit together. "What is it?"

"I still think I'm going to die."

My heart skips a beat, my hands trembling. "I don't understand."

"I let Jacqueline take control of my body, and she won't give me it back. She's letting Agent Rosaline kill me." Hunter shoves his hands in his pockets. "But I still want you to live. I need you to fight to wake up, Nadia. I need you alive, or I'll never find peace."

Tears pour from my eyes, dripping into the rainbow mist to disappear. Hunter reaches up and swipes his finger along my cheeks, and my heart aches. It's the worst pain I've ever felt. I'm not even sure I want to wake up from this dream. If I wake up, I'm afraid I'll never see Hunter again.

Anger grips at my heart. How could Jacqueline betray us like this? After Hunter let her live through him all these months, she's just going to give up and let Agent Rosaline kill him? *When her host body dies, she can jump to another...*

"Jacqueline was planning this all along," I say.

Hunter touches my jaw and trailing his fingers to my ears before tucking my white hair behind it. "I should've seen it coming. I was so stupid. Jackie only looks after herself. I knew I shouldn't have ever trusted her."

Cupping his face in my hands, I kiss him. I pull away and meet his hazel eyes. "I'm not letting her kill you, Hunter. I refuse to let you die."

HUNTER

I stand over Nadia's limp body and watch as her fingers curl and uncurl. A soft moan escapes her lips, and her eyes flutter open. Her eyes stare at me, but I know she can't see me. She covers her pink skin from the sun and forces herself to get to her feet.

Wobbling, she stumbles her way toward Agent Rosaline. It's eerie watching her strangle my body, and I turn away and stare at Dr. Sullivan as she sits on the snowy ground next to Evie and quietly cries. I know she's not crying over Evie, though. She's sad and guilty because she's letting Agent Rosaline kill me.

"Jacqueline." Nadia's voice drifts to me, barely a whisper. "Jacqueline, please. Don't do this to us. We can find another way."

I shift my gaze from Nadia to my body, and my eyes roll back and close. I watch as my hands fall from Agent Rosaline's shoulders and hit the ground with a thud. It's too late. Jacqueline let Agent Rosaline kill me.

The string tethering me to my body lightens, and I rush forward. I'm not going to let it snap. I'm not going to give up and just die. I've given up too much already. I'm not giving up my life. I want to live to see another day. I want to spend the rest of my life with my beautiful nightmare inflictor.

My body calls to me, and I sink back into it. My ears pop, a buzzing noise echoing in my head, but I can't open my eyes. I try to wiggle my toes without success. I focus on lifting my arms, but they're dead weight at my sides. *You can do this, Hunter. Wake up. Don't let yourself die.*

I'm alone in my own head again, yet I still don't have control over my body. It's like Jacqueline left it, and since she didn't give me control again, I can't take it. I just don't know how to do it.

"Hunter, please don't die. Hold on," Nadia whispers in my ears.

"I can't open my eyes," I say, though nothing comes out of my mouth. It doesn't work.

Something rams against it, sending pain through me for the first time since giving away control, and suddenly, my lungs burn and I gasp. Flailing my arms, I shift my body and kick my legs to fight off whoever presses their weight to my chest. My eyelids turn from black to red, and I open them, squinting through blinding sunlight.

I gulp in another deep breath, blinking as a silhouette hovers over me, haloed in pale light. Nadia's light gray eyes shine, her tears dripping on my cheeks, and she smiles. I open and close my mouth, my throat burning. I want to scream to the world that I did it, that I didn't die, but I just stare at Nadia's beautiful face.

"You did it, Jacqueline," Nadia says.

Nadia shifts and pulls me into her arms, hugging me to her, veiling me in her cascading white tendrils of hair. Fear rushes over me at her words, and I flick my gaze around until they land on Agent Rosaline kneeling two feet away from me. I flail in Nadia's embrace, swinging my arms in Agent Rosaline's direction.

Agent Rosaline tilts her head to the side and smirks. "Oh, knock it off, Hunter. I wasn't going to really let you die." Jacqueline's lavender eyes shine against her new body, and she runs her hand over her short, dark hair. "I actually like having you around."

I grind my teeth and tense my shoulders. Nadia runs her hands down my arms and twines her fingers through mine. I relax under her touch. "You could've warned me first."

"You wouldn't have agreed," Jacqueline says.

I flare my nostrils. "Of course I wouldn't have. You almost killed me!"

Jacqueline gets to her feet. "We can argue more later. We still have a few things to attend to. I think you should be the one to talk to Dr. Sullivan."

I blink my eyes a few times, composing myself, shock and relief still flooding through me. I'm alive. Nadia's alive. Heck, even Jacqueline's alive. I never thought I'd be so thankful.

Jacqueline holds out her hand for me, and I take it, letting her pull me to my feet. I glance at Nadia, who remains on the ground, pulling her hood up to shield her reddening skin from the sun. She waves me away despite the concern rushing through me. She looks ready to pass out, and all I want to do is get her out of here.

"Hunter," Dr. Sullivan says as I hobble up to her. "You're alive." Her eyes widen as she looks at Jacqueline standing behind me in Agent Rosaline's body.

"What can I say? I have a lot of fight in me."

"And you?" Dr. Sullivan asks Jacqueline.

Jacqueline shrugs. "Sorry, your agent is dead. I'm keeping her body. Maybe this one will actually stick."

Dr. Sullivan covers her mouth with her hand, and Evie gasps next to her. Shifting my gaze toward Evie, I twist my lips to the side. If stuff like this scares her, she's not going to make it long as an agent for the HPA. I feel bad for her.

I touch Dr. Sullivan's hand. "I want to make a deal with both of you."

Dr. Sullivan nods. "Anything. I owe you my life. You protected me when you didn't have to even after everything I've done to you. You know I don't want to see you dead."

I glance at Evie.

"Please, just don't kill me," she says.

I sigh. "We never wanted any of you to die. We just want to get away from all this," I say to Evie. I turn back to Dr. Sullivan. "Can you make it happen? I want you to guarantee the board won't come after us."

She's quiet for a moment. "But the council member."

Nadia clears her throat. "Tell them Mr. Soto was a shaman and a lot stronger than you anticipated. He used his powers against you and killed Agent Rosaline. He was so angry at us that he retaliated and killed us, too. Mr. Soto escaped and is on the run, but now you know what he is and what he looks like. I'm sure the board will be more concerned about recovering their precious council member anyway."

Dr. Sullivan nods. "You're right. I better call my agents and start a search party."

I help Dr. Sullivan to her feet and she slings her arms around me, kissing my forehead. "Take care of yourself, Hunter. I am truly sorry for what I've done to you. I do love you. Don't forget that, okay?"

I press my lips together for a moment. "You don't have to go back."

She twists her lips into a frown. "The HPA is my world, and your brother still needs me. I need to keep fighting. Not because of creatures like Nadia, but because of the one's like Mr. Soto. The real bad guys."

Dr. Sullivan pulls Evie to her feet and supports her weight. I watch my mom help Evie walk toward the entrance of the park, and then they disappear when they turn onto the side-walk. Shifting on my feet, I glance between Nadia and Jacquel-ine. I almost don't believe that we're all alive and that this can all be left behind us.

"You've changed your mother," Nadia says. "She knows not all of us are bad."

I smile. "I guess we've finally made a difference."

26

NOT BOUND TO DESTINY

NADIA

MY FATHER'S FROZEN clothes stick to him, his pale skin tinted blue, as he emerges from the river just minutes after Dr. Sullivan and Evie leave. He clenches his hands, ready to fight.

"It's over, Dmitri," Hunter says. "We won."

Tires squeal, and Jacqueline pulls up in the white Honda. She flings the door open, raising her arms to show she's unarmed, and steps closer. "Dmitri, good to see you again."

My father narrows his eyes, gliding up to her to grips her shoulders.

Hunter stumbles to his feet. "Don't hurt her. That's Jacqueline. She took a new host."

Frowning, my father looks at me. My teeth chatter, my whole body shaking. My skin burns in the sun, but I'm frozen to the core, and so weak. It's hard to keep my eyes open. Mr. Soto's image flashes through my mind, and I push it away. He's dead and gone, and I now know who the real monster was in the end.

I force my mouth to work. "I was so scared Mr. Soto hurt you." I close my eyes for a moment, the world shifting as my father picks me up and carries me to the car.

He kisses my head. "I was a fool. I should've been more prepared. The HPA was supposed to be the real threat. I'm sorry for letting you down, Nadia. He could've killed you."

"He tried," I whisper.

"It wouldn't have been the first time," Jacqueline says, coming up to the car door. "He wasn't the gentle, human-loving man you all thought he was. He murdered a lot of people."

Hunter slides onto the seat next to me, and I rest my head on his lap. "He didn't even try to run like we thought he would. All he wanted was to make you pay."

My father puffs air through his lips. He bends down to touch my cheek with his icy hand. "I'm just glad you're all okay. This should've never happened to begin with."

My lips crack when I smile, and I wince. "Don't blame yourself. We're all alive, and Dr. Sullivan will make sure the board will leave me and Hunter alone. We finally got through to her."

Hunter brushes my white hair from my face. "Only took

nearly dying herself for it to happen."

I relax in Hunter's arms. "But at least it happened."

HUNTER

Nadia closes her eyes, and I glance at Dmitri. He climbs in the front seat and pulls his phone from his pocket, making a phone call. Jacqueline gets behind the wheel, and Dmitri gives her directions. Instead of heading back to the warehouse, Jacqueline takes us into the city and to the building where The Haven is located.

Nadia's breathing slows, coming so faint that fear chokes my heart. She desperately needs to inflict a nightmare to get her strength back, and I'm worried she won't even have the energy to do that.

Dmitri jumps from the car and opens my door, scooping Nadia into his arms. "You two wait in the car. We won't be long."

I watch him disappear into the stairwell, and Jacqueline turns in her seat to look at me. Blood clumps in her short brown hair, and mud streaks her cheeks. She's as beat up as me, but neither of us complains because at least we're alive and out of each other's heads.

"Nadia will be fine," Jacqueline says.

It's like she can still hear my thoughts. Lowering my brows, I rub my forehead with my hand. "Get out of my head."

She smirks. "Oh, shut up, Hunter. If you'd learn to conceal your emotions, it wouldn't be so easy to read you."

I shrug and shift on the seat. She doesn't have to say it, but I know she's joking. There's a connection between Jacqueline and me—not like the one Nadia and I share—but a different kind of connection I'll never have with anyone else. Jacqueline drives me absolutely crazy, freaks me out sometimes, and knows exactly how to get under my skin. She's like the older sister I never wanted and got stuck with, but more than that, she's my friend. We've changed each other for the better in a weird and twisted way, and I don't think I'd change anything.

A silence falls between us, and Jacqueline taps her fingers on the steering wheel. "This is weird, huh?" she asks after a minute.

I lift an eyebrow. "What do you mean?"

"I just never thought I'd ever get a fresh start. It's strange. I don't even know what to do with myself," Jacqueline says.

I grin. "That's what's great about it. You can do whatever you want."

NADIA

Opening my eyes, I stare into my father's obsidian gaze. I feel like I'm a child again, like he's protecting me from the world. He shifts, and a breeze wafts around us. It tastes of whipped cream and caramel, and I inhale long, deep breaths.

My frozen fingers twitch with pain, and my muscles loosen. Warm, comforting energy seeps into me like my father has a glass full of everything good in life and slowly pours it over my head. I shift in his arms until he sets me on my feet as I take in the glorious nightmare.

Buildings burn and explode around us. Everything crumbles in my wake as I glide down the burning city street. The oranges and reds of the fire reflect off my pale skin, and I twirl around and tilt my head toward the stormy sky.

Fear laces through the air. I sense the dreamer not far from here. Voices echo, and I glide to the end of the block and around the corner. In the alley, I spot the dreamer and stop in my tracks. Cian shakes a chain-link fence but doesn't try to climb it. He spins around to face me, and I notice one of the lenses on his blue-framed glasses is cracked.

Yelling out, he tries to pull the fence up from the bottom, but there's no escaping this nightmare. I don't smile as I saunter closer to him, and as quickly as possible, I grip Cian's shoulders and destroy the dream.

I open my eyes and meet my father's smiling face. He hugs me against him, kissing my hair, and I glance at Cian asleep on a king-sized bed. He looks so small under the covers, almost child-like. My father reaches over and tugs a talisman from his neck.

"Thanks, my friend," my father says, tossing the talisman that put Cian to sleep on the night table near the bed and glides us from the small apartment.

I search the hallway and then look at my father. "Where's Hunter?"

"He's waiting with Jacqueline in the parking garage. It's not safe for them to be out in our world yet, but you needed sustenance." He grabs my hand, and we glide down a long hall and enter a stairwell.

"What about Alyssa?" The last time I saw her, she was sinking into the river with the water nymph. I wonder if she's upset I didn't go with her.

"She's on her way to the compound. It's where we're headed next."

I don't respond. I never thought I'd see the compound again since the last time I snuck in to ask for help for my father. I wonder if anything has changed. *Everything has changed. Mr. Soto is dead.*

I blink my eyes a few times as the events from today settle in my mind. "What happens now?"

"We move on with our lives."

HUNTER

Nadia twines her fingers with mine and leans into me. Jacqueline stands on the other side of her, and Dmitri sits at the table with the council. Peering over the crowded room, I recognize a few faces I remember from my short visit here while in Jacqueline's mind.

Alyssa sits in the front row next to a bald man with thick eyebrows. I only saw Mr. Augustine briefly at the warehouse, and before that, during the first attempt to break Dmitri out of the termination facility, but I'm glad he's here. We can use all the support we can get.

"What happened next?" Veronica Sanders asks. She's the ex-HPA scientist turned council member.

Jacqueline clears her throat. "Hunter let me possess his body, and I redeemed Mr. Soto."

"Why?" Ana asks.

"Because I save who I can."

Nadia smiles at Jacqueline, and I keep my face serious. I still don't believe Mr. Soto deserved peace after everything he did in his life, but I'm thankful Jacqueline stopped me from murdering him. I don't want people to know me as a killer.

"I see," Veronica says.

The young guy next to her with a shaved head and clean face yawns. He looks as bored as I am. "Let's move on to the HPA board member. I've heard enough about Javier."

"What do you want to know?" I ask, speaking up for the first time since I entered the room.

The guy tilts his head and stares at me for a moment. "Why did she leave you alive?"

I glance at Nadia and Jacqueline, but they don't say anything. Alyssa shakes her head from the crowd. I can't tell the council we're alive because the board member is my mom. I don't think the council or the creatures here are ready for that, and I need to protect her not only because she's my mom, but because it'll guarantee she keeps the HPA away from us.

I take a deep breath. "I saved her life."

"You did what? Why?" The guy's face reddens. "Didn't that woman try to kill you guys multiple times?"

I shrug. "I'm not a murderer, and we made a deal. Her life for our freedom. Nadia and I just want away from all this. From the board—" I look around the room. "And the council."

Veronica clears her throat. "We have so much to offer you, though. We can keep you safe."

Nadia laughs, the sound echoing through the room, and everyone stares silently at her. "We don't need anything, and we're pretty capable of taking care of ourselves." She stands, grabbing my hand. "Now if you'll excuse us, we'd like to just forget all this ever happened."

"It's not that simple," Veronica says.

Dmitri stands up and towers over the council. "It is, actually. It's their life, and I'm not letting any of you influence it. Do you understand?"

Nadia smiles at her dad, and I wag my eyebrows at her. After kissing me once in front of everyone, she pulls me along and we walk off the stage together. Alyssa meets us in the aisle, and we turn to Jacqueline, who hasn't left her spot.

Jacqueline looks at us and offers a small smile. "I'll catch up with you all later, okay? I want to stay here for a while and figure things out."

Nadia opens her mouth to argue, but I squeeze her hand and she nods instead. We leave Jacqueline and Dmitri in the auditorium, and when we step out into the crisp air, Alyssa slings her arms around both of us.

Alyssa digs into her pocket and pulls out her car keys, handing them to me. "I'm going to wait here for Dmitri."

"Let us know how it goes," Nadia says.

I wrap my arm around Nadia's shoulder and stroll with her through the compound and to the parking lot. Sitting behind the wheel, I start the engine. She stares at me with a brilliant smile on her face. Faint sunlight sets her pale blond hair aglow, and her indigo eyes look like two vibrant pools of water.

I lean over and kiss her. "Where to now? We could go anywhere."

"I just really want to go home," she says.

I nod. "Sounds like a plan."

NADIA

Flopping on my bed next to me, Hunter curls his arms around me. He plays with strands of my pale blond hair, and I listen to his heartbeat against my ear. I've never felt so relaxed and safe in my life, and it feels so good to lie here without worrying about whether or not I'll see Hunter again, if I'll die any minute, if I'll never get to see past the city... Everything fell into place like it was supposed to—the way I wanted it, so Hunter and I could be together.

Hunter closes his eyes and drifts off to sleep. Kissing him, I press my fingers to his temples and slip into his dream. He smiles when I shimmer into view, and I spin on my feet. We stand on a vibrant green hill overlooking a valley of rainbow flowers. The sun sets on a vast ocean in the distance, casting a golden hue over the land. The water reflects orange and red, and the puffy clouds look like pink and purple cotton candy in the yellow, sun-kissed sky.

Hunter strolls closer with his arms open, and I fall into him. Our lips brush together, sending tingles through me, making me smile. His soul, his very essence is nothing short of incredible in this moment, unlike anything I've ever felt before. It holds such love and joy, such hope, that I never want to be without him. And I won't.

Still smiling, I pull back and peer into his beautiful hazel eyes. I run my fingers along his cheek, cupping his face. He grins at me before kissing me again.

"Where are we?" I ask. "This place is beautiful. Maybe we could visit here in real life."

Hunter laughs. "This place is just for you. I created it my-self."

I kiss him again. "I love it. Your dream is so magical. You really are my dream boy, you know."

He pulls away but doesn't let go of my hands, twining our fingers together. His intensity warms me in a good way, his desire sending butterflies through my stomach. "It's our dream, Nadia. I'm not going to have another one without you."

I let him guide me forward, and I stare at our beautiful dream world in awe. I thought my life was over today. I was certain of it. I couldn't imagine what life would be like, even in a few hours, but now, as I stand here with Hunter amid our dream, I realize I was given a second chance. A chance to live and see places I could never imagine. A chance to make my own decisions and experience the outcome of them. A chance to plan for my future.

I now know that I wasn't destined for dreams, to never see the beauty that comes from the world of reality, a world I'm not either human or nightmare inflictor. I'm free to embrace both sides of me, sides that include Hunter, the one boy who loves me regardless. The one who sees all me, loves all of me. And I love all of him, too. My dream boy. My reality. I now know we're not bound to destiny at all. We get to choose how we want to live our lives. And right now, I want to live it like this—one day at a time, one dream at a time, surrounded by the people I love most.

EPILOGUE

ENDLESS POSSIBILITIES

HUNTER

THE ROAR OF waves hums in my ears. Lying in the sand, I soak in the hot sunshine overhead. I stare at the backs of my red eyelids and breathe in the salty scent of the ocean. Sea mist sprinkles over my warm skin, and cool lips brush against my cheek.

I open my eyes and grin at Nadia. She stands over me, shaking her wet, pale blond hair. Ocean water splashes my bare chest, and she laughs and plops onto the white sand next to me. Her indigo eyes shine in the bright sunlight, and she wraps a sandy towel around her shoulders.

"The water is amazing," she says.

She kisses me with salty lips, and I sit up and pull her onto my lap, letting her lean her cool, damp back against me. I rest my chin on her shoulder, staring at the stretch of blue water in front of us. I never thought I'd get to visit the beach again, let alone a white sand beach on a tropical island, and I don't think I ever want to leave this place.

"See any mermaids out there?" I ask.

Nadia laughs and shifts in my arms to face me. Her nose crinkles when she smiles, and I press my forehead to hers.

"Why don't you join me and find out?"

Sliding her arms around my neck, she kisses me deeply, wrapping her legs around my waist. I push to my feet with her in my arms, spinning on the sand, making her giggle. She leans back and gazes at the sky, her arms hooked to my neck. I don't think I've ever seen her so happy. I want her to always be like this. I'll make sure she's always like this.

I drop to the sand with her in my arms, and she leans back on the white sand. Pressing against her with my legs between hers, I kiss her again. She runs her hands up my arms and over my shoulders, making me moan into her lips. Her heart beats against mine, matching the rhythm, and I still can't believe this isn't a dream.

This is my life now, and it's a good one—a great one. One I won't ever take for granted.

"Nadi? You two should come inside for a bit."

Nadia kisses me once more, and I help her to her feet and turn to face Dmitri. He hovers on the small patio of the beach house and motions for us to join him. I pick up the wet, sandy beach towels and shake them off as I follow Nadia.

She leans into me and asks, "Think we'll have time to look for mermaids later?"

I grin and kiss her hair. "We have all the time in the world."

NADIA

I sit next to Hunter at the white wood table in the small kitchen of our beach house. It's been almost a month since Hunter and I reclaimed our lives, and my father announced that we should all go on a vacation. I never thought he'd pick this beautiful, Caribbean island, but I'm glad he did. The real beach is a million times better than the ones in the dream worlds. I'm tempted to ask to stay forever.

"Are you sure you three will be all right here alone for another month?" my father asks.

Alyssa giggles. "I'm sure we'll be okay for a year."

I suck in my bottom lip when I look at Hunter. His eyes shine as he grins at me. "I wish you didn't have to escort a dang council member back to the compound!" I yell toward the living room.

Jacqueline, wearing a lavender sundress the same color as her eyes, saunters in from the living room with a cell phone glued to her ear. She rolls her eyes at me as she hangs up the phone and sits down next to my father.

"I wish I didn't have to go either, but I have meetings with basically the entire supernatural world for the next three weeks." She rolls her shoulders and leans on her elbows. "I was just starting to enjoy the island living, too."

Only days after revealing herself to the council, Jacqueline was asked to fill in Mr. Soto's spot. She was the perfect person for the position with knowledge of the HPA and of the supernatural world. They loved her bravery, her selflessness, and her desire for change. Jacqueline has come a long way since the first time I met her. She's powerful and in control—far from the victim she was.

My father, no longer obligated to work for the council, chose to stay anyway. I'm not mad at him for it either. He wants to spend his life helping people, and now with the new order of things, he can.

"Don't worry, you'll be back," Alyssa says. "There are a lot of amazing vacations in our future."

Hunter holds my hand under the table and rubs his thumb on mine. I never dreamed of a life like this, where I could sit and laugh and talk about normal—mostly normal—things with my family. My life is better than I could have ever hoped for, and it's even better than what Hunter and I thought about in our dream world. Our life has a future, one that's in our control, and no one will ever take that from us.

Jacqueline grins. "I like that vision. Where will we visit next?"

Alyssa shrugs. "I don't know."

I glance at Hunter and then turn to the rest of my family. "Wherever we want. The possibilities are endless."

THE END

WELCOME ABOARD THE OCEAN JEWEL

CRISP SEA AIR BLOWS STRANDS of my blond hair across my face, veiling the view of the Ocean Jewel, the luxury yacht I'll be calling home for the next week. The three decked, two hundred and fifty-seven foot monster of a boat waits at the end of a long dock in the middle of Azure Waters' harbor with dozens of other boats around it, none of which are comparable in size or extravagance. I'm the last one on the dock, standing in the dead center as the deep, blue-green ocean surrounds me only feet away.

From twenty feet ahead, my best friend, Giselle Nash, waves a hand over her head, trying to grab my attention. When I don't move, she drops her bag in front of a man in a dark blue blazer and khakis—one of the crew members—and jogs my way without glancing at the dock beneath her. I tense, imagining her tripping on the wooden beams and falling into the sea, but she makes it to me without a problem.

She stops a foot away, placing her hands on my shoulders, and stares at me with her amber eyes. "You can't change your mind, Ava. We're already here, and if you turn around now, you'll regret it. Look at that thing." She points to the yacht. "We're not traveling to sea in a rowboat."

She's right. Yet I still can't suppress the fear that freezes me in place. You'd think that after all this time I wouldn't be so afraid of the ocean. It's been nearly eight years since the accident that swept my older sister away and left me almost drowned. I'll never forget the silent look of terror on Bailey's face as the ocean current broke us apart moments before she disappeared under.

"So, are you coming or not?" Giselle asks, shaking my shoulders, forcing me to draw my attention away from the yacht.

I open my mouth to say, "not" but instead, I say, "Yeah, just give me a minute."

With a deep sigh, my best friend spins on her heels. Her bronze hair flies behind her, and she skips down the dock and back to where our group of friends waits for what's supposed to be the best adventure of the year, thanks to Sapphire King's eighteenth birthday, an obnoxiously large trust fund from her grandma, and as a gift to all of us for graduation.

When the others climb the ramp to enter the deck, I finally find the nerve to start walking. My bag hangs heavy in my fingers, but before I make it halfway to the yacht, a boy my age, wearing the same blue blazer and khakis as the other crew members, jogs to my side to take it from me.

He meets my eyes with a smile that manages to ease my fear of the ocean enough to where my legs no longer tremble. I really needed this incredibly hot distraction. Scruff covers his handsome face, his skin bronzed with a deep tan gorgeous enough that someone like me, who doesn't get much sun, would pay a lot for.

"First time out to sea, huh?" he asks, amusement lining his eyes.

"That obvious? I haven't even been in the water since I was a kid," I say.

I expect him to ask why and get ready to tell him the same story everyone in Azure Waters already knows. But he doesn't say anything. Instead, the boy offers his free arm to me, and I take it, hooking my hand around the sinewy muscles of his forearm.

"I wasn't even going to come, but my best friend basically threatened me—mostly with a good time," I add to fill the silence.

His smile widens as he glances at me in the side of his vision. "I can promise she's right. The Ocean Jewel speaks true to her name. I even have fun, and I'm on the job."

As we reach the ramp that'll take us onto the Ocean Jewel, I slow down. Everyone has boarded, and no one waits for me. They're probably already heading to their staterooms or exploring the upper decks. Apparently, the sundeck contains a hot tub and pool, according to Sapphire.

This is my last chance to turn away and run when none of my friends are looking. I wouldn't even have to explain myself for a few days, and by then, they'll all have moved on.

As I start to turn away, the boy blocks my path. "Why don't you board before you make the decision to bail? We won't leave port for another twenty minutes or so. You can change your mind if you hate it. And if it makes you feel any better, I'm an excellent ocean swimmer and diver. We've never had a single person fall overboard, either."

"And I'm supposed to trust you? I don't even know your name." Crossing my arms over my chest, I hold myself, imagining being in the middle of the ocean with no signs of land. The thought unsettles me.

He holds out his hand, but I don't take it right away. "Carter Stevens, deckhand, steward, activities coordinator, cook—basically, I'm at your service..." His voice trails off, his eyes smiling though his mouth remains firm.

I meet his blue-green eyes that match the ocean around us and reluctantly shake his hand. "Ava Adair."

He cracks a smile, holding my fingers long enough to make me uncomfortable. Instead of releasing me, he pulls me forward onto the short ramp, the sudden movement causing it to shake under our feet. Using my free hand, I grip the single guardrail and shoot him a death glare that only makes him smile wider as he pulls me the short distance onto the yacht.

Without giving me a chance to glance at the calm ocean beneath us, he guides me up a set of stairs, and we cross the main deck and head into what he calls the saloon. The lavish room shines with metal, glass, and light wood, all gleaming to perfection. Two short, white leather sectionals face an eighty-inch television stationed in an entertainment center that also serves as a room divider to another sitting area with a few tables and chairs. The magnificence of the room is breathtaking. I almost feel like I'm in a swanky penthouse hotel room. Almost.

Instead of guiding me all the way around the main deck, he directs me to a small elevator past the sitting room and hits the call button. The door opens, and we step on and ride it to the upper deck where our staterooms are located.

Voices hum through another lounge area surrounded by a panoramic view of the harbor and the ocean that disappears into the blue horizon. Giselle waves her arms when she spots us, flicking her eyes to Carter before pursing her lips at me in a look that says I must've found the hottest crew member on the boat. I'd be lying if I didn't agree.

"I already picked out our room." She takes my hand and pulls me toward a short hallway where voices echo from within the opened doors of the staterooms. There are five rooms altogether, and another suite toward the bow of the yacht where Sapphire's parents will be staying since they're the ones chaperoning our vacation.

Carter follows behind us, still holding my bag, and I grin at Matty and Logan, who each sit on the end of a twin bed next to each other in one room, and then to Sapphire, who talks to Daisy and Chloe in her own room with a queen bed and a view of the ocean through the porthole. I poke my head into two more staterooms, both with queen beds, which Giselle and I could've taken since Giselle is Sapphire's cousin, but we agreed to share a room because there was no way I was sleeping on the ocean in a room alone.

Our stateroom is the last door in the hall, and two beds, identical to the ones in the room where Matty and Logan are staying, sit against each wall of the white and blue room. A long window allows sunlight to shine across the white-carpeted floor, and along another wall is a flat screen TV and built-in drawers. It's simple yet chic, and my fear of coming aboard disappears the moment I perch on the edge of the comfy bed.

Carter sets my bag on the other bed and flashes another smile. I don't think I've ever had someone smile so much at me besides Giselle. It sends my heart beating faster, and not because I'm about to embark on a luxurious vacation on a yacht.

He places his hand on the doorframe. "This is your last chance to get off," he says.

Giselle swings her gaze to mine. "You're not going any-where."

I lean back on the bed. "You're right. I'm not."

Carter hovers for a second longer. "Enjoy your stay aboard the Ocean Jewel, Ava."

Giselle smirks at me as she waves goodbye to Carter. Covering my face with my hands, I release a long sigh. This is less terrifying than I expected, and I'm glad I decided to come.

Giselle flops next to me, the bed small for two bodies. "He's cute. This is going to be a blast."

I grin. "Should we go explore the rest of the boat?"

"I bet we could get your hottie helper to show us around."

"That's exactly what I had in mind."

Without missing a beat, Giselle pulls me from the bed and

we fly into the hallway. Voices hum from the other staterooms, and I grin at Giselle when I see Carter talking to a man outside the elevator.

The man looks over at us and smiles. "Welcome. It's a pleasure to have you aboard the Ocean Jewel. How do you like it?"

I politely turn my gaze from Carter to the man. "It's lovely, thanks. We were actually going to just ask Carter to give us a tour."

Carter offers a warm smile from next to the man, sending my heart racing.

Before he can respond, the man says, "I'd be happy to show you two and the rest of your friends around. I'm Hank, by the way."

I force my mouth to remain smiling though I want nothing more than to frown. "That would be great, thank you."

Giselle sighs next to me but just shrugs when I look at her.

"Perfect, I'll be waiting in the saloon for when you're ready. We'll leave port shortly thereafter." Hank nods once to Carter before heading to the stairs instead of the elevator.

"You two have fun," Carter says, still grinning at me. "You'll get a better tour with the first mate, anyway. But I'd be happy to take you out on the water when we anchor after lunch."

Giselle grins. "Definitely!"

I shrug, disappointment creeping into me. The last thing I'll do is go out into the water, no matter how cute Carter is or how much he smiles. *Oh well.*

Voices sound from behind us as the others leave their rooms, and Giselle hooks her arms through mine. "Come on, Aves. Let's get the stupid tour over with."

I glance up to Carter. "I guess I'll see you around."

The dining terrace overlooks the sprawling ocean on the stern of the yacht opposite to where our staterooms are located. It's enclosed with floor to ceiling windows, which pop open to allow in the salty sea air. The sturdy wood table with seating for twelve sits on top a navy blue and gray rug that matches the curtains that could be pulled down, like anyone ever does that with such a startling, vast view.

A buffet table displays hot trays filled with all sorts of food from the chef on board. Warm dinner rolls steam from a basket, and the scent of garlic wafts through the air. My mouth waters as I follow Giselle. She grabs a white and blue ceramic plate from the stack near the start of the buffet. The others trail around us, and we all greet Ruby and Carlton King, Sapphire's parents and Giselle's aunt and uncle.

A familiar face pops up from his position behind a small bar where he scoops ice into glasses. Carter greets me with a dazzling smile, his ocean eyes quickly trailing from my face to the rest of me, taking in my strapless swimsuit cover. I won't be riding jet skis with the others, but my fear of the ocean won't stop me from hanging at the pool on the sundeck.

After a woman in her mid-twenties fills my plate with seared salmon on baby spinach, a side of garlic pasta, and one of the rolls, I set my plate down and head to the bar.

"What can I get you, miss?" Carter asks, taking on a more formal approach with Sapphire's parents behind me.

"Lemonade," I say, resting my elbows on the shiny counter. "And it's Ava."

As Carter stands in front of me, glass in hand, all I can think about is how good he looks in his dark blue polo since he's no longer wearing the blazer. He rubs a lemon wedge on the rim of the glass before dipping it onto a small tray of sugar. "Okay, *Ava*," he says as he sets the glass in front of me. "Anything else?"

"A Coke for Giselle."

He tips a glass of ice against the soda fountain and then hands it to me. "Enjoy your meal."

I try to think of something more to say, but Matty pushes up next to me, forcing my conversation to end with Carter. As much as I want him to ignore my friend, I don't want him getting in trouble on my behalf. We'll be on this yacht for a week, so I'm sure there will be plenty more chances.

I smile once more at Carter before turning my back and heading to where Giselle sits across from Sapphire on the opposite side of the table from her parents. I set the glasses down and take a seat next to my best friend.

"The bartender is checking you out," Sapphire says, leaning over her plate of salmon. "God, he's hot."

A warm blush blossoms up my neck. "His name is Carter."

Her eyes widen. "That was fast."

"What was?" Matty says, plopping down next to Sapphire before giving her a kiss on the cheek.

I shake my head, letting my hair veil in front of my face. "Nothing."

"The bartender," Sapphire says, causing me to blush even more.

"Oh, shit. Sorry, Ava. I totally messed that up, huh?" Matty wags his eyebrows before tearing into his roll. With his mouth full, he says, "I can go back and put in a good word."

"Oh, my God, you guys!" Giselle exclaims, throwing her hands up. "Shut up about it. Ava's got it under control."

Whatever *it* is, Giselle's right. I can handle it. I pick up my roll and chuck it at Matty, who catches it and takes a bite. "What she said."

Logan, Daisy, and Chloe join the rest of us, and I lose myself in my thoughts as Logan and Matty talk about the jet skis and share stories from last summer—stories I've heard a dozen times since I was the only one who stayed out of the water. My friends, while sometimes clueless, never make fun of me about my fear, but it also leaves me out of a lot of plans since we live in a beach community. They probably all took bets on whether or not I'd actually come.

"So, you're sure you'll be okay if we all go out riding?" Giselle asks. Even if I wasn't okay, I wouldn't say so. The way to guarantee people don't bother you about your weird quirks is to make sure it doesn't interrupt their own lives.

"Yeah, totally cool with it. Look at this place. I'm sure I can find some sort of entertainment." Leaning back in my chair, I gaze around the dining terrace, trying not to stare at Carter as he helps his coworker clean up the empty food trays.

Giselle bounces in her seat. "Perfect. You'll tell me if you're not okay, right?"

I exaggerate a long exhale. "Yes, Mom. Don't worry about me."

She hugs me before joining the others. They leave the table to head to the jet ski garage. Carter glances at me once, before following behind them, probably to help. I'd follow, but I want nowhere near the swimming platform that leads directly into the water.

Instead, I head to the elevator and ride it up to the sundeck and find a few padded lounge chairs surrounding a pristine, rectangular swimming pool with swimmer jets and a round spa on a raised platform. I scoop a towel from the cabinet under a covered lounge area and head to the lounge chair closest to the railing to get a better view of my friends. Carter helps them launch the jet skis into the ocean, and my heart sinks into my stomach when Giselle and Chloe take off at an unsettling speed. *They're wearing life jackets. They're excellent swimmers. It'll be okay.*

As much as I want to turn away, I can't. As Carter helps the rest of my friends onto the other two jet skis, I find that I'm gripping my knees for dear life. Laughter and playful screams echo through the salty air. The jet skis fly over the water, leaving glittering bubble trails in their wakes.

Giselle navigates the jet ski in figure eights before turning in a circle and jetting off again with Matty and Sapphire hot on her trail. I'm so afraid that if I look away from them for even a second, the ocean will swallow them whole like my sister.

A shadow falls over my shoulder, but still, I don't turn

away. "I can take you for a ride if you want when they're finished." Carter's voice causes me to jump, and I spin around and bump into his chest.

Ignoring his offer, I say, "Shouldn't you be down there watching them?"

His brows furrow when he catches the fear cross my face. "I asked Keith to take over. They're fi—" He snaps his mouth closed for a second before adding, "Ouch."

Spinning back to the railing, horror sweeps over me. I spot Giselle and Chloe bobbing in the water a few feet from their jet ski. Logan and Daisy are closest, but neither of them does anything except laugh.

"Oh, God. Come on, Giselle. Get back on," I whisper under my breath.

It must've not been low enough, because Carter makes a point to say, "They're fine, Ava. If they were in danger, Keith would get them."

"But how do you know they're not?" I watch Giselle struggle to climb back on with Chloe in the water next to her. I imagine a hundred horrible things that could possibly happen before Keith could even have the boat in the water. We're not in some lake. This is the same ocean that took my sister.

My hands grip the guardrail so hard my arms shake. Carter reaches out and touches my shoulder. "Hey, whoa. It's okay. Look." He points at Giselle as she helps Chloe back on the jet ski, proving my fear to be unwarranted.

Blinking away embarrassing tears, I pull myself from the guardrail, watching Giselle speed away again. I'm so mortified I can't even meet Carter's eyes. His silence speaks volumes, and all I can think about is getting away from him. Coming on this trip was a terrible idea.

"Excuse me," I say, nudging past Carter before he can block my way. "I need to lie down."

"Ava, wait up," he says from behind me as I stride toward the elevator.

I don't wait, though. Instead of getting on the elevator that could trap me and force me to explain myself to a boy I've just met, I fly down the stairs and head to my room, locking the door behind me.

I should've stayed home. If only I could magically transport myself to dry land.

ACKNOWLEDGEMENTS

THE DESTINED FOR Dreams series would have never existed without a few people very close to my heart, who have been here through my publishing journey, and who have supported me long before I ever started writing, and who will continue to support me through all my endeavors.

I'd like to thank my mom, Elaine, for all her love and support. Thank you for spreading the word about my books, both online and in real life. I appreciate you more than you know.

Thanks to Jan Moran, whose guidance through the writing and publishing process has been invaluable. You're not only my writing partner but one of my best friends, and I look forward to continuing this exciting journey with you.

As always, many thanks to my sister-in-law, Jamie, who reads every first draft...and second and third and—anyway, thanks for enjoying my novels from the roughest draft to the final version.

Thanks to my best friend, Jazmin Garcia, for always being there for me. Thank you for listening to me when I need someone to talk to—whether it's about my novels or about my personal life—you've always made time for me. Thanks for supporting my writing journey and for choosing my books as the special gift you give all your friends. I appreciate it.

Many thanks to the bloggers out there who have given my novels a chance, and especially thanks to Karen Laird, whose kindness and friendship helped me through some tough times. I'm very lucky to have met you.

I want to give a special thanks to my editors, Aleya and Jerika, from Ladies of Literature and my proofreader, Amanda Phillips. With your help, I've managed to produce a novel I'm proud to show off to the world. Thanks for your editorial guidance and for teaching me along the way.

Lastly, I want to thank my readers. Thank you for sticking with me through the series and for all your enthusiasm. Thank you for your kind words and your reviews. Reviews are very important for authors, and I appreciate the time you take to post them.

About Ginna Moran

GINNA MORAN IS a writer from sunny Southern California. She started writing poetry as a teenager in a spiral notebook that she still has tucked away on her desk today. Her love of writing grew after she graduated high school, and she completed her first unpublished manuscript at age eighteen.

When she realized her love of writing was her life's passion, she studied literature at Mira Costa College in Northern San Diego. Besides writing novels, she was senior editor, content manager, and image coordinator for Crescent House Publishing Inc. for four years.

Aside from Ginna's professional life, she enjoys binge watching television shows, playing pretend with her daughter, and cuddling with her dogs. Some of her favorite things include chocolate, anything that glitters, cheesy jokes, and organizing her bookshelf.

Ginna Moran loves to hear from her readers so visit her online at www.GinnaMoran.com. You can also find her on Facebook, Twitter, Instagram, and Snapchat (@GinnaMoran). To stay up-to-date on new releases, sign up to her newsletter. You'll not only get a FREE story, but you'll be able to participate in monthly giveaways!

Ginna Moran is currently hard at work on her next novel.

Other Young Adult Series by Ginna Moran

PARANORMAL
Destined for Dreams Series
Demon Within Series
Finding Nate Series
Spark of Life Series
Going Ghostly Series
When Souls Collide Series
Demon Watcher Series
Call of the Ocean Series

CONTEMPORARY
Falling into Fame Series

STANDALONES
Life After Lila

www.ingramcontent.com/pod-product-compliance
Lightning Source LLC
Chambersburg PA
CBHW051636180726

48284CB00006B/1755